THE
KORTELISY
ESCAPE

LEONARD ROSEN

THE
KORTELISY
ESCAPE

THE PERMANENT PRESS
Sag Harbor, NY 11963

For information, address:
  The Permanent Press
  4170 Noyac Road
  Sag Harbor, NY 11963
  www.thepermanentpress.com

Library of Congress Cataloging-in-Publication Data

Rosen, Leonard J., author.
  The Kortelisy escape / Leonard Rosen.
  Sag Harbor, NY: Permanent Press, [2018]
  ISBN 978-1-57962-542-9
    1. Love stories.

PS3618.O83148 K67 2018
813'.6—dc23   2018027960

Printed in the United Statesof America

For Linda. Again and again.

[B]ut this frighted me most, that the Angels gathered up several, and left me behind.

—JOHN BUNYAN, *The Pilgrim's Progress*

THE THREE ROSES

One: Grace Larson

The first time . . . the first time was when I stole Mrs. Del-Rey's lipstick.

She and Mr. Del-Rey must have flipped through the availables list like they were buying a used car or a washing machine from a catalogue. As we were driving back to their house, they sat in the front seat discussing my cheek bones, which they thought were well formed, and my hair, which they decided was too straight and in need of curling. I was four. Two weeks later, they were stuffing me into party dresses with crinolines and painting blush on my cheeks. They taught me to use Junior Miss lipstick, how to make that popping sound with my lips as I blotted away the extra on old envelopes. Mrs. Del-Rey even promised I could wear her very own "Fuchsia" by Maybelline on my next birthday.

When I didn't place in the Medford, Massachusetts, Tots Pageant or in States the following spring, the Del-Reys gave me back. Stealing wasn't a question of right or wrong at that point. All I knew was that I'd been promised something I would never get, so I rummaged through Mrs. Del-Rey's makeup kit before they hurried me out the door.

The second time was a belt. Mr. Elliot made a living off his foster children. He kept five of us cycling through his house in South Boston and was a big believer that discipline was the key to running a tight ship and developing good citizens. He would double up his leather belt and snap it to scare us into doing our chores with a smile. He never used the belt on me, but one day the DCF van came for us after the police found the oldest, Cameron, shivering beneath an I-93 overpass with welts across his back. I was five and knew exactly what I was doing when I stole Mr. Elliot's belt.

By the time they gave me to Mrs. Alcott nine years later, I had collected four more trophies of the homes I'd survived: Mr. Parker, the pervert (I stole his TV remote); Miss holy holy Carothers (the family Bible); the Daltons (a mini-bottle of rum—enough said); and the Healy sisters (a school photo of Alice, their first and—they'd never let me forget—*best* foster child). My rental parents called me moody. They didn't think I smiled enough or appreciated them sincerely enough. They complained I didn't talk at the dinner table. Each night I looked in the mirror wondering what was wrong with me.

One morning, Mrs. Alcott was peeling apples.

"Grace," she said. "No school today."

I hadn't heard of any holidays or teachers' meetings. "Are you sure?" I asked.

"Let's be quick about it. Go put on your dress."

I owned exactly one dress, which I wore to church and to DCF meetings when I was being trotted out to a new family. I understood what was coming and began looking around for something to steal.

Mrs. Alcott worked the paring knife in her brittle little hands, staring into the sink. "There's been a change," she sighed. "I thought it best to hold the news until this morning. No use upsetting the applecart."

This time, I was going to tell my case worker at the Department of Children and Families to put me in a motel and leave me alone to write computer games, about my only pleasure in life aside from math class and social studies. I knew which motel too: in Boston's South End near the cathedral, where I could eat Chinese every night, walk to school, then come home to find my bed made.

"They say it's your grandfather—which I do *not* understand. Sweet Mother of God, the man's just getting out of prison. I swear, Grace. Blood or no blood, they wouldn't give you to a murderer. Would they?"

"You mean this wasn't your idea?"

She waved a letter. "There's no arguing a court order."

When my mother was alive, I visited someone she called Dad at the federal prison in Danbury, Connecticut. After she died, no one in the system wanted me visiting jails anymore. It had been ten years since I'd seen this man, and the fact I'd finally be raised by a family member was supposed to make a positive difference in my life. I didn't see how. I had exactly one memory of my grandfather—putting my hand to the glass in a visitors' room as my mother held me up to the window. She'd lost her hair from the treatments by that point. The man held his hand to the other side and reached for me as best he could. "That's your grandpa!" she said, sniffling.

"I sincerely hope this works out for you," said Mrs. Alcott, sprinkling brown sugar over her apples.

"Time for a sound clip!"

"Grace, enough with that thing. This is serious."

I left her standing in the kitchen with her rolling pin, the key, she claimed, to a flaky crust, and returned with my laptop. Earlier that year, I decided to record details of my foster care placements. With so many rental families, I was on track to set a record for the world's least-wanted child. Maybe if I'd been prettier. . . . I tried, but I was done painting and twisting myself into Mrs. Del-Rey's kind of pretty. I liked school and did well, not that Mrs. Alcott noticed. Mainly she fussed over her miniature schnauzer. Each time she came home from work it was a reunion for the ages: "Daisy, Daisy! How's my little noodly noodles? You sweet thing, did you miss Mama? Come, give us a kiss!" Occasionally I got a *Did you remember to fold the laundry*? That counted as a good day.

"Turn your computer *off*," she said. "Always with the computer. Just stop and think about this. It's a big change for you."

As if I needed reminding. Getting booted back to DCF *was* a big deal, and now that I had a computer I wanted to record the moment. Who knew, maybe I'd write a long letter one day like those frontier women who kept journals about their adventures on the Great Plains. "Speak slowly and clearly," I said, wanting to catch every word. "Why didn't you tell me when you got the news?"

She waved the letter again, summoning us to the courthouse. "I told you, I don't believe in upsetting applecarts. . . . It's a lot, I admit, your being fourteen with all this tumult in your life."

As we were leaving, she pointed to my jeans, which were ripped at the knees, and to my T-shirt and my red high tops and started in on the importance of first impressions. "Your dress would be so much nicer. I'll wait while you put it on." When I didn't move, a light must have clicked on in the withered orchard between her ears. She sighed as if she'd suddenly realized she'd be my foster mother for approximately one more hour.

"Well," she said. "At least we can pray."

"For what?"

"A good placement, for starters. For your grandfather to be a decent man, despite being a criminal. I read once that criminals can have good hearts. Let's pray for that. And just in case, let's ask God to cradle His special little lamb."

I couldn't help myself and started bleating. "Ba-ah-ah. Ba-ah-ah."

"*Stop* that!"

"Don't pray for me, Mrs. Alcott."

"Why for heaven's sake not?"

"Because I never got cradled. Ever. And I'm not anybody's lamb."

"Grace. Haven't I—?"

"I mean it. Don't."

Just the same, she closed her eyes and asked *Jeez*us to show me a little attention. Despite myself I joined her in a hearty *Amen* because in truth I wanted a good placement. I just didn't see why the Lord would take a personal interest. We packed the Camry and were setting off when I told her I forgot something and needed to go back inside.

Mostly I felt numb as I surveyed the kitchen in search of something to steal. My eyes settled on the rolling pin—a wicked choice, I realized, but I didn't care. I stuffed it into my pack. Thirty minutes later we were standing before a brick building with white columns and planters thick with daffodils. Mrs. Alcott was tugging at my sleeve.

"Don't be upset, dear."

The woman had no clue. Getting a new rental parent mattered to me about as much as stepping onto a different crosstown bus. Maybe this new bus, driven by someone with my same last name, would be less boring than my present bus. In the end, all it could ever be was a box on wheels taking me down the road to my eighteenth birthday, when the system would spit me out.

Mrs. Alcott leaned close to plant a kiss on my cheek.

She smelled of dead leaves and schnauzer. I leaned away.

Two: Nate Larson

If you like having time on your hands with a minimum of commitments, prison is just the place. They give you a cot, a toilet, a roof over your head, and food. Your only real job is to survive. The rest is easy.

I sat at the edge of my cot working two decks of cards, one in each hand, sliding the decks open and snapping them shut at different tempos. I flashed the backs of the cards, flashed the fronts, shut the fans, opened them, first right, then left. I heard a beat in my head: *Ha-cha-cha. Ha-cha-cha, Snap! Snap!* Once, I saw a flamenco dancer working a pair of lace fans as she lifted her arms and spun, making a whirlwind of her dress. I'll never forget it: red dress, black edging, black fans, black hair—her floor stomps like gunshots. She used her fans to hide and reveal her lips and eyes—but only when *she* decided. *Ha-cha-cha. Ha-cha-cha, Snap! Snap!*

Absolute mastery is a beautiful thing.

"Very nice, Larson. I hear you're putting on a magic show next week."

A voice, a uniform, on the far side of my cage.

"Just my luck—on my day off! Maybe you'll show me a few tricks. My kid just got an Amazing Kreskin magic kit for her birthday. You know, the works all in one box: cape, wand that turns into a scarf, top hat, and disappearing ink. Maybe you'll teach me a little something I can show her."

"Sure, Jim. No problem."

"C'mon. Your visitor's here."

I'd seen the woman I was to meet many times on the evening news and in the papers. She'd usually be standing behind a podium at the federal courthouse, backed by the Boston Harbor and a big blue sky. That a United States attorney would bother with me was some kind of joke. The woman could snap her fingers and summon the national press. She'd brought down politicians and hedge-fund billionaires. If she wanted a meeting, it could only be for one thing, and I wasn't interested.

Just the same I agreed, if only for the entertainment value.

The guard removed my cuffs and opened the door to a gray bunker of a room: no windows, only one door, which I hated. Hunt looked no different than she did on television, though she was shorter than I expected. She had hard blue eyes and a hard, thin little body. She wore a blue suit and was all angles, all cheekbone and chin and nose, her hair chopped. Handsome, boyish. Chilly. There was no denying she'd look good in political ads if she ran for governor one day. And, by God, she would have gotten my vote because she'd let her hair go gray. Any pol who did that *had* to be honest.

"I know why you're here," I told her. "Sorry I can't help."

She forced a smile. "And a big Department of Justice hello right back at you, Mr. Larson. I drove an hour from Boston for this meeting. If you've already decided to screw me, at least have the courtesy to kiss me first. Let's talk."

The interview room reeked of men desperate to cut any sort of deal for their freedom. I wanted out no less than anyone else, but the price had to be right and what she was asking— what I knew she was going to ask—was too much. The room was dismal: two metal chairs, joints welded, chained to ring bolts in the floor on either side of a table, also welded and secured. They'd even thought to cage in the fluorescent lights so prisoners who were having a bad day couldn't rip out the bulbs and start stabbing people. Gray floor, gray walls, gray table and chairs, no windows. Welcome to life at FCI Danbury.

"I mean this sincerely," she said. "You're the victim of an honest-to-God miscarriage of justice. For me to even come here and say so is no small thing. You may have noticed the federal government's not in the habit of apologizing. But I am when there's a reason, and I'm genuinely sorry for what happened to you. Let's make this right."

"I'm touched, Miss Hunt. The answer's still *no.*"

She straightened the folders before her. "If I've learned anything in this business, it's that reasonable people change their minds. You got tangled in a bad law. Only the politicians supported the Three Strikes sentencing guidelines. Great optics, right?—taking career criminals off the streets. The evening news eats it up. Your first two offenses weren't even crimes, Mr. Larson. *That's* the real crime here. The judges knew it too."

"Are you done? At the rec room they're showing reruns of *Gilligan's Island.*"

It took me a decade at Danbury to learn how to breathe with the boulder American justice had rolled onto my chest. When the judge pronounced it, my sentence—twenty-five years to life with a minimum of twenty-five served—sounded like a joke given what I'd done or, rather, not done. The system ate me alive. More than once I prayed to be back in Ukraine under Stalin or Khrushchev or the long line of thugs who succeeded them. At least in the Soviet Union you never fooled yourself into thinking you'd get a fair trial. After a few years, I began making my peace with the facts: a wretched law had

put me behind bars, likely for the rest of my days—and no one
was coming to the rescue.

"Buying Percocets on the street was . . . *misguided*," she
said, looking up from a file. "You ever hear of doctors? Why
didn't you get a prescription? Forgive me, but this could have
been a legal purchase if you had just waited until morning."

I struggled to hold back my bitterness, but on it came,
at first a trickle and then a little more until I thought *why
not* and let it run because bitterness feels so good—until it
doesn't, the way raking your fingernails across poison ivy feels
good until it sets your skin on fire. This lady wanted news?
I'd give her a bellyful: "Nora spent that whole day throwing
up blood. You ever see that? I asked one of her doctors for a
pill—for something, anything to get me through *my* pain so I
could stay with her. The doctor said, 'She's the one who's sick.'
I didn't have time to shop around. I was in that much pain,
holding my wife's hand, cleaning her vomit when the nurses
were too busy. You ever help somebody you love to die? It was
two in the morning. I needed to get numb fast."

My hands started shaking more than usual.

"Why not go to a bar?"

"The bars were closed."

I should have lunged across the table and throttled her.

"She was young. It was tragic, but the system's the system,
Mr. Larson. What was the undercover cop supposed to do, *not*
run you in? Even the judge was sympathetic. You got straight,
unsupervised probation, which was the right call. But it was
still a felony. Still Strike One and a brand-spanking new criminal record. No justice system can walk away from evidence.
You bought the pills illegally."

I stood to leave.

"Hear me out. You've got time. At least fifteen more years
by my count."

"You're a real charmer."

"Yes, I am. I also deal in facts. You're sixty-six. You've got Parkinson's. You walk like you're seventy-six. The air in this place is damper than in my cellar, which has a dirt floor, and I'd bet a hundred bucks some kind of mold is already growing in your chest." She scanned a second file. "Strike Two. Good God, the prosecutor was having a bad day. Probably had to make his numbers."

Innocent doesn't begin to describe what happened. I was helping a neighbor move and found some loose ammunition for a historic gun her husband owned, a rusty old thing. I thought nothing of putting the bullets in a pocket. That afternoon, a cop pulled me over for a broken taillight. He saw a drug conviction on his computer, told me to empty my pockets— and out dropped the bullets for an antique gun that wasn't mine and didn't fire. Felons can't own guns or possess live ammunition.

Who knew?

She shook her head. "They weren't your bullets. You had no intention of committing a crime. You were helping a neighbor. I wouldn't have brought that case. My predecessor was . . . aggressive."

I asked the guard to cuff me.

"Still, there was a law and you broke it. The second judge didn't send you to prison either—again, the right call. I can get you out of here, Mr. Larson. And let's not forget, there's Grace to consider."

The guard had already walked me a few steps down the corridor. I stopped, not quite believing what I'd heard. "You'd drag a child into this? Perfect. Now I know what I'm dealing with."

She set the folders aside and stood, keeping the table between us. "Look, I'm decent enough. I check my kids' homework every night. I go to PTA meetings. I volunteer at my church. But I happen to commute to and from hell every day of the week, and in case you hadn't noticed, you're living in hell right now. You're up to your eyeballs in flames, Mr. Larson, and I can get you out of here even though Strike Three . . . Strike Three was the real deal." She reached for the last folder. "Not twenty-five to life real, but real enough. What were you thinking, the insurance company wouldn't want its money back?"

"*Gabby*! You didn't read about Gabby?"

She ran a fingernail across the table.

"Ovarian cancer. After what happened to your wife? The same cancer? I cried when I read that, a single woman in her twenties with a four-year-old. I actually cried. You and your family got dealt a miserable hand. But other men get beaten down and don't go scamming insurance companies. Fifty thousand dollars is a lot of money. That was Strike Three, a real one, and you were *out*. I read the sentencing memo. The judge wanted no part of giving you twenty-five to life, but he had no choice. You got caught up in a bad law, and here we are ten years later. You should have been out by now, and I'm prepared to help. But you need to cooperate. You know how this goes: You have to give to get. Work with me."

"There was a clinic in Sweden that used an extract of—"

"I *understand* all that. If it was my daughter, I'd have gone to the ends of the earth, too, looking for a cure. You'd already mortgaged your house to fly your wife to Mexico for treatments when her chemo failed. And let me guess, big brother Dima wasn't much help. He had all his money tied up in . . . *business*." She spit the word. "So you made a false insurance claim."

"Baseball's a stupid sport."

"Excuse me?"

"If Abner Doubleday didn't make three strikes an out, I wouldn't even *be* here. Why not a four-strikes law, or six?"

"Testify against your brother," she called as I walked away. "I'm going to get him on tax evasion, and you know exactly where the money went. He's guilty of a lot more, but I can't prove sex trafficking yet."

She was right. She couldn't.

"It doesn't bother you he built a highway from Ukraine to your grocery to traffic girls? The Justice Department's aiming to shut down major trafficking rings. Your big brother's whoring teenagers, Mr. Larson. They're not much older than your granddaughter. Where's the outrage? My gut tells me you're a decent man."

"I used to be."

"I want him gone *now*. Testify for me and I'll get you custody of Grace. And for God's sake, get the child tested. If my mother and grandmother died of a bent BRCA gene, I'd want to know. It's the year 2000! There are things she can do. . . . Surgeries. If you don't take the deal, you'll die in here."

Not likely. I had her exactly where I wanted her.

Three: Grace Larson

An officer in a dark brown uniform, with a gun on his belt, showed me to a library at the courthouse and directed Mrs. Alcott to the room next door, where she was to meet for "the handoff" with a supervisor from the Department of Children and Families. It wasn't much of a library. People had carved their initials into the desk and bookshelves, and the law books looked about a hundred years old. Through a half-open door, I could see one leg of a chair and one of Mrs. Alcott's legs in her thick support hose and blocky shoe. On the floor beside her was a handbag with brass-button feet, sitting at attention like the good pet she wanted me to be.

Mrs. Alcott needed a daughter, but I was already someone else's daughter—or used to be. No matter how much I tried, I couldn't make my real mother go away even if I didn't remember her. On our very first day together, Mrs. Alcott asked me to call her *Mama*. Or *Ma*. Or *Mom*. "Anything along those lines, dear."

She was trying so hard. When I called her Mrs. Alcott, a wall went up between us.

I heard footsteps along the corridor before I saw a form take shape through the frosted glass of the door. I closed my eyes. When I opened them, there stood a grizzled old man whose last name and, apparently, blood I shared. No choirs sang. The clouds didn't part. My grandfather looked exactly like a bum rattling a paper cup for nickels. The skin below his eyes sagged. He had crooked, yellow teeth and dark blotches on his cheeks and hands. It was nearly painful to see him smiling, wanting to make a good impression. How was that even possible when he looked like he'd just taken a nap, underground, in a cemetery?

"Grace, is that you?"

I slumped in my chair, staring at my laptop. I'd taken a picture of myself and swapped it for the head of Ayala, The Princess Warrior—a game I'd built in the computer club after school. At that exact moment, I was rising above a battlefield thick with trolls bashing each other with axes.

"Grace?"

I peeked over the screen.

"Do you remember me?"

"No. Not really."

"Of course, you don't. You were so young the last time we met. Four years old." He eased himself into a chair using the armrests. "What's that?"

Seriously? At least Mrs. Alcott knew what a computer was. How was I supposed to go home with someone who didn't know a laptop from a typewriter? More mornings than not, I'd wake with the laptop still on my chest from playing games or programming the night before. I *lived* with my laptop.

A little countdown app I'd built flashed the number of days remaining until my freedom: 1,423—just shy of four years. On the morning of my eighteenth birthday, I would quit the foster care system forever. All I had to do was survive this ridiculous old man and all the other rental parents DCF threw my way once he returned me. What would I be stealing from him, I wondered.

"It's been a long time," he said. "I guess you've had a few homes."

"I guess."

"I've thought about you."

"Well, I forgot about you."

"Makes perfect sense. You're growing up to be so pretty!"

"*Don't* call me that."

Mr. Parker, the one who stank of cigarettes and breathed on my face when he tried kissing me goodnight, called me pretty. I was his pretty little love-bug pony rider. Come, sit on my lap, Grace. *Giddyup!* The perv.

"I can't compliment my own granddaughter? Is it okay to say you remind me of your mother? Same blond hair, hazel eyes. Same moxie."

The only thing left of my mother—aside from an image I couldn't shake of her dying in bed with tubes in her arms and neck—was a snip of her hair. She'd put some in an envelope and gave it to me once it started falling out from the treatments. I knew from photos that her eyes could look green one day and gray the next, depending on the light. In fact, we did look alike. That was the only piece left of her.

"Don't talk about my mother," I told him. "And I don't have *moxie*, whatever that is. You left. You just left."

"Not exactly. I got sent away. Maybe it's better we don't talk for a while?"

In the next room, Mrs. Alcott was winding up for a fight. I knew all the signs, first a question or two she really didn't want anyone answering: "To a criminal? An actual *convict*?" And then someone who was prepared to contradict her, which was usually my role. Another voice, just as determined, answered: "A former convict, Mrs. Alcott. He's served his time, he's rehabilitated. That's why it's called a penitentiary. In any event, it's out of my hands."

"*Former* only because someone wheeled and dealed to get him out of jail. Who decided that she should go to him? And if it's out of your hands, then point me to somebody who *can* talk. I demand to know—"

"Ma'am, with all due respect, no one owes you an explanation."

My grandfather rapped the table with his knuckles. "Do you like stories, Grace?"

Stories. Stories? Coming on the heels of the storm gathering in the next room, he may as well have asked if I liked water parks or french fries with mayonnaise. I couldn't have heard him right. I was okay losing Mrs. Alcott. But trading her in for this?

"I most certainly *do* deserve an explanation! I cared for this child. I still care!"

"Grace? What about stories?"

"What? Sure. Everybody likes stories."

"Mrs. Alcott, I can assure you we all have the child's best interests at heart."

"Here, Grace. The story's *here.*" He rapped the table again. "I want to tell you about an uncle of mine. He was a gifted magician, and he made his way around the world performing and searching for magic. He devoted his life to it and wound up in Mongolia. This would have been before the Chinese revolution. He lived in yurts on the high plateaus, and he worked with the herders tending sheep and goats. It took him fifteen years before he made his way back to Boston, and he'd seen some amazing things. He sat me down one day and asked if I wanted to see his mystery coins. I have them now. Do you want to see?"

In the next room, Mrs. Alcott banged on a table, and through the open door I could see her standing—really going to bat for me. I was beginning to feel bad about stealing her rolling pin. My grandfather cleared his throat and when I turned back to him, he was holding a red velvet bag with a braided drawstring. He jangled the little bag, and the coins inside clinked. He spread them on the table. I studied them, without a clue what I was looking at. "Before he died, my uncle gave them to me, along with several other tricks from all over the world. I always liked these coins the best. They're ancient, you know. Very rare."

They were etched with strange markings. Who knew? Maybe goat herders *had* made them. I felt the old man's eyes on me. For about a year men had been turning their heads as I walked down the street. Some whistled. Some said things that reminded me of Mr. Parker. My grandfather wasn't staring that way. He concentrated all his attention on my eyes, and he gave me no chance not to watch him.

With a lightning move, he swept the coins from the table and counted them off, one . . . two . . . three . . . and four. He took one and dropped it into his shirt pocket, where I heard it jingle against a paper clip or a key. Then he made a fist around the three remaining coins. "If you use your imagination," he said, "you can feel and maybe see how the coin will fly away from my pocket and come back to my hand. Tell me, why would a coin do this?"

"Coins don't *do* anything," I said.

"These coins do. They're brothers."

"They're not alive. How could they—"

"Good question! They were minted on the same day seven hundred years ago by high priests way up in the mountains. They poured liquid metal at four thousand degrees into identical molds, then made strange markings on them. Mind you, these people spent every night studying the stars."

I thought he might be crazy.

"They etched everything they knew about everything: stars, mountains, sheep, goats—all these strange markings you see here. Only the herders understand that language, but they taught it to my uncle. All their wisdom. The coins share what's known as coin blood, and they will *not* be separated. Watch the attraction. *Watch me!*" With a knobby finger, he traced an arc through the air from his pocket to his fist, making a whistling sound. When right hand touched left, he opened his fist and counted off one . . . two . . . three . . . and *four* coins.

"But you *took* one!" I said. "I saw you."

"Exactly."

"What's the trick?"

"Sorry. Only if you become a—"

"What a phony. That coin didn't float through the air. You hid it."

"If you're so smart, you try."

He placed the coins in my hand, and the moment I began counting, he stopped me.

"You need a story," he said. "Patter. You can't just start counting coins and expect things to work."

"It's what you did. You counted out—"

"No, I told you about my uncle."

"Who cares?"

"If I didn't tell you about him and the goat herders in Mongolia, then it would have just been a trick. No yurts, no mountains, no stars. People forget tricks, but they remember magic. There's a difference."

I looked around for the court officer. I wanted to go back to Mrs. Alcott.

"Well?"

"Well, what?"

"You need a story."

I counted the coins in my hand and mumbled four words.

"What's that? I didn't hear you."

I mumbled again, louder. "I said *mother, father, daughter, son.*"

"Excellent! What about them?"

"The father went to war and got killed." I took one of the coins and moved it to my pocket. Then I did what the old man had done: I clenched a fist around the remaining three coins so hard I could see my knuckles. "The mother and her children cried. They went to a priest, who said, 'Abracadabra, he's come back to you.' The mother said, 'Dead people don't come back.' The priest said, 'They do this time. Go and see for yourself.' So they went home, and there he was."

I opened my fist and counted out the coins: one . . . two . . . three . . . *four.*

Four? How did I do that?

He examined my hands, front and back. He looked between my fingers, then into my eyes. "You have a gift," he concluded, leveling his stare at me. He was very serious. "If I gave this trick to a thousand strangers walking down the street, maybe two or three would end up with all four coins in their hands—after ten or more tries. You did it in one. You've got a gift."

He dropped the coins in the pouch and slid them across the table.

"Yours, my dear."

"I'm *not* your dear," I said, unable to summon much heat. When I looked to the next room, Mrs. Alcott was gone.

A woman entered the library and delivered a large envelope with papers to be signed. "I need your signature here, here, and here, Mr. Larson. Fill in the date here. May eighth." She turned to me. "Hello, Grace."

She flipped her business card onto the table with a look of total disgust, as if she didn't want to risk touching him. "I'm Jacqueline Roberts," she said. "Your case manager. And I don't mind saying this whole business stinks. Am I being clear enough? I don't know what you did to get custody of this child, but it stinks of backroom dealing. I had the US attorney's office calling, a clerk for a federal judge calling, and somebody on a special crime task force from Washington. These people never get involved in my work, but for you the phone didn't stop ringing. I've been in this business for thirty years. I've seen everything—except this. What did it take for you to get custody of this child?"

"I'm not a child."

"Your first mistake is your last," she continued. "Then she's DCF's. Just so you know."

"I am *not* a child!"

"Of course, you aren't. Anyone can see that."

She was tall and thick. She had beautiful copper skin and wore gold bangles on her wrist. She had an accent and smelled of jasmine.

"Mr. Larson, you call and check in every Monday morning. I'll be keeping a log. I'll also be visiting—sometimes announced, sometimes not. I can tell you from the start, I'm not happy about this traveling magic show of yours. School's over in six weeks, then you're taking Grace on the road for the better part of July and August? She's maturing now and there are considerations. For instance, how many rooms will you have?"

What magic show? No one told me about a magic show.

He held up a finger. "One room is what I can afford."

"You and a fourteen-year-old in the same motel room? Not even close. Two rooms."

He nodded.

"And what about conversations a young woman might need to have?"

He had no idea what she was talking about. Miss Roberts handed me a card. "You call when you need to talk," she said. "Really, don't you think a part-time job here in Boston would be better? I'll leave you with a brochure that lists several programs. You could be with children your own age. Do Service Corp, maybe—you know, volunteer work."

The truth was I wanted to learn more magic tricks since I had such a gift. I looked at the lady. "You said two rooms, right?"

She collected the papers and stuffed them into a file. "Monday mornings," she said, pointing us to the exit. "Call. Think of me as your parole officer. One slip and you're history. Need me to write that down for you?"

When we reached the courthouse parking lot, he apologized. "I should have told you straight off about the summer, but I wanted to meet you first. School's out soon and I thought we'd have ourselves a little adventure. I've booked a traveling magic show through some beautiful country—starting in New Hampshire, up through Vermont to Willoughby and Canaan, all the way to the Northeast Kingdom. We'll end up not even five miles from Canada—way, way up there."

"You weren't going to ask me, were you?"

He didn't answer.

"You *weren't*. You'd decided everything without me."

"It takes a long time to set up a tour, Grace. I wrote more than a hundred letters from prison. I had to start before we met. I promise it'll be fun."

"What if I said *no*?"

"I figured you'd say *yes*. In any event, I need an apprentice. Before I advertise for the job, I thought I'd ask you. Interested?"

I pretended to think it over.

"What would I have to do?"

He explained, and none of it was very exotic. I'd help set up and take down props. Carry stuff. Also help with one very difficult trick, an escape. He did offer one carrot though. Free magic lessons. As many tricks as I cared to learn.

I agreed.

With all the fuss Mrs. Alcott was making and with Miss Roberts barking so much, I'd forgotten about the coin I'd put in my pocket. I fished it out. "Wait a minute," I said. "There are *five* coins. It *was* a trick!"

He grinned.

"The coins in the bag aren't the same thickness. The thickest one was actually *two* coins, and when I squeezed my fist, it separated. It wasn't *real* magic!"

"It was," he said.

"Tell me one thing about it that was real."

He touched my cheek with a knobby finger and said: "The look on your face when you counted out the fourth coin. That was real."

Four: Nate Larson

The Department of Children and Families would never release a teenager to someone living in the motel I'd called home the first month after my release. I went to work on the problem the first day out and applied to rent thirteen furnished apartments in and around Boston. But every time, the landlords denied me when they learned I was coming straight from prison. It probably wasn't legal what they did, but they knew no one was taking anyone to court. I needed a place fast, and at the last possible moment I met Frank Maloney. He'd posted an ad in the Arlington *Advocate*. The *Globe* hadn't been much help, so I went to each town's local paper and found the place on Marathon Street just a block off of Mass Ave—a two-family, the rental unit on top. I called ahead to explain about FCI Danbury, just to get that out of the way so I wouldn't be wasting my time. When I was done, Frank told me he had a cousin who'd been sent to the state lockup at Walpole.

"Which means I'll listen," he said. "At least we can talk."

When he greeted me at the door, I felt like a midget. Frank Maloney was not just a large man—a former dock worker, half-foot taller and a hundred pounds heavier than I was. He was a Gibraltar of a man. I could also tell that his size was the least impressive thing about him. Frank listened when I

spoke, never interrupting. He chuckled when he scanned my
rental application and read the section labeled "Employment
History." The form left twelve or so blank lines, waiting to be
filled in with company names, pertinent dates, and phone
numbers. I'd scrawled *Guest of the Federal Government* across
the form. When I saw he appreciated my sense of humor,
I told him everything—not only about my years at Danbury
but about the years running the grocery in Somerville with
my brother. I also explained the deal I'd cut with the Feds,
since the monthly checks they'd be sending would cover my
rent.

He heard me out and wanted to make sure he understood:
"You mean you're going to testify against your own brother?"
He waited a few moments to digest that then asked what Dima
had done that was so awful.

"The charge is tax evasion," I answered.

Frank wasn't a lawyer, but he had the instincts of one. "Tax
evasion? *Tax* evasion? Shorting the government every April is
a national sport. Unless he hid millions, it couldn't be just tax
evasion. What did he really do?"

At that point I was grateful Hunt had brought the charge
she thought she could prove rather than the one she wanted
to bring, human trafficking. I doubt my prospective landlord
would have been so understanding about that.

"The Feds used tax evasion to get Al Capone. Your brother's not a mobster, is he?"

This time I lied and told him I only knew what I was told.
It was clear Frank had doubts, but he said nothing when he
realized we were getting to sensitive territory, which made me
respect him all the more because he was going to be my landlord, not my priest, and he knew the difference. He sized me
up the way a rancher might inspect a horse at auction. "I'm
almost convinced," he said, finally. "But tell me something.

You wrote on the application you're a professional magician. Is that true?"

I nodded. "Learned in prison. Going on tour this summer."

"That's a new one," he said. "I've heard of guys who got their high school diploma behind bars. I read about one man who became a Muslim priest. But magic? You'd better do a trick for me, Mr. Larson. You know, prove it. Fool me and the apartment's yours."

He was serious.

"That's a lot to hang on one trick," I said. "Sometimes tricks fall apart."

"Let's hope yours doesn't."

"So if my application read *trumpet player,* you'd have made me play?"

"What I'm saying is that I need to know you are what you say you are. If you lied about that, you could lie about anything. You don't have a work history. There's no one to call for references. How else do I check you out?"

I never went anywhere without a deck of cards or a few coins in my pockets. That way, I could practice while I waited in line at a store or when I was stopped in traffic. People who meet magicians are always asking them to perform, so Frank hardly surprised me with the request. What got my attention was the size of the bet he was willing to place. The apartment was already mine. He just didn't know it yet.

I produced a deck and fanned the cards with a little flourish to whet his appetite. When I said, "Pick a card," his radar switched on. Like most people, he couldn't resist the dare of those three words. Once Frank picked a card, he was a goner.

"Study it," I said.

He studied it.

"Can we agree I haven't seen or touched your card?"

We agreed.

"Okay, then. Return the card to the deck anywhere you like. I'll close my eyes."

Done.

"Now I want you to write down the number and the suit of your card on a scrap of paper. I want you to fold that scrap in half and slip it into your shirt pocket. Again, I'll look away so I can't read the motion of your hands."

We were seated in his living room, a coffee table between us, and I chose this particular trick because I knew he'd have to cross the room and go to a desk or go into another room for paper and pencil. Either way, he'd turn his back on me. Sure enough, he pushed himself out of his chair and went to a hutch, five or six paces away, and opened a drawer. This gave me the seconds I needed. He returned, grinning as he folded a piece of paper and slipped it into his shirt pocket.

Frank thought he had me. At my invitation, he shuffled five or six times then cut the deck. When he was done, I spread the cards facedown on the table in such a way that by flipping the first card in line I could push through the deck and flip the next fifty-one until they all showed, faceup. It's a nice little effect. I marched my fingers down the line of cards, past the three of clubs, then reverse-marched back to the three.

I asked him to unfold his piece of paper.

"Son of a *gun*! How did you—?"

"Let's sign the rental agreement, Mr. Maloney."

"Call me Frank. I was going to rent it to you anyway. Maybe you *could* make a living off this stuff. How'd you do it?"

I told him what I tell everyone, because everyone asks: "Can you keep a secret?"

"Sure."

"So can I."

I crossed my arms.

"Ha! Come off it. What's the trick?"

"You really want to know?" I lowered my voice, and he leaned close. "God talks to me," I whispered. "The magic just happens somehow. I wake up in the morning and I see things. I let my mind relax and I hear things. I can't explain it."

"And I'm the Pope. Do it again."

"Can't. Come to my show in July—the start of my tour—and you'll see much more."

As we were signing the lease, he asked if I thought Grace would have any interest in walking their dog before and after school, for twenty-five dollars a week. I agreed without knowing what she'd say because I needed to keep the man happy—which meant *I'd* walk the dog if it came to it. He took me back to the kitchen and gave me two sets of keys, one to my apartment and one to his. "I'm not stupid," he said when I hesitated. "If anything goes missing, I'll tell the cops I've got an ex-con living upstairs. So whether or not you steal from me, you'd better hope no one else does because all fingers will be pointing at you. The keys are for Grace when she walks Lucy."

I liked this man.

A block from the house, I pulled into a lot and squared the loose cards I'd slipped back into my pocket. I tapped them on my leg, then on the dash, and worked them into their sleeve. From my other pocket I took the second deck I'd used, its back patterned identically to the first. I squared those and slipped them into their sleeve. The second deck had fifty-two cards, ace through king, four suits; the first deck, fifty-two cards—every one a three of clubs. It was a C-level trick, maybe C+. It might puzzle Frank for a night or two. But soon enough he'd come knocking at my door and we'd have a good laugh.

— • —

ON THE Sunday before I was to take custody of Grace, I was napping, struggling to push a dead weight off my chest in a closed, dark room when Frank called. What a mercy to be shaken from that dream: thrown into a hole with blood and smoke and guns, a grown man crying, then gurgling, then silent.

"You told me you didn't have any friends," Frank said over the phone. "There's a guy down here who disagrees. He just knocked on my door."

At the downstairs landing I had to stare a few moments to be sure it was Bobby Bianchi chatting up my landlord. If I looked thirty years older for the decade I'd spent in prison, Bianchi looked like someone had kidnapped him, plugged a live air hose into his ear, and walked away. He'd been hand-some once. Now his lips and pug nose were set in a soggy marshmallow of a face with two chins and a third on the way. A sizable gut hung over his belt. Still, in all that tonnage I saw signs of the man I knew, mainly in the scrapes on his knuckles. Bobby could tell a joke but had a temper. He could butcher a side of beef with cleavers and then, one careful snip at a time, prune the bonsai tree we kept in the front window of the grocery.

When he saw me, he bounced a little on the balls of his feet, grinning. He'd lost none of his charm or Sumo quickness. His hair was still thick and black, his eyes still the color of sharkskin. Despite the weight, he looked good and had come bearing gifts: a casserole in one arm and a neatly wrapped package, the size of a shoebox, in the other.

"Hey, Nate!"

"I'll take it from here, Frank. Appreciate it."

I pointed him upstairs and followed, noting the upgrade to his wardrobe. He used to wear sweat suits. Now he wore crisp khakis and a long-sleeved shirt with a little graphic over the breast of a jaunty green pepper with pencil arms and legs, winking and giving a thumbs-up sign. Embroidered beneath:

The Green Grocer. So now we had a logo? We shook hands
again, embraced again, and came close to sniffing and circling
the way dogs do. He surveyed my little apartment and took a
deep breath. "Goddamn," he said. "It smells like 1960 in here.
My grandmother had a couch just like that. Don't tell me the
doilies are yours."

In fact, I was grateful for any such touches of home, even
the doilies and the crocheted welcome mat at the landing. Compared to prison, my apartment was a palace, and I wasn't complaining though I was nervous about what Grace would think.
To a fourteen-year-old I imagined the place would feel like
some saddle-backed motel. The chairs and tables were scuffed
and bony. The stuffing had gone mostly flat in the couch. The
beds sagged. The wallpaper in *every* room had little blue wind-
mills. And at the windows Lola, Frank's wife, had hung lace
curtains to match the doilies—sewed them herself. I'd spent
three frantic days trying to make the apartment presentable to
a teenage girl, as if I had an idea what that meant. Aside from
painting her bedroom and the bathroom, I was lost.

Bobby handed me the casserole: "Just a little something to
celebrate your freedom. Tuna-noodle, with condensed Campbell's cream of mushroom soup for the glue, plus onion rings
for a little crunch. It's my go-to dinner since the wife left. You
got a microwave? You plop a few spoonfuls of this into a bowl,
nuke it, and you got yourself a meal. You got vegetables—
mushrooms. Carbs—noodles. And all the protein you need
in the tuna, plus dairy. I use whole cream. Doesn't taste right
without it. In a pinch you can live on tuna-noodle casserole.
I read they found some of this stuff in King Tut's tomb. Ha!"

He dropped himself onto the couch and propped a foot
on the coffee table. "You got iced tea? Some chips and dip
maybe?"

I handed him a plastic cup and pointed toward the sink.

Dima and I had hired Bobby when I was convicted of insurance fraud and was awaiting sentencing. We needed a reliable number two at the store, someone who was willing to look the other way when business took my brother to Eastern Europe and especially when he returned with young women. Anyone we hired would need to overlook the details of Dima's business dealings, which meant we were likely to interview people who preferred not to talk much about their past. Dima and I were seated on a bench outside the store one day when this barrel-chested bruiser came rumbling across the street. He unfolded the page he'd ripped from the *Globe's* Help Wanted section, compared the address on the storefront to the circled address in the ad, then glared at us as if he were picking a fight.

"You know anything about a job?"

He wouldn't say much about his work experience except that he'd been a "produce specialist" in New York and had come to Boston in a hurry. "For the schools," he added. "I got a daughter." He insisted we pay him in cash—no taxes, no social security withholdings, no paper trail. That was fine with us. "Hire me," he said, "and I'll work like a horse."

In fact, Bobby worked like a team of horses, and he certainly knew his produce. He could trim crates of romaine lettuce or savoy cabbage in no time, setting up appealing displays. He could stack peppers into pyramids so neat that Dima had to ask him to be a bit less careful because people didn't want to buy any and wreck the symmetry. That was the bright side. He could also send people running with his temper. Two weeks into the job, some kid in a stocking mask tried holding up the store. Bobby happened to be behind the counter, sipping a fresh, steaming cup of coffee. He threw the coffee in the kid's face, jumped the counter, and beat on his knees with a crowbar until Dima came running from the meat locker and pulled him off. I doubted that kid would ever walk again. Yet this same man insisted we sell hand-cut flowers, arguing that they sent a clear message to our customers that The Green Grocer understood the word *fresh*. Truly, he was a rose in a fisted glove.

Bobby still hadn't let go of his box.

"What's up with Dima?" I asked. "I can't get through to him. I'm heading over there tomorrow."

"What's up with Dima is that he got old. He's doing about as well as you might expect after hearing his brother was going to testify for Eleanor Hunt. Maybe that's why he won't pick up the phone. Why would you send your own brother to prison?"

"I'll explain tomorrow, when I see him."

"No, you won't. Our lawyers are worried it'll look like witness tampering, the two of you together. You're working for the enemy now, bud. Suppose you went missing before the trial. Their star witness. How would it look?"

I pulled up a chair.

"Relax, you dope. I'm not testifying against Dima or anyone."

"We heard you signed—"

"I *did* sign! Why am I *not* going to sign? Don't tell me you thought I was actually going to sell you guys out. I'll run to Canada in August, before the trial starts. I'll be in northern Vermont. Canada's just a few miles away. I've got the maps. Give me a little credit, Bobby."

"I *knew* it! In that case, here's another present."

He produced an envelope and slid it across the coffee table. "From Maxim Petrov, who's . . . working with us now." I peeked inside and found a brick of hundred-dollar bills.

"That's fifty thousand dollars. Maxim's going to be happy with the news you're leaving. No one wants this trial. He wants you to take this money and leave now. Go set yourself up somewhere."

"Who's Petrov?"

"Let's call him a partner. You were gone. We needed help."

"What kind of help?"

"The kind that matters."

Bobby rubbed his thumb across his fingertips.

"And no one bothered to—?"

"Maybe you forgot, bud. They sent you off for a minimum of twenty-five. Even you figured you were leaving the lockup in a box. Dima wasn't as strong after you left. The store was failing. We either needed to close or take in money to update so we could compete with the newer, bigger stores. I approached a guy I knew in New York. He comes from a connected family— the Petrovs of Brighton Beach. He asked me to tell you to take the envelope and have a good life. His exact words."

"Some guy I never met wants to give me fifty thousand dollars? What's he want?"

"That's not fair. Maxim's generous to his friends."

I slid the envelope back across the table. "Tell him to go bang his head on a curb. Use those exact words."

Bobby stared at the table.

"Nah. I don't think so. If you leave now, Hunt's case falls apart. No one bothers your brother, no one starts poking into our business."

I stood. "Thanks for the visit, Bobby. Tell Dima I'll see him soon."

"Are you hearing me?"

"Are you hearing *me*? I'm spending the summer with my granddaughter doing magic tricks. We're going on a little tour, and we're going to have a good time. Then I'll go to Canada on my schedule, not Petrov's. I don't know the guy, and I don't want his money. Why should I let him own me?"

Bobby tucked the envelope in a pocket and handed me the box. "Nate, you really should be thinking this one over. But if it's your final word, Maxim wants you to have a little something anyway. He's that kind of guy. And don't worry, it's not a bomb."

I slid the box back across the table. "Take it with you. I've got no interest in knowing this guy."

"Too late for that. He's in the family now."

Bobby slid the box back to me and lumbered to his feet. "Throw it away for all I care. I can't take it back. Hey, it's good to see you. I mean it, and I'm glad you're running. It's not right you should testify against your brother."

Halfway down the stairs, he paused and turned. "Everything changed after you went away. Listen to me. This Wednesday, don't show for your meeting at DCF. Don't take custody of the kid. You don't know her yet. Ditch her while it's easy."

"How did you know I was getting her on Wednesday?"

"Nate," he said, "I'm begging you to leave."

Five: Grace Larson

The house on Marathon Street had flower beds in front and to one side, a driveway to the other. I'd lived in cute little houses before, where the lawn was mowed and the trash barrels were tucked neatly away. Which revealed nothing about the foster parents who lived there, aside from the fact they liked things clean and neat. Which can be a curse. Try keeping your bedroom looking like an ad from a magazine all the time. I gripped my suitcase and computer bag, my heart banging as we approached the front stairs because I wasn't sure I could do it again, live in yet another home with yet another stranger. Did it even make sense to try when I had just four years left in the system? What if he turned out to be like Mr. Parker? I could do this only one way, which was to pull a curtain over my life and show him nothing aside from a polite *Yes, sir* and *No thank you, sir.*

"We'll be living upstairs," he said. "Our landlords live on the first floor, so you can't play loud music or have drunken parties."

"I don't drink. You thought I drank?"

"It was a joke, Grace. The Maloneys are nice people. They have a dog, Lucy. You like dogs?"

"Mrs. Alcott had a schnauzer. I hated that thing."

Upstairs, he walked me straight to the kitchen table, where he pointed to one of the few things he'd brought from prison: a checkerboard painted very carefully on an oil cloth. "In jail, people have lots of time on their hands," he said. "Mostly, I did three things: I played checkers, I read, and I practiced magic."

I was staring at a gift-wrapped box on the counter.

"A present? You got me *another* gift?" I immediately wondered what he wanted from me. None of my rental parents had ever done that. He was setting me up. Once again, I thought of Mr. Parker.

"Sorry," he said. "It's mine. I forgot to throw it away."

He dropped the box into the trash can. "I don't like the person who arranged for me to get this. Checkers is more interesting."

"You're not going to open it?"

"I'm not. But here's what I will do. Every night you and I will play checkers, and the winner gets to choose carryout dinner. I don't cook. And unless you do . . ."

I was still eyeing the trash can.

He pointed to two bowls beside the oilcloth: one with whole, shelled peanuts and the other with halves. "House rules," he said. "You eat the peanuts you jump, and winner chooses takeout. Up the street we've got Chinese, burgers, pizza, falafel, and something called Tandoori."

That year, we'd spent a week on a checkers unit in math. Our class would meet in a lab where we played checkers on a computer. My teacher must have seen some talent in me and suggested I join the computer club, which was how the school came to loan me a laptop. I'd even built my own version of checkers on it. That meant I had to write rules and strategies of the game into a computer program. And *that* meant I had to study those rules and strategies—truly understand them. The old man didn't have a chance.

I opened the fridge, which was empty save for crusty squeeze-bottles of ketchup and yellow mustard, a half-eaten package of bologna, and a quart of milk. The cupboards were empty too—not a single box of pasta or cereal, though he did have paper plates and napkins and a plastic bowl with crimped packets of salt and pepper.

He took a seat at one end of the checkerboard. I sat opposite, elbows on the table and chin on my fists. "We'll need soy sauce," I told him, making the first move.

"Why's that?"

"Because I'm going to embarrass you. And when I do, I'm ordering Chinese."

— • —

I MET the Maloneys and Lucy that first evening, when they returned home from work. Lola had a government job with the Social Security Administration. Frank worked at the docks in Charlestown. She was a sliver of a woman, smaller still when standing beside her husband. He must have played football in high school. She didn't even come up to his shoulders. Then there was Lucy. All that dog wanted in life was to yap and lick my face. After we stepped into their kitchen, as my grandfather was making introductions, Lucy dragged a leash across the room, dropped it at my feet, and began pushing at my leg with a wet nose. Lola was nearly as excited to have a real, live teenager living upstairs. She fussed over me and wouldn't let me call her Mrs. Maloney. She promised to bake any kind of cookies I liked. She told me how pretty I was, and the way she said it left me no room to snap at her because she *meant* it and was so happy to have another "gal" around. It all felt so new and strange, how happy they were. "If you like to garden," she said, "I've got extra gloves. I grow flowers, snap peas, and green beans. See this thumb? You can't tell for looking, but it's *green*, dear. I can grow anything. Do you like to garden?"

"I never have, Ma'am. Not really."

"Stop with *Ma'am*. I can teach you how to garden as long as you're willing to get dirty. You mind dirt? What about cookies? I make chocolate chip, oatmeal raisin, snickerdoodles. What's your favorite?"

"I'm watching my weight, Mrs.—"

"Please. It's *Lola!*"

All this time, Lucy was nosing my leg.

My grandfather enjoyed the fuss they made over me. "You'd think they'd never met a teenager," he said. The short climb winded him, and that night, our first night, he went to bed early. He looked exhausted, and his skin was even blotchier then before. Rental parents went to hospitals and died like everyone else, I knew. When you moved in to a new place, you looked for signs. When it happened, DCF would send a van to haul us back to the dormitory in South Boston. Even without major health problems, rental parents were quick to send us packing. They'd get a bad cold or a migraine and decide they didn't want to deal with us, that we weren't worth the few hundred bucks the state sent them every month.

I knew right away I could use my grandfather's shaky health to my advantage. If for whatever reason I wanted to leave, I could call Miss Roberts and say he was too old and wobbly to care for me. It would only take a word—any small lie would do, maybe that he nodded off at red lights or forgot to kill the flame on the kitchen stove every once in a while. I kept that plan in my back pocket, expecting the worst because that's what life usually served up.

On the positive side, I had my own room and a connection to the Internet. Frank was big on progress and believed everyone, everywhere should be connected to the web. So that evening, I played computer games at the kitchen table, relieved that when the old man said goodnight he didn't try kissing me or parade around the apartment bare-chested, in boxer shorts, like Mr. Parker. Thirty minutes after the light went off in his room, I poked at the box he'd thrown away. It was nearly killing me not to know what was inside. Gifts were precious things, and I didn't understand how he could just throw this one away.

Lola heard me as I tiptoed down the front stairs, so I could open the box somewhere in private. I didn't know who in the house slept soundly or would wake and find me out. Or even care. I wasn't happy to find her standing in the foyer in her housecoat, waiting. "You okay, dear?" I felt like a burglar.

"Are you spying on me?"

"I heard a noise . . . I just made chocolate chip cookies to leave for you in the morning when you walk Lucy. Want to have one with me while they're warm? New carton of milk too. I didn't wash the spatula yet, but you'd have to fight Frank for the dough."

From somewhere in the living room behind her he called. "Hi there, Grace. Where you going?" He stepped to the door and rested a hand on her shoulder. Three or four of Lola could have fit inside him.

She glanced at her watch and glanced at the box in my arms. Frank was about to say something else and she stepped on his foot. They followed me to the porch, and I walked far down the street and sat on the curb by a parked car, just beyond the wash of a street lamp. When she thought I was out of hearing range, she said, "You do *not* ask teenagers nosy questions. You let whatever she has to tell us come out on its own. Over cookies. Were you ever fourteen—or did you skip that year?"

I rattled the box, which weighed no more than a pound. I heard something, or rather many little somethings, shifting inside. It sounded like chattering or rustling, the noise dry leaves make on a sidewalk, in the wind. I peeled back the tape with my fingernails and carefully removed the gift wrapping—pictures of baseballs and baseball gloves and bats. Little boy wrapping. Thin as it was, the wrapping had blocked a sweet smell. Chocolates? Or maybe my favorite, fresh-dipped strawberries.

Remembering what the old man said about the person who gave him the gift, I slid the box off my lap. At a full arm's length, I raised the lid an inch, another inch, and two more. Then, sensing movement, I jumped away. The next thing I knew I was bent over the curb, throwing up the dumplings I'd eaten for dinner. *Cockroaches?* There could have been a hundred, maybe a thousand. They scrambled in every direction, and I threw up again when I got a good look at what they were eating: a piece of rancid meat.

I stumbled and gagged. I brushed off my clothes like a crazy person to make sure I wouldn't carry any bugs into the house. I brushed my teeth to wash away acid in my mouth and took a long, hot shower. Who could have done this? And who was my grandfather to even *know* such people?

Bleary-eyed and dressed in my uniform at seven o'clock, I waited for him to drive me to the Cathedral School. He rose early, and by the time I was ready he'd taken the trash to the curb and would have noticed the gift-wrapped box was gone. He was old but he wasn't stupid. He'd seen the circles under my eyes. I would have bitten his head off if he asked what happened. But like Lola, he said nothing.

Six: Nate Larson

Three days after my granddaughter moved in, I made a mistake that nearly ran her right out of the house, back to DCF. I'd had years in prison to mourn my wife and daughter and contemplate the cancer that took them both. Eleanor Hunt got my attention when she called after me at the end of our first interview. There are tests, she said. Surgeries. A woman would always want to know her odds. I'd been locked away for a long time and some categories of news, like advances in medical technology, had slipped down a black hole. So it was a surprise to learn that there was, indeed, a test that could settle whether or not Grace had inherited a mutated gene from her mother and grandmother.

I didn't want to scare the child. If I asked outright to swab her cheek for DNA, what would I say? "Oh, it's just a little something to learn whether or not you'll die young and in pain"? I was not being sentimental. At the end of August I'd be running to Canada, alone, in order to sink Hunt's case against my brother. Just the same, I wanted Grace to have accurate news. I wasn't any sort of grandfather to her and never would be. But I could still do the right thing.

The prison library gave me access to journal articles so complicated I had to read with a medical dictionary beside me.

Eventually I discovered that women with the BRCA1 mutation whose close relatives died of related cancers had a high risk of developing cancer themselves and should be tested.

By the time of my release, the test for BRCA1 had been available for several years, so I ordered a kit that consisted of a cotton swab, a plastic tube with a screw-top cap, and a mailer. I made my mistake on the third morning.

Grace told me she liked sleeping in on weekends and that I shouldn't wake her before noon. That first Saturday morning proved her right. She woke at eleven, so on Sunday I rose at six, figuring that would be safe, and set the DNA kit on the kitchen table. I found an unwashed glass she'd used the night before, with dinner, and prepared the test. Just as I was swabbing the rim of the glass, I looked up and found her standing at the edge of the kitchen.

"What are you doing up?" I asked.

"I had to go to the bathroom. What are *you* doing?"

I stuttered. She walked over to the table and read a few lines of the instruction sheet I was following.

"You're testing my DNA?"

She waited.

I said nothing.

"Why?"

I wouldn't tell her the truth. At fourteen, she didn't need a *maybe* hanging over her neck while she waited for test results.

"You're testing to see if I'm really your granddaughter, aren't you? You want to make sure before you go to all the trouble of taking care of me. What? DCF's not paying you enough to get me off their hands? What kind of sick jerk are you? Rental parents—you people are the worst!"

"Grace—"

"I'm leaving."

"It's not that. I promise."

"Like your promise means anything? I've known you two days!"

She stood before me with bare feet, in a T-shirt and pajama bottoms, her hair a mess, her eyes red. I was caught in a time warp. This was Gabrielle, my daughter, standing before me, furious at whatever teenagers get furious about every other day. "I know you're my granddaughter," I stammered. "It's not that."

She crossed her arms.

Out of the blue, a word, a name, formed on my lips and rescued me. "Remember that uncle I was telling you about," I said, giving myself a few seconds to improvise. "The one who gave me the coins?"

She said nothing.

"He told me that going way, way back, he and Houdini shared a great-great-grandfather in Eastern Europe. That made them cousins."

"This is stupid."

"No. Wait. If Houdini was my great-great-somebody's cousin, that makes him my cousin. You probably know more about DNA than I do, but your mother got half her DNA from me, which means you have a chance, possibly, of sharing DNA with Houdini. I was going to get you tested and surprise you with the news, if it was positive. I'm sneaking around now because I didn't want you to get your hopes up and then be disappointed. As a magician, I take this relation to Houdini very seriously. Even with this attitude of yours, he just *might* have been your relation too. Wouldn't that be useful to know? You can believe me or not. But since we're just getting to know each other, what *do* you believe in?"

"I believe in my eighteenth birthday."

"Very clever. And why's that?"

"Because that's when I can walk out on you and DCF and everyone else!"

"Terrific. Now I've waited too long to take a proper DNA sample, so this test is ruined. I paid two hundred dollars. Thanks for nothing," I said. "Now you'll never know."

I dropped the swab and the mailer in the trash as she stormed back into her room.

"I don't care about Houdini!" she yelled.

But I still did. I made a note to call an old friend.

— • —

THE GREEN Grocer that I helped my brother build was a clean, simple neighborhood store where people could shop instead of climbing into their cars and driving thirty minutes to a supermarket. We knew our customers and knew our inventory. Fresh vegetables, fresh fruit, fresh seafood, fresh meat and cheeses: we were the grocers down the street you could depend on for quality and convenience at a fair price. We were on a first-name basis with our neighbors. We cared about their kids and remembered to ask after elders who'd fallen ill.

Bobby was right about one thing: the world had changed— at least the immediate world around the store. The triple-deckers that had cramped us in were now gone, replaced by The Green Grocer's larger footprint and an expanded parking lot. Inside, the aisles were wider and the display cases newer. The lights were new, the shelving was new, and there was now a misting system that kept the produce looking as if someone had picked it that morning. Buying and tearing down the triple-deckers alone must have cost this Maxim Petrov fellow a fortune. Why would he have done that?

Bobby found me admiring the fresh fish, and he wasn't pleased.

"Nate! Didn't I tell you to stay away?"

"Look at this," I said, pointing. "It's hard to keep blue fish looking this good. Nice! And the rest of the place— everything's first-rate, Bobby. Congratulations."

"I told you that our lawyers told us to—"

"I don't really care. I came to see my brother."

"In that case, he's not here."

I doubted that. Dima used to work fourteen-hour days, starting at five each morning.

"I'll tell him you stopped by. I promise. Now go."

A thin man, my same height, approached. He carried a clipboard. He, too, wore khakis and a shirt embroidered with a smiling green pepper. The thin man must have noticed what, from a distance, looked like a disagreement. Bobby was always waving his hands when he got agitated.

"New customer, Bobby?"

Mostly he was smiling, but not his eyes.

"Maxim Petrov. Welcome to The Green Grocer. And you . . . must be Dima's brother. Great news that you won't be making that court date in August. Bobby told me all about it. But we shouldn't talk about that here. In fact, we shouldn't be talking at all, according to the lawyers."

"In the event something happened to me."

Petrov laughed. "What do you have in mind? I've got connections everywhere!"

"Nice job," I said. "I hardly recognize the place."

"My brothers and I run groceries just like this out of Brighton Beach, in New York. The concept is to go bigger than a Mom and Pop corner store but smaller than supermarkets. If it works in Queens and Brooklyn, why not Boston?"

Bobby had stepped aside as Petrov approached. The Bianchi I knew was not in the habit of making room for anyone, and I knew at once what was what. In prison, I'd met every sort of criminal: scammers, white collar crooks, leg breakers, rapists, pedophiles, and men who'd buy you coffee and then slit your throat because they thought your watch would look good on their wrist. About the only useful thing that came of my time at Danbury was knowing a player when I saw one. Old-school guys puffed out their chests and promised a quick settlement if you crossed them. That was Bobby. Petrov was a newer breed. He'd hold an elevator door for you, then let it close on your arm as he cut open your kidneys.

"I told him to stay away, Maxim, and here he is. You don't know Nate."

"I'm getting to!" said Petrov. "Relax. How could it be a problem to meet Dima's baby brother? We'll cut him a break, Bobby. A man goes to prison for ten years, he's not thinking straight. You've got to ease back in slowly, Nate. What you need is a little candy. Takes the edge off."

"How much?" I said.

"How much what?"

"How much did you leave for Dima? He used to own it all."

"The man's got no family. No kids to support."

"Bobby, I was asking Maxim."

Petrov leaned close and lowered his voice. "The Green Grocer was a dump, and your brother needed help. We put up plenty to buy those houses and tear them down, then rebuild. My family invested big-time, so maybe you should change your tone. You might even try thanking me."

"You didn't answer my question."

"Dima's set for his retirement, all expenses paid until he dies. He's hanging on, the old goat. He's costing me plenty. But I'm a fair man."

"What percentage did you take?"

"Are you listening? I *saved* his decrepit ass. He's out on the street without me."

A woman stepped behind us at the fish display, pushing a stroller. "The blue fish, please. A pound. No, make that a pound and a half. And a bag of ice to keep it cold, if you don't mind. I have some errands."

Petrov brightened and turned to greet her. "I picked that up from the pier this morning, Ma'am. That was caught off Cape Cod yesterday. You won't find fresher fish in the city." They chatted as the clerk weighed and wrapped her dinner. Off she strolled with her baby, another happy customer. Petrov had charmed her. I was stuck on *decrepit ass*.

"Wait here," he said. "Give me a minute."

Bobby looked like he needed blood pressure meds. When Petrov left, he was pinching the bridge of his nose. "Are you *trying* to pull his chain? I wanted to make peace between you two. The money in the envelope is still yours. Take it."

Dima's new partner returned with a young woman I'd seen on my first pass through the store. She'd been stocking the yogurt case, and I had paused a few yards away to consider how beautiful she was and what a gargoyle I'd become in my time away. She wasn't much older than twenty. I could have been her father. I could have been her grandfather.

"Sveta," said Petrov, "meet Dima's little brother. Nataniel, meet Sveta Zelenko. She's Dima's most recent arrival from Ukraine."

I felt ridiculous standing beside her. Somehow she saw past my age and extended a hand, looking directly at me—past the loose skin at my neck and the bags under my eyes and the weary decade I'd spent in prison. She said in very good, accented English: "If you're Dima's brother, you're my friend because Dima is my friend. I am most happy to meet you, Nataniel!"

"Got to love it," said Petrov. "Listen to that English. *Most happy*. She sounds like the queen."

"Of what?"

"I don't know. England. Sheba. Dima found her before things got bad with his brain. She's been here a year."

"I'm glad to meet you too," I said.

I turned to Bobby. "If Dima's so lost in his head, how could he have gone to Ukraine—"

"It was his last trip. Thirteen months ago . . . when he could still function."

"Tell you what," said Petrov. "I admire your brother's eye. Bobby tells me he always brought the best ones home. Smart, good-looking. He had a genius for it. Go on, get out of here you two. You're both from Ukraine, right? Go to lunch, drink vodka. I don't know, talk about the old country. *Nostrovia*, right?"

Petrov practically pushed us out the door. Sveta handed him her apron and asked that he keep her time card punched in. "Do this, Maxim," she said. "I don't want to lose my hours. I'm saving up for another class."

— • —

YOU DON'T have to live in prison very long before you understand how nasty the world can be. On leaving Danbury, I thought nothing could shock me. But when, not half a block from the grocery, Sveta, who looked as if she could have led a youth group into the mountains that morning, slid a hand up my thigh and pointed to the Somerville Motor Lodge, I jerked the car to the side of the road.

She thought I was parking so we could take our romp at the motel. She opened the door. "They charge by the hour," she said. "Maxim has an account. It's clean. They know me here."

I grabbed her wrist.

"Get in."

"I have a big love for America, Nataniel. And a bigger love for Dima. If you and Dima are brothers, this means I love you. It will be my pleasure. Truly." She looked so nearly convincing I might have followed her inside—until her smile cracked just a hair.

"What did my brother say you would do in America?"

"Work," she answered. "Learn English, work at the store, then go off to make my life."

That sounded right.

"Did he say you'd do this kind of work?"

She shook her hand loose and rubbed my leg again.

"I'm very good at what I do."

I removed her hand.

"Work," she said, "is work. In Ukraine, I had nothing. Dima found me living on a subway grate. He gave me America."

"He told you to do this?"

"Dima is a sweet old man. No. Maxim told me."

"Do you have a family?"

"My parents and two sisters. Most of my money goes to Maxim. But what I earn at the store is mine, and I send my sisters money so they can go to school and not live on subway grates. The winters in Kiev are cold."

I tore through Somerville, then through Boston, headed to a restaurant on the South Shore, unable to speak without raging at how Petrov had hijacked my brother's life's work. I didn't stop until we got to Odessa, famous among Ukrainians living in Greater Boston. The restaurant—with its *bublik* and pork dumplings, the food I'd loved as a child—calmed me down. We talked, and I learned her parents had cut her off for reasons she didn't care to discuss, though if the stories of other girls Dima rescued were similar, she'd gotten tangled in drugs, an unwanted pregnancy, or both.

When we returned to the grocery, having made no stop at the Somerville Lodge or any other motel, Petrov was working one of the cash registers. Sveta passed him by without a glance, and he checked his watch and winked at me. "You old goat! Gone two and a half hours? I'd figured you for fifteen minutes, max. Come here."

He removed an envelope from his apron, the same one Bobby had offered. "Take it," said Petrov. "Take it and leave."

I told him what I told Bobby.

"And if I sweetened the offer—say, to seventy?"

"I'd tell you to stop bothering me. I'm going to spend the summer with my granddaughter. I won't testify. I'll run when the time comes, but I'll run on my schedule, not yours."

"You know," said Petrov. "If a man asks three times—"

"Don't even start. I've had it up to here with three strikes."

I turned my back and left.

Bobby caught up with me in the parking lot. "Dima's at his apartment with a day nurse. Give me some time to get him ready to see you, okay? It's gotta be out of sight. Really, the lawyers mean it about this witness tampering thing. Everything's hard for Dima now. Tonight I'll tell him you're out of prison, and he'll forget by tomorrow. I'll tell him every day for a week, and he'll forget."

I said nothing.

"Hey, don't you have a magic show coming up in a couple of weeks? I could talk about that, show him pictures of magicians, then bring him."

Traffic roared down Broadway.

"Petrov's sunk his claws into all of it," I said. "Thirty years of work, Bobby, and he walks in here and hijacks Dima's pipeline? Is that what they do in Brighton Beach, traffic girls out of grocery stores? How could you let it happen?"

"It happened, all right? You try talking to the Russians. I admit I went to the wrong people. But we needed money, and you know I couldn't go to a bank. The Petrovs got one look at this place and decided they needed to expand north, into Boston. And Maxim, the one they sent up here to run things? Don't even *try* talking to him. He got sent up twice, the first time for nearly killing a guy with a baseball bat. Family business. Second time, who knows? I didn't just *let* it happen. I opened the door a quarter-inch, and a flood poured in."

Bobby kicked at a curb.

"On top of it all, your brother's mind blinks on and off like a lighthouse. Sometimes he doesn't remember me. I'm sleeping in the second bedroom now. It's worked okay since my wife kicked me out. He's getting worse. He'll talk for an hour like nothing's wrong then stare at a wall for the rest of the afternoon. And he has accidents. I love the old coot, Nate. I can't stand what's happening to him."

I had misjudged this man.

"You never signed on to change diapers," I said. "I'll take over." But how could I? If I stayed to care for Dima, then testified, he'd go to jail. If I stayed and didn't testify, Hunt would send me back to prison. If I ran, I'd be no help at all. I didn't know how to fix this.

"I'll take care of him," said Bobby. "What you need to do is leave."

"And never see my brother again?"

"Listen to me. If they convict Dima, they'll come for Maxim next. Maxim's made up his mind, and that puts us on opposite sides. If he's feeling generous, I'll throw you onto a ship or train to get you out of here before the trial. The case against Dima's got to collapse. He's not a subtle man, Nate. I've been running interference for you, and it's not going well."

"You're forgetting Grace."

"And how's that working out? My Ella drives me nuts. Everything's an argument with her—clothes, boys, makeup, and I only get to see her twice a month. What kind of memories is she going to have—always at each other's throats? Maybe I'll take her to your show, along with Dima. It'll be fun, right?"

"Wholesome family entertainment," I promised.

As I drove back to Arlington, I wondered if I had it in me to fight a younger, stronger Petrov. I had learned many things in prison, among them this: When you need to take someone down, never telegraph it. Just set him up, use your knife, and disappear. *Listen to me*, I thought, driving along the Mystic Valley Parkway. *Good old Nate talking like a player*. Why not? Dima had saved me too many times to count. It was my turn to save him.

Seven: Grace Larson

"Did you *really* have an uncle?" I asked.

He was standing at his mirror, producing a rose from his back pants pocket, then vanishing it into that same pocket. He didn't break his eyes from the mirror as he answered me. "Sure I did. His name was Nestor. Nestor Lazarenko."

"You mean Larson."

"Lazarenko was our Ukrainian name. Dima changed it."

We had been living together a few weeks. Ever since he mentioned the possible Houdini connection in our family, I'd been reading up. It was insane what Houdini could do: get locked in heavy chains, nailed into a box, and dumped into an ice-cold river only to bob to the surface a minute later, waving and smiling. Once he made a six-ton elephant disappear on stage in a crowded theater. He was a master, and I wanted to know if the family connection was real.

"Your uncle said he was related. Or was that just part of your story for the coins?"

Nate stepped away from the mirror and joined me at the kitchen table. "That's what Nestor told me. Houdini was born in Budapest. My grandfather's grandmother was also Hungarian. This would have been in the 1870s. The family split. One branch—the Weiszes—came to America. That was Houdini's branch. Houdini was a stage name. One of his cousins moved to Ireland—that was my uncle's branch."

"So if you're related," I said, hesitating, "I'm related?" I could almost stomach the thought of the old man's blood running in me. He set up the checkerboard and looked across the oilcloth.

"If Nestor was telling the truth, then you're related. Sometimes I couldn't tell with him because he was always joking. But I believed him about this, not that I'm 100 percent sure. I can live with that."

An hour earlier, Lola had called and asked us to leave our front door open because she had a surprise for us. She arrived with dessert. "It's Frank's birthday, everyone! This is my first German Chocolate Cake. The batter didn't taste like much, but I believe it's going to be excellent. How are you, Sweetie?"

She kissed me on the head. Since Mr. Parker, I didn't like people touching me, but Lola was different. She invited me to bake cookies. We weeded the garden and planted snapdragons, which had just begun to flower. I liked the Maloneys, Lucy included. Frank arrived wearing a silly birthday hat with streamers at the top. He was carrying paper plates, forks, and a carton of milk.

"You don't look a day over ninety," said Nate. "I was just telling Grace that she's related to Houdini. Maybe."

"No way," said Lola. "Really? Could that be?"

Lucy jumped onto my lap.

As she sliced and served the cake, Lola wondered aloud how anyone could prove a thing like that. "I suppose you'd use family Bibles," she said. "You know, study the front pages that record births and deaths. Official birth records would be better, but how would you go about finding them?"

"There's a much better way," said Frank. "I was reading an article about DNA in the *Globe* magazine the other week.

What Grace needs to do is take a cotton swab, roll it inside her cheek, and send it off to a lab. Then the lab sends her a full report. I don't know about the Houdini part. They'd have to have some of his DNA, too, for a comparison."

I could almost hear my grandfather saying *I told you so* for trying to get some of my DNA off a glass a few weeks earlier. He excused himself and returned with one of his notebooks. He tore out the page and handed me my laptop. "Go to the Internet," he said. "I copied this notice down from one of my magic magazines. The Houdini Society of New York is looking for all living relations. Apparently they're offering some sort of college scholarship."

I went to the web address he'd written down and, sure enough, found the Houdini Society. Information on the front page explained how they had preserved a lock of Houdini's hair and had run a DNA test on it. There was a lot of technical information none of us could follow, but it more or less came down to this: The society ran a scholarship fund with money from Houdini's estate. Teenagers who could prove their relation to the Houdini family would get their college tuition paid for at their home-state's public university. I copied the address and phone number onto a scrap of paper and read from the screen. "It says to click here for directions on how to submit a DNA sample."

Frank and Lola were getting excited about the scholarship. "Four years of tuition?" he said. "That's nothing to sneeze at. Grace, you should do this."

I thought so too.

The one I wanted to hear from most remained silent. He took a big gulp of milk, waited a few moments, and said, "You could be disappointed. Maybe Nestor was just telling me a story. I happen to believe it, but maybe it's better you don't do this thing. As long as you don't check, it'll always be true at least a little. Right? Getting the wrong news would upset you."

"I'm calling."

The Maloneys agreed I should.

Sure enough a man answered and told me all about the scholarship. I asked about the hair and the DNA and gave him my address. When I hung up, I looked to each of them, not quite believing what I'd heard. "It's real," I said. "There *is* a scholarship fund. On the website, they have the address of a lab in New York that sells DNA kits. They'll send a kit to us. It's two hundred dollars."

The adults discussed the pros and cons, and mostly it came down to the expense and whether or not I was willing to take a chance on being disappointed. I was definitely willing, but I didn't have two hundred dollars.

Lola and Frank had been married a long time, and Frank must have caught her meaning when she glanced at him across the table. "All right," he said. "We'll pay for the kit, and we'll take it out of your wages for walking Lucy. A no-interest loan. Deal?"

Deal.

Two weeks later, on a Saturday, the DNA kit arrived from a lab called Genographics in Schenectady, New York. We gathered around Lola and Frank's kitchen table as everyone watched me swab the inside of my cheek, seal the swab in a plastic tube, then seal the tube in a prestamped mailer.

"Science is amazing," said Lola.

I took a bow. "I'm going to be famous!"

"You already are," said Frank, smiling. "Only no one knows it yet."

I wasn't sure which made me happier, the possibility I had a great magician's blood in me or the possibility I might go to college for free. I was only in eighth grade, but I'd already visited the guidance counselor and signed up for information sessions for the University of Massachusetts in Boston. Long after everyone went to bed that evening, I fell asleep reading the college catalog and descriptions of the computer courses I would take. That Harry Houdini, my great-great-great somebody three times removed, might pay for it was the best news I'd ever heard.

My imagination flew outside my bedroom window, around the world, and straight back in. Every day after school I ran to the mailbox to see if an envelope had come from Schenectady, New York.

— • —

ONE AFTERNOON, the old man was seated at the kitchen table, playing with wooden dolls he called his Matryoshkas: seven dolls, one smaller than the next, that fit into each other. Each was painted with a rosy-cheeked girl with button lips and big eyes, and each was hollow inside so that it could be opened to store the smaller dolls. He played with them almost every night after checkers and often during the day on the weekends. Sometimes he danced the smaller dolls around the way I had when I was younger. He spoke to them in Ukrainian and sang songs. I didn't know what to make of it, except that it was strange to see someone his age playing with dollies.

After a month of living together, I hadn't really made up my mind about my new home and rental parent. True, I enjoyed watching him practice magic. I definitely enjoyed beating him at checkers, which meant we ate Chinese five or six nights a week. And unlike Mrs. Alcott, he didn't bother me about spending too much time writing and playing computer games. Mostly he left me alone. That was the good news. But as a DCF kid, I knew that bad news was always around the corner. In fact, I distrusted harmless rental parents even more than evil ones. The evil ones kept you on guard. The harmless ones sucked you in. You ended up liking them. Liking led to being nice, and being nice never worked because whether you were friendly and well-behaved or not they gave you back. You'd think everything was going great and, wham, back you'd go to the DCF dorm in South Boston.

I was programming one of my computer games when he asked about showing me a trick. I grunted and kept my eyes on my screen.

"What do you think? C'mon, it's a good one."

"I'm busy," I said.

He turned back to his mirror and I peeked over the edge of my laptop, watching him practice, moving like a dancer. He saw me in the mirror and caught my eye. "All right," I said, deciding to be generous. "I mean, you already interrupted me."

He asked me to sit on the couch and returned from his bedroom wearing his suit, the one the guards returned to him when he left prison. It was too large, but he explained that for this particular trick he needed the extra room. He cleared his throat and ran his fingers through his hair. He took a deep breath and bowed to me. "*The Three Roses*," he began. He set his right palm faceup, parallel to the floor, just as waiters do when they carry dinner trays. He held this position for a few seconds, then passed his left hand before his right. "Miss Larson," he said, pulling away his left hand. "I give you a rose."

Somehow he'd placed a rosebud on the tray of his open palm. For all the world, it looked as if he'd snatched it from thin air.

"Nice! Really nice!"

"When I was a boy," he continued, "I attended Saint Mark's Catholic School in Boston. One day, in Bible Study, Sister Marguerite said, 'We learn from the Apostle Peter that life is a pilgrimage: We come from God, walk this world of storm and stress, and return to God.' She drew a white line on the black-board. 'Consider the span of our lives,' she said, tapping the line with her chalk. 'This is our road, shorter for some, longer for others. We may suppose that before birth and after death all is blackness, black as this board—in which case we make our journey from nothing to nothing. But what if there were something before and after that was *not* blackness and what if this something lay hidden just beyond our view? Wouldn't we search every day to find it and know it? Wouldn't our search change everything?'"

Again he passed his left hand before his right, and when he withdrew it this time I shouted, "*You couldn't have!*" because somehow he'd placed a second rose on the flat of his palm. He addressed the flowers, not me: "To make good friends along the road is a gift because friends are our fellow travelers. But to find your dearest one, your life's partner, is a miracle because through the sacrament of love two may become three. I loved someone once. Her name was Nora, your grandmother. We had a child, Gabrielle, your mother."

He covered his right hand with his left a third time, and when he withdrew it a third rose appeared on his palm. I jumped off the couch. "*How* are you doing this!"

He held very still. He said nothing. He moved nothing, not a muscle, aside from his left hand, which had covered and uncovered the roses. Once at school we watched a film of the Pope at his window at the Vatican, blessing crowds in twenty-three languages. My grandfather moved his hand just as the Pope had moved his.

Benvenuto. Bienvenue. Welcome.

"You and I are like the roses," he said. "We're born. We bloom. We enjoy our season of beauty, and we wither and die—like Nora and your mother died . . . too soon. When the snows came for them, it broke my heart, Grace. They left me alone on the road." Again one hand covered the other, and when it withdrew, a single rosebud remained.

"Every story we will ever tell ends the same, with love following love to the grave." He made a last flourish, and the third rose disappeared.

I was speechless.

He broke his pose and became a regular old man again. "So," he said, "what do you think? Should I open the show with it? I'd change the details about Nora and Gabby, of course. This particular patter was just for you. But that's the trick, *The Three Roses*. Does it work? Come on, be honest."

Did it work? I fought tears. I wrestled for the right words because I thought my grandfather should perform not just for me but for queens and presidents. For kids in libraries and old ladies in rest homes and bums on the street and men with shaved heads who chanted all day and people in office buildings in their suits and ties. Who wouldn't love *The Three Roses*? Who wouldn't want their jaw to drop?

"It's perfect," I said. "Don't change a word."

I had a thousand questions but at that moment needed to leave to compose myself because I'd suddenly realized something as I listened to *The Three Roses*. This old man, if he was *really* my grandfather, was the one person on earth who could possibly have hurt as much as I did when my mother died. Watching him perform his magic and hearing what he said about becoming two with Nora and three with my mother was like discovering half of my heart beating in someone else's chest. Was it possible DCF had placed me in the home of someone who truly cared? I didn't want to care. For a time, I sat on my bed unable to speak. An hour later he slid something under the door: his notebook for *The Three Roses*.

THE THREE ROSES

STEPS:

1. BEGIN WITH
   EMPTY PALM.

2. DIVERSION: MAGICIAN'S
   FOCUS ON PALM DRAWS
   AUDIENCE ATTENTION TO PALM

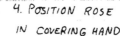

3. WITH AUDIENCE
DISTRACTED, PULL ROSE #1
   FROM POCKET.

4. POSITION ROSE
   IN COVERING HAND

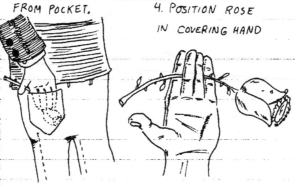

5. DEPOSIT ROSE ONTO
PALM AND PULL COVERING
   HAND WITH FLOURISH.

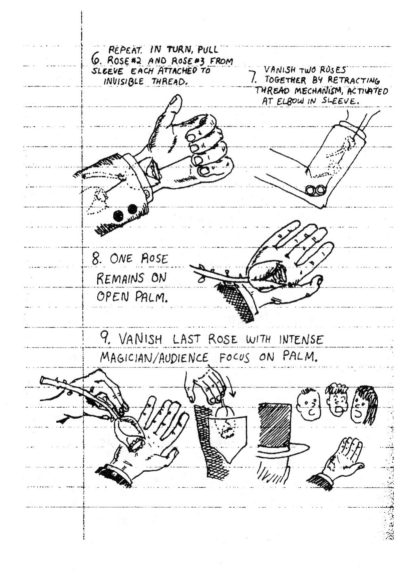

REPEAT. IN TURN, PULL
6. ROSE #2 AND ROSE #3 FROM
SLEEVE EACH ATTACHED TO
INVISIBLE THREAD.

7. VANISH TWO ROSES TOGETHER BY RETRACTING THREAD MECHANISM, ACTIVATED AT ELBOW IN SLEEVE.

8. ONE ROSE REMAINS ON OPEN PALM.

9. VANISH LAST ROSE WITH INTENSE MAGICIAN/AUDIENCE FOCUS ON PALM.

Eight: Nate Larson

Miss Roberts had warned me she'd visit unannounced, but when she called to say she'd be inspecting our home in thirty minutes, I panicked. I'd just gotten off the phone with a lawyer from Eleanor Hunt's office, who wanted to begin coaching me on the upcoming trial even though we had more than two months to prepare. But I was headed out of town, as he reminded me, and I was in no position to argue or bargain. We arranged a meeting at the courthouse for the next afternoon.

I was recovering from that call when the second one from Miss Roberts came. For ten years I had lived rough in prison, and I didn't change my habits when I moved to the apartment in Arlington. Grace didn't mind that we sorted laundry by throwing dirties into different corners of our bedrooms. We'd collect the piles off the floor once a week in duffels and head out to the coin-op on Mass Ave. That night was laundry night, which meant our bedrooms looked like a typhoon had blown through them. The kitchen was no better. We kept a garbage pail lined with a thick plastic bag for our Styrofoam empties from each night's carryout. We kept no food in the cupboards, no veggies or milk in the fridge, no dish soap, no scrubbies to wash dishes we never used, nothing that on a quick inspection would confirm our apartment was anything more than a squatters' camp.

A single bag of Utz potato chips, family size, sat on the counter.

"She's not going to like this," I said.

"What's the plan, Nate?"

I froze, unable to think of a plan.

"If she comes and sees this . . ."

"Well, you've got to do *something*."

When it became clear I couldn't, Grace ran to the hook by the phone and grabbed the key to the Maloneys' kitchen door. She also grabbed the trashcan. "I'll take care of the kitchen," she yelled, headed downstairs. "You make the beds and kick all the dirty clothes underneath. Run a towel over everything in the bathroom. Clean the sink, and leave the toilet seat down."

"Do we have fresh towels?"

I stood there, staring.

"I'll take care of that too." She looked at my watch. "Twenty-eight minutes. Go."

I did exactly what my granddaughter ordered me to do. I straightened the living room, vacuumed the rug, plumped the pillows. In four trips, she'd hauled upstairs just about every bit of food in the Maloneys' refrigerator and cupboards, all of it in a clean trash can liner. Meanwhile I cleaned the bathroom and made sure the laundry disappeared. What saved us was that Lola had bought frilly dust ruffles for the beds, perfect for hiding dirty clothes.

By the time we finished, Grace had transferred to our fridge Tupperware containers filled with tuna salad, cooked rice, and sliced ham and cheese. The apples went into the fruit bin and the romaine and carrots into the veggie bin. She even brought a bowl of Jell-O. She'd taken it all, including the

contents of the Maloneys' spice cabinet. The final touch was
the plate of homemade cookies Lola had set on the counter
for Lucy's afternoon walk.

With three minutes to spare, Grace went to the shelf where
she kept the books she'd read during school that year and
grabbed *To Kill a Mockingbird*. When the doorbell buzzed,
she began to read. "Come here," she called to Lucy, who followed her upstairs. The dog jumped into her lap. "All right,"
she said, looking at me. "Catch your breath, count to ten, and
try to look relaxed."

The doorbell buzzed again.

As I turned toward the stairs, my granddaughter wore the
most quizzical look—as if she'd surprised herself by her own
whirlwind. I greeted Miss Roberts at the landing and offered
a few pleasantries. She had none for me. Up we came to find
Grace scratching Lucy's soft ears and eating a cookie. "Hi," she
said, looking up, alert. "You ever read this?" She pointed to the
book. "I'm at the part when Atticus sits up all night in front of
the jail to keep the mob from lynching Tom Robinson."

"That *is* a good scene. How are you, Grace?"

"Fine, Miss Roberts. And you?"

Who *was* this child?

Roberts produced a clipboard and a checklist. After
explaining what she was about to do, and getting me to sign
a document giving her permission to do it, she ran her hands
along the kitchen countertops and opened cupboards and the
refrigerator to find both well stocked. She poked her head into
the bedrooms and the bathroom. That part of the inspection
didn't last ten minutes, and I heard her making encouraging
Um-hm sounds as she checked her way through her list.

"Well, then," she said. "You pass the first part of the
inspection. About the worst thing I can find is the diet soda
in the fridge. It has aspartame. It's not good for Grace—either

the additive or that she's watching her weight. She's thin, you know."

"I am not."

"I honestly didn't notice, Miss Roberts."

"Well, maybe you should pay more attention. If it weren't for all these ads with bone-skinny children with their come-hither smiles . . . You know what I mean. Grace, when's the last time you had a checkup?"

"I don't remember. And stop calling me a child."

I retreated to the rear porch when Roberts asked if she and Grace could speak in private. It made me nervous, having no control over what Grace would say. But ten minutes later Miss Roberts called me back in, and I found them laughing and smiling.

"I talked with a school counselor last week. They told me your granddaughter has done well—in fact better now that she was living with her grandfather. I wouldn't have guessed it, Mr. Larson, but I suppose some credit is due."

As she was leaving, she reminded me she'd visit again, both announced and unannounced. "And let's pencil me in one of your magic shows this summer," she said. "I've gone on record that it's a bad idea, Grace going on the road with you. Now I want to see for myself. If I was wrong, I'll say so. Do you have a calendar with tour dates and locations?"

I handed her a flyer.

The woman *tsked* as she read through the list. "A magic show . . . All right, very likely I'll make the last show, in Canaan, Vermont. I have a cousin who lives up there, and she's been inviting me forever to visit. Let's see what Grace puts up with on the road, Mr. Larson—especially if you have any plans to do this again next year. I'll say this much. If you can make those weeks of traveling as comfortable and safe as what I've found here, you just may convince me."

"Feel free to come any time, Miss Roberts. You know I'm trying to do the right thing."

"Maybe you are," she said.

I walked her to the door. When I climbed back upstairs, Grace was reading.

"It really is my favorite part of the story," she said, "Atticus sitting up all night. He's such a good father. . . . How'd we do?"

"How do you think we did?"

She shrugged.

"She almost believes I'm a half-decent foster parent."

I gave her an opening with that. When she offered nothing, I winced but tried not to show it. "Hey," I said.

"What?"

"Let's invite Lola and Frank for dinner. We've got plenty of food." She waited one beat, then two before giggling. I laughed. When she laughed harder, I thought I heard river ice crack and buckle as something that resembled affection flowed between us.

Nine: Grace Larson

I used to think happy families spent every day congratulating themselves on how happy they were. With the Del-Reys and Mr. Parker and the others I was so desperately *un*happy that I thought of little else. Yet when I started living with Nate and realized I could basically do what I wanted, I didn't jump for joy at every moment. Being safe and not bothered by anyone was just how things were. I got used to it. Nate and I communicated best by not talking. For the most part we occupied the same space, at work on our separate projects in plain sight of each other. He'd be standing at his mirror, practicing. I'd sit at the kitchen table bent over my computer. Sometimes we wouldn't speak for hours on end. Then we'd eat Chinese carryout when I beat him in checkers. We didn't even talk after I saved him from Miss Roberts. She would have taken me that very day if she'd seen how we really lived. I could have let Nate panic, done nothing, and moved on to a different family. But I helped him, and I wasn't sure why.

We didn't talk about that either.

After weeks of watching him practice, he described an escape he wanted to perform as the finale of his show. "It sounds horrible," he began, "but hear me out. It's rigged, though the audience won't know that, and it's not dangerous if you've got dependable help. I want you to be my helper."

He called it *The Kortelisy Escape*, and it was worthy of Houdini. The basic idea was to tie him up in a straitjacket so he couldn't free his arms, then wrap his head in plastic—the clingy kind with labels that warn parents to keep kids away. Somehow, he was supposed to escape, which to the audience would look impossible.

That was the point.

One volunteer would bind him tight in the jacket, then plastic-wrap him. Two more volunteers would then step onto the stage holding a curtain made of black velvet on a long pole, which they would raise as high as they could so that no one, themselves included, could see what was going on behind. The last view of my grandfather the audience would get before the velvet curtain went up was of an old man curled onstage, not moving and not breathing but staring directly at them—his eyes pinned open by the plastic. In introducing the escape, my grandfather would say: "If something goes wrong, the curtain's here so you won't have to watch a man suffocate." Of course the real purpose of the curtain was to keep people from seeing me crawl from a hidden spot backstage, commando style, in order to cut holes into the plastic, then unbuckle him. The different venues with their different sight lines would present challenges to keep me hidden, but Nate said he could figure that out. My job was to crawl to him and, when he was safe and could finish the job himself, crawl back undetected.

"This is the stupidest thing I ever heard," I said, the first time he described the escape.

"No," he answered. "It's not stupid. All the great ones tempt death—and they survive. In case you're interested, I *don't* intend to die onstage."

Still I hesitated.

"It's how magic works," he continued. "You get the audience to care, you put yourself in danger, and you make them anxious—in this case that I'll suffocate. Then you make them wait, which means you let them suffer. And *then* you release them. *Suddenly.* After ninety seconds, the audience will be tearing their hair out. That's when I'll jump from behind the curtain, very much alive."

Before we practiced on him, we practiced dozens of times on a junked soccer ball. Nate had cut a hole in it as a substitute mouth. He promised he wouldn't do the escape unless I was 100 percent comfortable with my part. He said I could call it off up until the very moment he gave instructions to his volunteers from the audience. All I had to do was knock the handle of my knife against the stage floor. He would hear the knock, and he'd end the trick by escaping from the straitjacket only. He'd still need my help, but the unbuckling posed no danger and was easy. We practiced until I was bored silly and Nate was satisfied I wouldn't leave him to suffocate. At first, he wrapped his own head in plastic because I wouldn't do it. Little by little I grew confident enough to help. Eventually we had the routine down to twenty seconds—ten for the wrapping, which started the clock (Nate would instruct the first volunteer to wrap as quickly as possible), and ten more for me to release him.

— • —

THE MYSTERY Lounge is a large, windowless room located two steep floors above the Hong Kong restaurant in Cambridge, Massachusetts, opposite Harvard University. For six nights a week it's a comedy club. But for one night comedians give way to magicians for a different sort of entertainment. I was disappointed on seeing it at first—Nate and I had visited a few days before the show to check things out. I had imagined it would be a proper theater with hundreds of seats that would be filled for Nate's debut. He was related to Houdini, after all. *I* knew how good he was, and I expected great things. As it happened, the lounge was a big black empty box with a narrow little stage and was packed with long tables at which people would drink beer and eat Chinese carryout from the restaurant downstairs.

Nate said he didn't mind competing with food and alcohol. I didn't believe him. "We're rookies," he said. "And rookies always start rough. We'll be playing in theaters soon enough," he promised. "Don't get discouraged."

The truth was nothing could have discouraged me at that point. School was out, the summer days were warm and long, and I had about the best job of any kid I knew. A magician's apprentice? The kids at school were cutting lawns and babysitting. I even had my own uniform: a black leotard, with black stretch booties, black gloves, and a black hood to hide my hair. I needed to be stealthy, Nate said, so people wouldn't see me slinking along the floor to free him during the escape.

Ten minutes before our first show was to begin, I counted seventy-three people—a terrific "house," as he called it. The manager at The Mystery Lounge had printed flyers, in addition to ours, and placed ads promising an escape more terrifying than any that had been seen since the days of Houdini's *Torture Cell*.

Nate was ready.

I was ready, though I was nervous.

He opened with *The Three Roses*, and already a few minutes into the show he'd brought the audience to its feet. Strength built from strength that night. He forced pennies to float and spin. He bent spoons with his mind. He chatted up a volunteer onstage, stole her watch without anyone realizing (he used a double-grasp handshake—very smooth), then retrieved that *same* watch from a locked box suspended from the ceiling.

His ten-minute warm-up left people laughing and amazed. He paused, sipped from a bottle of water, and ran his hands through his hair. "Settle in," he told the audience. "Please, get comfortable. I've started with a little magic, and we've had some fun. But the truth is I don't do magic for fun. What I do up here is a matter of life and death for me, and the best way to explain is to tell you a story. It's mystery of sorts. Can I tell you?"

The audience applauded. He owned them.

"It's not usually done," he continued, "but I'm going to wrap all the magic I've got left tonight in a simple little story about a young woman named Rachel."

He took a deep breath.

"Ukraine, 1934," he began. "The countryside. Farms, scattered villages, forests. Rachel Lubovsky is seventeen years old. She's a girl and a woman, still in many ways a child, and she lives in dangerous times. Europe is gathering itself for war. It's late autumn as we find her walking along a dirt road, alone, approaching the village of Kortelisy.

"Tonight I want to tell you about the miracle at Kortelisy, where I was born sixty-six years ago. You should know two things about our little village. The first is sturgeon. In the lake and the river that fed it lived big fish with delicious eggs. We know these eggs in America as caviar. Villagers had fished sturgeon for longer than memory could reach. Left alone, these fish could grow into monsters."

Nate reached for a plate on one of his tables.

"Observe this cracker, ladies and gentlemen. On it, I have spread a thin layer of cream cheese. And on this cream cheese

I've spread a layer of caviar—little black eggs, lightly salted. Watch closely as I make this cracker disappear."

He took the same stance he'd taken for *The Three Roses*, the cracker resting on the flat of his right palm. He set his legs and waved his left hand as if he were about to turn the cracker into a mouse. Then came the flourish. But instead of covering his open palm, he picked up the cracker and popped it into his mouth. He crunched it, swallowed, smiled, and reached for a flute of champagne which he removed—three-quarters full—from an inside pocket of his jacket.

The audience roared.

"The lake at Kortelisy was famous for something else," he continued. "Young lovers walked its shores and many of them, inspired by its beauty, made plans to marry. At the very same lake, young men and women who were not so lucky in love ended their sorrows by throwing themselves from the cliffs. It is in this sad condition we find Rachel: cast out, alone, and prepared to end her misery.

"Why?

"It's an old story. In her own village, Rachel loved a soldier from a nearby garrison. He had a beautiful moustache and coal-black eyes. He had a gun and a saber. He wore a fine uniform. He dazzled Rachel and, without any thought of marriage, left her with child. On learning he was to be a father, he volunteered for a remote outpost on the far side of Ukraine and disappeared."

Nate produced a doll of a little soldier with black pants, white tunic, and a vest—which he had sewn very carefully in the weeks before the show. The doll had a moustache and wore an officer's cap. He set the doll on his palm, tossed it into the air with one hand, pointed with the other and watched, along with everyone else, as it exploded into a cloud of glitter.

"When Rachel could no longer hide her secret, she confessed to her parents. Her mother wept. Her father pointed to the door. 'Get out,' he yelled. 'You've disgraced us!' So she took to the road and tramped from one village to the next, living off scraps tossed aside for dogs. Ailing and beyond hope she could ever care for the child, she knew the end had come. She remembered stories of Kortelisy, of its lake and cliffs. *I'll go there*, she thought, *and end this misery*.

"It was late afternoon, and a haze of wood smoke had settled over the village. She followed a path that circles the lake to this day and climbed a rocky trail that ended in a promontory high above the water. Darkness fell. Rachel cried for the soldier and cried for their unborn child. She forgave her parents and then, asking the Lord to forgive her, she leapt!

"Down she went. Down!!"

Nate reached high into the air with one hand while the other—at his waist—held a black disk. He flicked that disk and it became a magician's top hat, open-end up. In the hand aloft he presented another doll, this one a woman in a peasant dress. When he released her, she fell. But just before reaching the open maw of the hat, the doll stopped in midair, hovering. Floating. "Something's wrong!" said Nate. "Rachel has leapt from the cliffs. She wants to die but death won't take her!"

Defying gravity, the doll floated back up into his hand.

"Earlier that same evening, a farmer and his son named Dima pulled their boat from the underbrush and paddled out to fish for sturgeon by the light of a full moon. According to the old men of Kortelisy, the biggest fish rose in the cool evenings before winter set in. Let's watch them pulling at their oars.

"The night is still. The moon is up. They're rowing and rowing when, all at once, they hear a tremendous splash. Sturgeons are huge fish known to break the surface in spectacular displays, like whales in the ocean. Thinking this must be a fish of legendary proportions, the father didn't hesitate. In he dove after the dark shape, groping for what might be the biggest sturgeon in living memory. He reached into the murk for anything he could grab and wrestle to the surface. Imagine his surprise when he grasped—a hand! The farmer called to his son. This was no fish! They rolled her into the boat, unconscious but breathing. They rowed to shore and loaded her onto the cart they'd brought for their big catch.

"'Back so soon?' called the wife as they carried Rachel through the doorway.

"For three whole days, Rachel lay unconscious in a bed pulled near the fireplace. When she lost her child on the second day, these good people knew just what to do. This was a farm, after all. They had delivered calves. They had splinted broken bones of animals and men. They understood the dangers of this world. They fixed what could be fixed and said prayers for what could not.

"On the fourth day, Rachel woke. She looked about the unfamiliar room and saw the farmer's son reading a book by the fire not ten paces away. On a stool before him lay three metal rings. As the boy read, he reached for them. Waving the solid rings in the air, he passed one ring through the others, steel passing through steel. He linked and unlinked them just like this."

Nate performed his *Chinese Linking Rings*, passing steel through steel. I stood behind the curtain listening so intently I'd nearly forgotten that an audience was out there beyond the stage lights.

"Rachel watched this boy read from a second book. He took a coin and made it hover in midair. It rose from one hand and flew to the next, floating and spinning just so." Nate performed his floating coin trick.

"Then, with a wave of his hands, it disappeared!

"*What is this strange place*? thought Rachel. Her last memory was of death and the onrushing lake. *Is it true*? She thought. *Have I died*? She coughed. She tried to speak, her voice rough. 'Sir,' she called. 'Young man, am I in heaven?'

"Rachel already knew the answer. Before she jumped, she was filthy and aching. Now here she lay in a feather bed with fresh clothes, her hair washed and smelling of flowers. And here she saw coins dancing in midair! It is so, she decided: she had died and gone to heaven.

"She felt beneath the covers. Her belly was flat, and she thought, 'My child? What's become of my child?'

"Just then, an infant began to cry. Unsure whether to fetch his newborn brother or tend to this strange woman, Dima ran from the room and returned with his mother. The farmer's wife reached for her own newborn and, lifting her blouse, nursed the child.

"'Good lady,' said Rachel. 'I threw myself off the cliff and woke to find this young man performing miracles. And there, in your arms, is my child! Bring him to me. Praise God, I'm in heaven! I've come home. You must be angels.'

"The farmer entered the room and surveyed this strange scene. He didn't have the heart to tell Rachel he'd pulled her from the lake and that she was alive. Dima hadn't the heart to tell her that he performed no miracles but had saved all his money to buy books on magic and was studying to leave his village and become a great magician in Kiev. And the farmer's wife? She hadn't the heart to tell Rachel that she had miscarried and that *this* beautiful child nursing in her arms was Dima's brother."

Nate broke out his cups and ball and began peppering his audience with questions: "Where is Rachel? In the village of her birth? No. They threw her out." He circled the cups clockwise and counterclockwise, lifting one cup and the next, flashing the ball then hiding it. "Is she here in Kortelisy? It's possible. But Rachel thinks she's in heaven. Perhaps it's all a dream. Does *any* of this exist?" Nate lifted all three cups—and the ball was gone!

"*Where* is Rachel?"

The audience cheered.

Again Nate circled the cups, then paused.

He lifted two cups. Empty.

He lifted the third to reveal *five* balls: "Five!" he said, "Count them. Rachel lives with her new family in heaven: farmer, wife, son, infant—and Rachel herself!"

The audience was up, clapping and whistling.

"No one would contradict Rachel's happiness. As she recovered her strength, she helped with chores on the farm, surprised that even in heaven people worked for their bread. She accepted this new life because she now had food, a kind family, and shelter. She sang as she sewed. She milked cows and helped with the harvest. If she pricked her finger, she bled—even in heaven. At night, she watched Dima practice his tricks. Once she saw him command a table to float through the air."

Nate floated a table onstage.

"The farmer thought her mad, but he had come to love her as a daughter. 'Let her think what she wants,' he said. 'What harm can come of it?'

"The years passed. It was 1942 and the child, now eight years old, grew up believing he had two mothers. No one minded, least of all little Nataniel. That's me, friends. Nataniel Lazarenko, the son of Ukrainian farmers come all the way to America to tell his story. Mama Rachel doted on me, a little boy who wasn't her child—not that she knew it. So did Mama Anastasia, my real mother. Could a woman have been more generous, sharing me this way? Could a child have been more blessed?

"Like most places, the village of Kortelisy had its kind souls and scoundrels. Kind or not, everyone kept a soft spot in their hearts for Rachel Lubovsky. The baker, a famous sourpuss, stopped arguing with his wife long enough to tip his hat when Rachel entered his shop. So did the dry goods clerk, who would stop adjusting his tie in the mirror long enough to show her the latest bolts of cloth from the city. Rachel was so pure in her love of everyone she met in heaven that no one could think to pierce the sweet halo of her madness. When in her company, the villagers treated each other with the same kindness she showed them so that she would continue to think she had died and gone to heaven.

"To think of it: a conspiracy of love! At first, all their courtesies were make-pretend. But then something strange happened. Even in Rachel's absence, the villagers began treating each other with affection. It started one day when the baker kissed his wife on the cheek for no reason at all. The dry goods clerk bought a meal for a beggar at his door instead of calling for the constable. Then farmers began leaving wheat and barley unharvested in the corners of their fields to provide for the poor. Some sort of contagion had broken loose. Everywhere kindness followed kindness until the village of Kortelisy was bursting with it. Then one day it happened, something altogether unknown in human history: Kortelisy became heaven on earth.

"No angels flitted about, playing harps. No manna fell from the sky. Just the same, the villagers knew what had happened. Petty arguments and fears melted away. Jealousies vanished, all for the love of a girl named Rachel Lubovsky. The spell she cast without ever casting it was complete. In that tiny place, far across the world, she had changed everything.

"This, my friends, was the *Miracle of Kortelisy*. When you leave tonight, remember that once there was a heaven on this earth. I know it's true because I saw it. I lived there. I may be a magician, but there's nothing magical in thinking it could happen again. Here, for instance. Tonight. Help me perform the biggest and most potent magic of the evening: Right now, turn to your neighbor, someone you've never met, and say, *Hello.*"

That was my cue. I was on.

Ten: Nate Larson

In seven hours I was scheduled to debut at The Mystery Lounge. I hadn't slept the previous twenty-four, and by early afternoon I was a jittery mess—though I tried looking calm for Grace to help manage her nerves. "I'm going to take a nap," I said. "Or try. You okay here?" She was lounging on the living room couch, her computer propped on her belly.

Sleepless nights can kill a man, and they were killing me. When I didn't sleep, I felt trapped in my body. In the mirror each morning I saw the stone faces on Easter Island: grim, paralyzed, unable to wave or shout when actual, living people sailed by. I didn't know if doctors had a word for my condition, but I suspected my blood had begun retreating deep into my organs to keep me alive, which left the outward-facing parts of me the color of junk marble. On good days, when I had logged two or three hours of uninterrupted sleep, I was quick enough with my hands to do magic and could work my way through an hour-long show. When sleep wouldn't come, I'd steal time during the day with ten- or fifteen-minute naps, often seated upright at the kitchen table.

I closed my eyes, and once again demons overran me. I was eight, living in the forests of Ukraine with Dima and the partisans, some thirty fighters who divided their time between hunting for German soldiers and hunting for food. There were other children, and when the adults left us to stalk wild boar or German patrols, we'd stay behind and tend camp. Early one morning, before first light, I woke to the sound of gunfire.

"Wehrmacht! Up! Out! Now!"

Dima yanked me from my sleep sack and ran me across an open field, to the edge of a forest. He flung open the door to a root cellar we'd dug into a hillside, shouting over the gunfire: "Stay here and don't move. Take this revolver. If anyone, *anyone* but me opens this door, kill him. Understand? Point the gun at his chest. Cock the hammer and pull the trigger, the way I taught you. Say something, you blockhead!"

I couldn't.

My brother slammed the wooden door, leaving me alone in the cellar. I heard gunshots and screams muffled by the walls of earth. *Pop pop pop.* Then a burst: *brrrrrrrrrr.* The sun rose. Light streamed through the edges and cracks of the cellar door. An explosion rattled the shelves and I smelled burning wood. I heard screams and shouts and then bigger guns and concussions that hurt my ears. Someone began pounding at the door and threw it wide.

Daylight blinded me. A figure stepped forward.

"Dima?"

"*Aufstehen! Hände hoch!*"

"Dima?"

I felt for the gun in my lap. A uniform? The man wore a uniform and a helmet, but he was lit from behind and I couldn't see clearly. He pointed a rifle. He yelled strange-sounding words. I pointed the gun. I pulled the hammer. I closed my eyes and squeezed the trigger. The roar stunned me, and the muzzle flash scorched my fingers.

The man clutched his chest as I trembled, and he nearly laughed as he said: "*Ein Kind?*" He fell into the cellar, pinning me to a shelf of cabbages. We lay that way for what seemed hours. Unable to wriggle from beneath him, I listened to him die. First came gurgling sounds, then tears, then words: *Gott, Mein Gott.* Then a name. *Gisela, Gisela.* Eventually the sounds stopped. When Dima threw open the door and pulled the corpse aside, he found me shivering and turned to the crowd behind him: "Behold the little fighter! He lives!"

They washed the soldier's blood from my face and clothes and forced vodka on me. The liquor made me sick that night. I screamed and I wretched, and every night since dreams of the soldier have sickened me.

Ein Kind? Mein Gott!

I wondered how the angel of death, who claimed that man's soul, knew not to take mine. After all, his body and my body were pressed together for hours. How could the angel tell us apart? Did he receive special training on how to pluck souls from a battlefield? I was convinced he'd touched us both and was headed to hell before he realized I was alive. Back we came to the forest to return my soul to my body, but he was in such a hurry he left me to fit the parts together myself.

I've been trying ever since.

At the kitchen table, I opened my map of Vermont. With a thick carpenter's pencil, I had drawn my route to freedom: a line linking six stops on my summer tour, six circles, six shows starting in Boston at The Mystery Lounge. We'd head north to Portsmouth, west to Concord, and north again, ending in Canaan, Vermont. From there, I'd drawn a short, final line to the Beecher Falls border crossing. It would take but five minutes to reach Canada and put the nightmare of testifying against my brother behind me. I'd already bought a fake registration for my car along with stolen plates. The forged passport had cost me plenty, but all was in order and I had everything I needed to run.

I looked to Grace in the living room, where she'd fallen asleep clutching her laptop. As it rose and fell, I wondered what I'd say to her when the time came for me to run. Nice knowing you, kid? Wasn't it a fun summer? Be sure to write?

I folded the map.

It was four o'clock. The show started at seven thirty, and it was time to deliver on the work I'd long planned. Before she drifted off, Grace had taken my Matryoshkas and set them in a neat line on the coffee table. Lord knows she'd watched me fiddling with them, and I enjoyed the thought they might entertain her too. Sixty years is a long time for anyone to hold on to a childhood toy. The only reason I still had my Matryoshkas was because I'd taken them with me the day Dima and I left Kortelisy to retrieve a broken axle. "One toy to keep you from complaining all the way there and back again. One," he said. "That's it. We've got to go." I ran to the house for the dolls my father made the winter before from the wood of a linden tree. Our parents told us not to be late getting home, that there were reports of German soldiers in the district.

It was the last we saw them alive.

I reassembled the dolls, fitting each neatly into the others, and curled a strand of hair behind my granddaughter's ear. The monsters from her miserable past had left her alone that afternoon. I wasn't so lucky. "Wake up," I whispered, my hand at her shoulder. "Let's do some magic!"

Eleven: Grace Larson

In the two months I lived with Nate, I'd seen him at his mirror rehearsing every trick he performed in his first show—yet he'd never mentioned Kortelisy, the actual place. Whether or not the miracle he described happened, the audience loved his patter, and so did I. Which left me confused: why would he name an escape after a place that was so wonderful? If Kortelisy was heaven on earth, I didn't understand why he or anyone would want to leave.

"I need a volunteer!" he called. "Some brave soul to assist me as I tempt death. Time for some thrills, ladies and gentlemen. A proper magic show needs an escape, and here comes mine: It's called *The Kortelisy Escape!*"

I waited behind the curtain, ready to do my part.

"Bring up the house lights, Mr. Manager."

He shielded his eyes and scanned the room, then pointed. "Ah! A friend! Mr. Maxim Petrov is in the house. Ladies and gentlemen, we're fortunate indeed! Let's have a big round of applause for Maxim! My escape demands an assistant who's fearless, and Maxim's our man. His name says it all!"

He was gesturing to a table in the far corner of the room. I saw a girl my age, a very pretty woman, and three men, one of them very old. The one who must have been Maxim was protesting. He wanted no part of Nate's egging him on. No one at the table cared, and they were laughing and pushing him toward the stage. The pretty woman and the girl seated to either side of him began to applaud.

"Please, a warm welcome for Mr. Petrov!"

He was a thin man, dressed in tight-fitting jeans and a sport jacket, smiling nervously the way the other volunteers had that evening. He wasn't happy.

"Friends, here's how this will work," said Nate. "I've hired an off-duty Emergency Medical Tech for the escape. Mr. Barnes?" A man in a short-sleeved, khaki uniform was leaning against the wall by the exit. He saluted. "You know CPR, Mr. Barnes. Correct?"

Another salute. "Recertified last week!"

"And you have the portable device that will jump-start my heart in the event of a catastrophe?"

Mr. Barnes held up a little box. "Powered and ready to go!"

"Friends," Nate continued, "I've prepared and signed a document for the house manager and owner of The Mystery Lounge stating they are not responsible should something go wrong with *The Kortelisy Escape*. Mr. Crowley—where are you? Could you please confirm?" From the sound booth at the rear of the room, a man with a bad toupee waved a sheet of paper and gave a thumbs-up sign.

"As for you, Mr. Petrov, I've prepared another document stating that you are not responsible for any harm that may come to me through this escape. Let's fill in your name, and I'll sign. Are you ready?"

Nate filled in Petrov's name and then signed the document.

"To make sure you understand the gravity of what you're about to do, I want you to perform a small escape of your own." Nate produced a Chinese finger trap, a woven cylinder that cinches tight once your pointer fingers are inside and you try pulling them apart. I loved that trick. I couldn't do it the first time Nate tried it on me.

"Stick out two fingers, Maxim. Your pointers."

My grandfather set the cylinder over Petrov's fingers and said: "Ready, set, pull!"

The harder Petrov pulled, the tighter the trap cinched. The audience roared when Nate produced giant hedge clippers from his equipment box. He opened and closed the shears, making guillotine sounds. "What do you say, folks? Shall I cut Maxim's fingers loose? One little snip should do it! You know, there's always a price to pay for freedom. Isn't that so, Maxim? One snip is all."

The audience clapped, and Nate explained that the best strategy for an escape, any escape, is to relax. "No matter how dangerous the moment, clear your mind and relax," he said. He plumped the woven cylinder while it was still on Petrov's fingers and removed the trap. "Relax, Maxim. Here's where you get your revenge on me."

Nate wriggled into a straitjacket and asked Petrov to buckle the straps.

The stage was wider than it was deep, and from behind the curtain I stood close enough to hear Nate wheezing. I could also hear Petrov talking as he pulled the straps tight. "This isn't funny. Whatever you're doing, I don't appreciate it."

"It gets better," my grandfather whispered.

"I need two more volunteers," he called. "Two people to hold a curtain that hides me in the event I don't make it. It's ugly watching a man die. Suffocation is the very worst." He chose a couple seated in front and directed them to the side of the stage, to a pole with a black velvet curtain attached.

"Now watch carefully, everyone, as Maxim wraps my head in plastic. I won't be able to breathe, and, as you can see, with my arms and hands bound tight by the straitjacket, I won't be able to pull the plastic from my nose and mouth. *How*, you might wonder, will I survive?"

I knew what was coming, and even I was nervous.

Petrov shifted the box of plastic wrap between his hands as he might an iron bar, getting a feel for it. It was a store brand that had the words *It clings!* on the box in bright yellow letters. Petrov leaned close. "You are out of your mind, Larson. If you want to die so bad, I'll be happy to arrange it—someplace more private."

Nate turned to the audience. "I nearly forgot, friends . . . my panic bell. You see the pedestal with the can on top? That can's filled with paper clips. If I get in trouble, I'm going to kick it over. It'll make a racket, and Mr. Barnes, our EMT, will leap onto the stage and save me if he can. I'm in better shape than I look. I can hold my breath for ninety seconds."

That was a lie.

"The papers are signed. I, and no one else, am responsible for the stupidity you're about to witness. I'm about to be suffocated, ladies and gentlemen, of my own free will. Who would do such a thing? Mr. Theater Manager, are we set?"

The man from the sound booth shouted: "We're good to go!"

No one was laughing now. The girl from the table at the back of the room called, "No, Maxim. Don't do it!"

"Do it," said Nate. "Show us what you're made of."

"This is sick," someone yelled as Petrov began wrapping my grandfather's face in plastic. I crouched at the base of the curtain wearing my ninja outfit, which disappeared into the black of the stage curtains and the stage itself. I wore a zippered leotard top and bottom with a black hood, gloves, and slippers. At my waist I wore a black bag with my tools: a serrated knife and funnel.

We had practiced hundreds of times. I was ready.

In the seconds after the volunteers raised the pole and curtain, I slid along the stage floor, cut a hole in the plastic wrap with my knife, and inserted the narrow end of a funnel into Nate's mouth so he could breathe. He nodded, our sign that he was okay. Then, just as we rehearsed, he turned onto his side, away from me, and I unbuckled the four leather straps of his straitjacket. From a hidden pocket he removed a scissors with a flat safety end on one blade, which he used to cut though the plastic wrapped around his head.

From start to finish, the release took twenty-five seconds, a little longer than in practice. Then the fun began, though a strange sort of fun. Free of his straitjacket and breathing easily, Nate scooted past me, behind the curtain, to a door that led to a hidden corridor built when The Mystery Lounge was a dinner theater. That corridor circled the room behind a wall so that actors could enter from the rear as well as from stage right or left. We wouldn't be able to do this for every performance, but The Mystery Lounge was laid out perfectly. I spent the next twenty seconds making thumping noises on the floor—the sounds of a someone caught in a death struggle. It was a wicked trick to play on the audience.

All the while, from the far side of the curtain, the off-duty EMT had been calling the time in fifteen-second intervals, in a steady count to ninety. At "Forty-five seconds!" I returned to my hiding spot backstage and let the audience imagine the worst.

At "Sixty seconds!" people began to yell.

At "Seventy-five seconds!" I heard a woman sobbing.

"Ninety seconds!"

Just as the EMT jumped onto the stage and the panicked volunteers dropped their curtain to reveal nothing but an empty straitjacket, Nate burst through the door at the rear of the room, bellowing: "What are you staring at? The man you're worried about is right here—fit as a fiddle!" Caught in a wild swing of emotions, the audience turned and erupted with applause. "Thank you!" He waved as people cheered. "Thank you! Thank you very much! Nate Larson's Tabernacle Tour of Magic is launched! Tell all your friends!" he called. "Tell your family that the tour makes its next stop in Portsmouth, New Hampshire, next Saturday night!"

Everyone, save one man, had turned his way to cheer and clap. He was leaning against the wall beneath the exit sign, staring at the stage. I had opened the curtains just enough to watch Nate in his moment of glory closing out the show. That was plenty wide for Maxim Petrov. Never mind I was still wearing my ninja suit, which was supposed to make me invisible. His eyes cut through the narrow opening and pinned me. He smiled, then waved, and mouthed three words.

I see you.

Twelve: Nate Larson

When Dima visited me in prison, we'd embrace the only way possible, by placing our hands against the security glass in the visitors' booth. It was a cold comfort, being close yet unable to touch. Now the glass was gone, and I hurried across the room to my brother.

"Ho!" he called, our old greeting. "Ho, Little Brother!"

For some people, the words *Hail Mary, full of grace* call them home to themselves. Others say or hear *Blessed are you, O Lord*. The words that anchored my life were *Ho, Little Brother*. For as long as I could remember, this was Dima's greeting. Even when they put me behind bars for a decade, he'd speak those words into the phone on the far side of the security glass to remind me there'd been life before prison. We rushed into each other's arms, I trembling at the weight he'd lost. I could see the bones of his face. Through his jacket, I could count his ribs.

"The lawyers told me not to come," he said. "Lawyers! How could they keep me from a show given by Nataniel the Magician! Did you see us in the corner? Bobby found us a table. You have such a talent, Little Brother!"

Bianchi stood near, arms folded, watching. He'd kept his word.

"It's hard to see from the stage, Dima. But I knew—"

He held me at arm's length for a proper inspection. "What happened, Nataniel? You got old. Isn't he old, Bobby?"

Bianchi extended a hand. "Great show, bud. I'd like you to meet my daughter, Ella."

She was older than my granddaughter by a few years, with a budding woman's body though still a child's face. Seeing her, I recalled Gabrielle, whose change had come at fifteen. Such a bewildering and beautiful age! I smiled at the thought that Grace would get her turn soon. But she wasn't there yet. She still favored floppy T-shirts and ripped jeans. The contrast with Ella Bianchi couldn't have been sharper. Bobby's daughter had applied makeup for her big evening out. She'd chosen clothes to accentuate her curves.

"And, of course, you remember Sveta."

Sveta. Her fingers were interlaced with Petrov's. It sickened me to think of her in that man's bed. He began wagging a finger. "I missed my chance up there, Nate. Next time the plastic'll hold and we'll all get to say pretty words over your coffin."

My brother swayed like a tree, planted in one spot.

"Nataniel, you got so old. How is it possible?"

"I went away, Dima. Ten years is a long time."

With the lights up, The Mystery Lounge looked like a cave, its walls and ceilings and duct work all painted black. The cleaning crew had arrived and begun with their mops.

"No," said Dima. "Older than ten years."

That was true. I *had* aged more than a decade in my time at Danbury. But my brother had crossed an even grimmer divide. There's young old and there's old old. Dima had lost weight. He was losing his balance—he had grabbed onto tables and chairs to work his way across the room. His booming "Ho, Little Brother!" had gone reed thin. Even his hands looked wrong. He'd once had powerful hands that worked plows and cleared fields, hands that in wartime had killed soldiers and snatched me from harm's way too many times to count. Now they dangled at the end of his arms like dead weights on a chain. His eyes were worse. He was lost. He was a man studying a scrap of paper with an address for the wrong corner in the wrong city. Eleanor Hunt had no business putting my brother on trial even if he was guilty of tax evasion.

"Nataniel the Magician! Everyone cheered, Little Brother! And this must be Grace!"

At least a dozen people had lingered after the show, asking me to sign flyers and discuss the finer points of magic. With the last of them gone, Grace stepped from behind the curtain, not wanting to give anything away about *The Kortelisy Escape*. She still wore her ninja black and was tugging at the zipper of her leotard, which, I noticed, had nicked the skin at her neck.

"Your lovely assistant," said Petrov, introducing himself. "You helped your grandfather with the escape. Right?"

"Sorry. Magicians don't tell."

"Come here, child. Give your old uncle a kiss."

Grace took half a step back when she saw Dima.

"It's okay," I said, nudging her. "He won't bite."

But she looked as though he would.

"Nataniel, did you know that Grace and I met once? After you went away, Gabby and this one came out to my farm for the Fourth of July. Do you remember, child? Bobby's Ella was there too. And here she is, all grown up. You were so young, the two of you. Pretty as buttons. Do you remember the tractor ride? The hay wagon?"

"Not buttons," Petrov corrected him. "They're prettier than buttons. They're gorgeous young women now. Is there anything anywhere to match a sixteen year old who's—"

"Grace, do . . . you . . . do you . . ."

Dima lost the thought, lost his sentence. Before he realized he needed help, Bianchi was at his elbow. Bobby, I realized, was the only one who stood between my brother and a nursing home. And here I was preparing to leave for my summer tour and then leave for good in August? I hadn't failed only Grace by getting sent to prison. My brother was fading, and I had done nothing and could do nothing to help him.

Sveta gave my granddaughter no chance to resist an embrace, then turned to Ella. "Look at you two! America grows such tall, pretty girls. In Ukraine, we grow women short and thick. We all look like a grandmother at thirty! You," she announced, hooking arms with them, "are my new American sisters! I adopt you!"

"You're breaking my heart," said Petrov, sucking on his beer. "You adopted *me*."

Dima had begun eating leftovers off a nearby table. Bobby snatched the plate away as Petrov slipped an arm around Sveta's shoulders then worked a hand down her back, to her hips. He pulled her close and said, "Nate, I didn't appreciate what you did to me onstage."

Bobby stepped between us. "Save it, Maxim. We're having a good time here."

"Hey—can't anyone take a joke? Did you see? I wrapped him like Sunday's leftover dinner. That was good fun!" Sveta was a born diplomat. She sidestepped Petrov and walked Grace and Bianchi's daughter across the room, which left Petrov smiling with his nice white teeth. "Just so you know, the fifty thousand's off the table. Now you leave because I want you gone. Tell me you know how to spell *gone*."

"Sure," I said. "A-u-g-u-s-t. Grace and I have some magic to do first."

I headed back to the stage to pack my things. Sveta and the girls had claimed a corner, and I watched Grace sitting opposite her new friends, positioning herself so the light was to her advantage, at her back. She was prepping *The Vanished Card*.

"What kind of stupid are you?" said Bobby, catching up to me. "You met the guy for ten minutes at the store. You have no idea who he is or who his people are, and you haul him onto the stage to make a fool of him? Russians don't like insults, especially in front of their women."

"He turned Sveta, Bobby. He makes me sick."

"She didn't exactly have a choice. And you don't either." He had parked Dima at a nearby table and went to retrieve him. "Tell him yourself, Nate." He stepped aside and moved my brother close. "Go on. Tell him you're leaving."

My big brother could have been a cardboard cutout.

"We'll speak alone," I said.

"Sorry. I change his diapers. There's nothing I can't hear."

"Nataniel, how are you! Nataniel the magician!"

We embraced once more. "We got old," I whispered. "Imagine, two old Lazarenkos." He patted me on the back, and I mourned him gone. But then, just as Bobby had warned me, a light suddenly flashed in his eyes. On/off. Off/on. He was back with me for the moment. It was terrifying.

"Dima?"

"Bobby does everything for me now. Did you know?"

Bianchi glanced back at Petrov. "You two shouldn't even be talking. If Eleanor Hunt saw this, she could use it against us in court when you disappear. I'm sorry, Nate, but no more visits. I can't allow it."

"And it's up to you to allow or not?"

"Be nice, Nataniel. Bobby helps me."

"Tell him, Dima. Tell him you and I can talk alone."

An urgent look in my brother's eyes, then: "Bobby, take me to the toilet."

I was nearly desperate watching Dima shuffle away. He'd been strong. He'd saved lives during the war and after, and this was his reward—to need an aide propping him up at a urinal? Across the room, Grace was mid-trick. I could see Sveta and Ella leaning in, watching. She was holding their attention. *That's my girl*, I thought.

When Dima returned, Bobby took a few steps back, giving us a measure of privacy. I led my brother to the corner table, where he chased the remains of his dinner with a single chopstick.

"Talk to me about the court case," I said.

"Court case . . ."

"The indictment. Eleanor Hunt. Tax evasion. They're putting you on trial."

"Right! It's terrible. Those people!"

"I won't testify against you, Dima. I would never do that."

"Of course you won't. Bobby says you're leaving. Where are you going, Nataniel?"

"Away."

"Have a good trip! I thought you were in prison."

"I got out." I patted his hand. "When I run, the government will send people to find me. I can never return to Boston. What will happen to the store?"

"Maxim takes care of everything. It's gotten hard for me. Sometimes I can think and sometimes I can't. Sveta—look at her. The last of my Rachels! A year ago, I took Maxim to Kiev to introduce him to my contacts—the passport and visa people, the customs agents, all the people I bribed over the years. He said he wanted to learn my work. He wants it to continue. Isn't that great? I could still find my way a year ago. But not now. Now Maxim will go alone to Ukraine to find girls. He speaks good Russian. He'll make his way."

Across the room, Ella and Sveta shrieked when Grace chose their cards. I could just hear her saying, "Sorry, a magician performs a trick only once." And then: "I'm related to Harry Houdini. No one knows yet. But it's almost definite."

I turned back to my brother. "Maxim is not continuing your work."

The light in his eyes was blinking off again, and I gave his arm a shake. I didn't know if I'd have another chance. "Tell me. Did Petrov force you to sell the store?"

"No. I *gave* him the store!"

Forty years, gone.

"Nataniel, Rachel . . . she didn't jump off a cliff. Papa and I found her in a ditch by one of the fields. She'd fainted. She didn't want to kill herself."

"I *know* that, Dima."

"And we never fished for sturgeon. The lake was too far away. Why didn't you tell about the soldiers? You confused me. I get so confused."

"I'll help you."

"You're leaving. Why? I want to go home with you."

I heard a crash, then shouts and a scuffle. When I looked up, Bianchi was bent over a kid in the cleaning crew, a fist raised just inches from his face. He'd grabbed a handful of shirt and was spitting mad. "She's too young to date you, you little twerp!"

Ella was beating on his back. "Daddy, stop. *Stop* it!"

Petrov wandered over for a ringside seat. He pointed and started laughing when the manager appeared from the kitchen, holding a cast-iron pan. "Enough!" the man yelled. "All of you, out to the sidewalk. I'm calling the cops in two minutes if you're not gone. Hey, Larson—nice friends. Get out!"

"Daddy, *why?*"

Ella was crying.

"The little punk . . . He said he wanted to buy you a few drinks and then—I won't repeat what he said. You're too young to drink. Or date people like that. Ever."

"I'm *sixteen!*"

"And for this you beat a child?" said Dima, startled back to his senses. He insisted I walk him across the room. "What, Bobby, you never talked big, puffed out your chest as a boy? You and Ella, drive me home now."

It wasn't my fight, and I didn't much care how it ended. What I cared about was Dima melting away. I cared that Petrov had turned Sveta into a whore and that she was sliding down a hole from which she'd never return. That week, I'd had business cards printed. Grace urged me to add "Related to Houdini" somewhere on it, but I didn't. I fished out a card and gave one to Sveta. "Call if you need help," I said, as Maxim finished off his beer.

"Nataniel?"

For a moment, Dima's old voice . . . enough of it to feel the full weight of what I was about to lose. Not only would I be giving away my granddaughter when I crossed to Canada; I would be giving away any chance of seeing my brother again, not that he was long for this world. I faced an embarrassing truth: at sixty-six, I still needed a big brother. How could this be? I fell into his arms, looking for the old Dima. I wanted Grace to meet the man who saved me, who fought Nazis, who talked a feverish child past immigration officers. I wanted her to know about all the Rachels he saved. To my granddaughter, my brother and I must have seemed ridiculous old fools. But she never ate the rabbits and squirrels he snared to keep us alive in winter, never needed him to make a tent of his body to keep from freezing to death. Years ago my heart had cracked in a root cellar, in a forest, during a war. Most of the blood had run dry. But every now and then it flowed, and when it did I hurt.

"Little Brother," he said, the light in his eyes flickering. "Kortelisy was no heaven on earth. Where's the pain in your story? The death? The soldiers? Did you forget? Open your eyes for once and see the world as it is!" He grinned. "Come, let's bless each other the way Papa used to. Do you remember?"

I remembered.

We held the other's face in our hands. We kissed each other's eyes, then each other's forehead. "Go and live," he said.

I wanted to live. I truly did. But I'd forgotten how.

Thirteen: Grace Larson

One day when my mother was sick, she took me to a farm outside Boston for a little vacation. The day started well enough with a picnic and a hay ride but ended with a woman in tears and Dima screaming at me to *Get out!* I'd forgotten why mostly because I didn't *want* to remember. Whatever happened had to have been awful given how sick I felt on seeing Dima again. Nate brought it up twice the next day, how rude I'd been. I told him I didn't care. What I wanted to talk about was his show the night before.

"The audience loved the Rachel story," I said.

"You think?"

"I do! And *The Kortelisy Escape*! What a great night."

We sat on the glider at our apartment on Marathon Street, in the shadow of an oak that was way older than the house. Sometimes I'd go to the back porch to sit alone and listen to the wind through the leaves. The glider was a rusty old thing. It screamed every time it moved, like I was pinching it.

"Nate?"

He slowed us down.

"I just finished *On Eagles' Wings*. Want to see it?"

I'd been making promises about letting him see the computer games I built, and I was finally ready to show him my latest. I figured I owed it to him, all the hours we spent on our separate projects working not even ten feet from one another.

He'd been away for so long he didn't know what a mouse was or a cursor or even what *click* meant. I introduced him to the basics so that he'd be able to play without my help. The screen was blank. When he hit the space bar, a cursor appeared on a spiral staircase that wound up into a tower. I raised his finger and brought it down on the mouse, showing him how to move the cursor around the screen.

Through the speaker we heard footsteps and clanging metal.

"They're after you," I said. "Hurry up."

"Who's after me?"

"Soldiers. Go on. Go up the stairs."

"How'd you make the sounds?"

"I used my computer at school. I carried it up and down the stone steps. It's a recording."

"You did all this?"

I paused to show him the program I used to build my games, Naturmkr. "The software does most of it." I said. "My job is to supply pictures of the main characters and whatever sound effects I want." There was a whole library of photos and sounds I could choose from in the program, and I also grabbed my own material by recording it on my computer. The program did the rest, after I made some basic decisions. Did I want my game to take place in a forest or in the mountains? Was this going to be a chasing game or a rescue game or both?

He cursored up the staircase and found himself standing before a window shuttered with rough wooden planks. Sunlight streamed through the knot holes and around the edges. The sound of footsteps was getting nearer.

"Nate. You'd better open the window."

"*Open* it?"

"Click on it."

I raised his finger, lowered it on the mouse, then released. The shutters burst open to reveal a green valley and, in the distance, a mountain pass.

"It's beautiful!" he said.

I had snapped the photo from a library book at school.

"Jump, Nate. Click anywhere outside the window. Either that or turn and fight."

"How do I fight?"

"You click all over the place as fast as you can—and use your special powers, which you haven't collected yet. I'll show you later. But if you played the whole game . . . watch out! They've got weapons."

He saw the problem at once. "If I jump, I'll fall into the moat."

"Or you might sprout eagles' wings and fly away. But you won't know until you try. That's the point of the game, right there. You collect your powers along the way, then use them when you get into trouble."

"Did I collect any?"

"Maybe. Click on the window and find out."

He did and fell into the moat. The screen went blank.

"What happened?" he asked.

"You died, Nate. It's no big deal."

— • —

WE WERE packed and ready to leave early the next morning, a Tuesday, for the Saturday night show—which would give us plenty of time to get to Portsmouth and do a little sightseeing along the way. With so many things to look forward to, waiting felt like a punishment. I could barely remember wanting anything more than to begin that trip. It was going to be the best summer ever. Finally the time grew near enough for me to count the hours.

The doorbell startled both of us.

Nate was busy at his mirror turning silk scarves into a wand, so I ran down to the landing . . . to find Miss Roberts with a man and a woman in police uniforms standing behind her. I was cautious as I opened the door.

"How are you, Grace?"

"You didn't call. I thought you were supposed to call."

"Is your grandfather home?"

"He's upstairs."

"Grace," he yelled. "Who is it?"

"We'll just follow you up, dear."

"Why are the police with you?"

On their belts they carried a gun and handcuffs and extra bullets.

"Hello, Mr. Larson."

He saw them in his mirror and turned around, setting his trick aside. "You were just here," he told Miss Roberts. "You told us we passed the inspection. You're supposed to call before you come. That's the rule. Why are you here?"

I ran to him, and he set a hand on my shoulder.

"This is different, I'm afraid. Grace, you'll need to pack your things."

"Don't you move," said Nate.

Miss Roberts crossed the room and delivered an envelope. "Someone filed a complaint," she said. "When we get a complaint like this, DCF takes custody until we can confirm or dismiss it."

"What complaint?"

"A serious one. Abuse."

"Nate?"

He pulled me closer. I leaned in to him as he tore open the envelope and read a few sentences.

"*Inappropriate touching?*"

The police tried wedging me away, but I maneuvered between them and buried my face in his chest. Nate held onto me—the first time I let him hold me—and I held onto him because they'd come to take me when, for once in my life, I wanted to stay. I was getting crazy inside, holding on as if I'd fall out of a plane if I let go. "Nate? *Na-ate?*"

The police woman grabbed my hand.

I shook her loose.

"*Where* are you taking me?"

"To the DCF dormitory."

"I hate that place! *NO!*"

I grabbed Nate's arm but eased away from him as I thought a terrible thought—that maybe this was all a show. That maybe he was done being a rental parent and had given me back, in secret. "Why are you doing this, Nate? Why are you letting this happen? I don't understand. I don't *understand!*" The cop picked me up and carried me across the room.

"Don't," said Miss Roberts. "Don't struggle. We're here for your safety."

I thought I was losing my mind. Had he given me back? No . . . she said they were taking me. I tried to think. I could have kicked and screamed. I could have fought them. I didn't. Instead I got very, very cold. I hated Miss Roberts, I hated the cops, I hated Nate, I hated every adult I ever met, I hated everything about my life. When could *I* decide how and where I wanted to live? I was done, finished with DCF and everything it touched. Yes, Nate was better than the others, but what good was that if he couldn't protect me? I went to my room for my suitcase, which was already packed and waiting for our tour to begin. Our tour. Now I would have to forget the tour and forget the summer.

With the cops there making sure he didn't interfere, and with Nate unable to see down the hallway to the bedrooms, I marched right to his night table, grabbed his Matryoshka dolls, and dropped them in my computer bag. *Perfect,* I thought. He'd miss them. Let him walk around in my world for a while.

He was screaming at her now, demanding to know who made the charge. "Grace, tell them. Have I ever . . . touched you in a bad way? Tell them. Tell the truth! Ask her, Miss Roberts. Take her to another room like you did last time. Ask anything you want."

I knew all about bad touching from my time with Mr. Parker. Nate had never asked me to pick up my T-shirt and dance in circles for him. He never ordered me onto his lap, late at night, for giddyup rides. He never touched me the wrong way, not unless getting kissed on the top of the head was a crime. What did it matter anymore? Any of it? Rental parents, all of them, existed for only one thing: to ruin my life.

"I'd never . . . *EVER* . . . I would *NEVER*— This is my *home*. She's my granddaughter. *YOU CAN'T DO THIS!*"

But they could and they did, and I didn't care.

Downstairs, the dog was howling.

Miss Roberts saw my suitcase and backpack.

"You're ready then?"

"Who filed the complaint?"

"Mr. Larson, I'm not allowed—"

"You were just here. Did you see *anything* that was a problem?"

"That's true, I didn't."

"Who filed the complaint?"

She opened a briefcase, then a folder, and flipped a few pages.

"Anonymous. Anonymous filed the complaint."

"Anonymous? I know exactly who *Anonymous* is, and this has nothing to do with child abuse."

"It makes no difference," she said, turning me toward the stairs. "When we get a complaint of abuse, we investigate. You won't be able to see or contact your granddaughter until we complete our work. This will take three or four months."

When I looked back, I saw an old man with tears wetting his cheeks. He reached for me, but I was already across the room, already gone in my head. I should have cared. But why care when all caring brings is pain? I'd forgotten the first rule, and I was determined never to let that happen again.

He was a rental parent. Rental parents come and go, and now it was Nate's turn to go.

THE PERSISTENT QUEEN

Fourteen: Grace Larson

When I have a nightmare, it's always the same nightmare, courtesy of the Massachusetts Department of Children and Families. In this dream, an arm—there's no body—is swinging a bloody hatchet, chasing me down a corridor at night going *Chop chop*, aiming for my neck. Both the arm and the hatchet belong to Ryan J. Cropsy, a foster kid who got lost in the DCF dorm and never made it out. If the house matrons ruled the dorm by day, the nights belonged to Cropsy. Janine Murphy told me all about him. She was the only girl either of us knew who'd logged more nights in the dorm than I had. She was the least-wanted of the least wanted. I was five and she was eight when she sat me down to explain what happened to kids who wandered the hallways after lights out. "Never," she said, "go to the bathroom at night."

Of course, Janine rigged things so I would.

A few days later, before bedtime, she called me over to her bed and pointed to a trunk in which she kept food stolen from the dorm's pantry. It was the younger girls who stole the goodies because only they could shimmy up through the drop-ceiling panels and into the heating ducts. Once inside those, it was a straight shot to the kitchen and all the food we could ever want. Many of the girls had done this, including Janine. It was a test to get in to our little sorority.

That night she offered me pretzels and slices of pepperoni. Then, just as pleasant as could be, she asked if I wanted some apple juice. I drank several cups and went to bed. The DCF dormitory, a former hospital, is a two-story brick building with long, tile-lined corridors and large rooms. I shared a bedroom with five girls. Everyone was asleep that night when I woke feeling like a dam about to burst and unwilling to risk going to the bathroom.

Janine had carefully cut the face off a box of Arm & Hammer baking soda to paint the clearest possible picture of how I'd die if I went to the bathroom alone, after hours. On the box she'd drawn a hatchet to replace the hammer in the famous drawing. "Hammers don't leave enough blood," she explained. "Cropsy needs blood because after he kills you, he washes himself in blood until the rest of his body begins to appear. At first, he's just an arm. The more he washes, the more of him appears until he's whole again and he looks just like the kid who got lost, dressed in his little suit, waiting for someone to take him home. But no one *ever* takes him home, Grace. He's still waiting. It's horrible!"

That night, I wet my bed.

In the morning, our house matron made a point of calling me "Little Miss Bedwetter" in front of the other girls. When Janine finally stopped laughing, she told me all about the drop-ceiling panels and the heating ducts and asked if I wanted to join the club.

I joined and within a month was tormenting the new arrivals.

I turned out to be a natural climbing through the drop-panel ceiling and making my way to the pantry. Once I pushed the panels out of the way and climbed up, I would grab and step onto pipes that were bolted to the real ceiling, which could support my weight. It was like a highway up there. The girls who'd gone before me had even pasted signs on the heating ducts: *Grab here. Step here. Pantry this way.*

It never felt good telling the new girls that Cropsy would get them. But they, and I, were easy targets. We had no mothers or fathers, at least any sober or fit enough to care for us. We had no neighbors or cousins to take us in. We had only each other, and I assumed we would live as sisters. If that was true, it was only in the worst way. We were more like dogs at the pound desperate to be claimed by a good family without even knowing what a good family was.

I had two advantages. The first was blond hair, which for some reason interested rental parents. They thought I was pretty, which seemed such a stupid reason to like a child. My secret weapon, though, was that I was always running at school, trying to exhaust myself before taking the bus back to the dorm so that I'd get to my cot and just collapse. All the running flushed my cheeks and made me look healthy, my second advantage. "Show us that one!" they'd say, pointing to my photo in the Availables book. "What a pretty name, and what a pretty face to go with it!" Once they took me home and got to know me, they gave me back. Eight times it happened, including Nate, and I didn't care if he *was* my grandfather. I was sick of being advertised like a used sofa, sick of being on my best behavior in the hope someone would like me enough to let me stay. The moon shot was adoption. No one ever dared to hope for that.

After Miss Roberts checked me into the DCF dorm, try as I might I couldn't forget the image of Nate reaching for me as I turned down the stairs. He looked so desperately sad, and if I was going to move on I needed to forget that. So I convinced myself that Miss Roberts and the police showed up as part of a trick to make me believe DCF was reclaiming me when it was actually Nate who wanted me gone. Sometimes I wondered what real parents did when they got tired of their children. All parents must hate their kids at some point because kids can be so obnoxious. But only rental parents get to give kids back. That was the problem, and the solution seemed clear enough. Run. It would be an easy thing to take a bus to the train station instead of to school one morning.

I could be gone before anyone thought to look for me.

The only good news in my life was the new computer game I'd begun to write, called *Chopped!* Meeting Nate's brother at The Mystery Lounge is what gave me the idea. I had only the haziest memory of what had happened so long ago on his farm, aside from the fact that afterward I began crying so violently my mother contacted her case worker at DCF to make sure Dima could never become my foster parent. I wouldn't talk about it, and my mother didn't know any details beyond my saying *no* when she asked if he'd touched me. She was dying at the time and was on a mission. With her own mother dead from cancer and her father, Nate, in jail, with no one willing to take me in, she arranged my care with DCF as best she could while she still had the strength.

Somehow, sadness over my mother and the memory of something terrible at Dima's farm got tangled in my head. The only way to move on was to do what I did best: build a game. The story practically laid itself out: I'd use the Naturmkr program not to find and rescue some helpless girl, my typical goal, but to find Dima and chop off his head as thoroughly and completely as I had killed off Mr. Parker in my previous games.

The more I worked, the more details I remembered of that day at the farm, which Dima had rented to grow vegetables for the grocery. There was a garden and a path that wound its way to a shed with a yellow door. I remembered collecting butter-cups for my mother as I walked along the path. I remembered hearing a girl crying, an older girl. I remembered approach-ing the yellow door. The crying got louder and I heard the girl saying *Please, Please don't!* I reached for the handle and turned it. When I opened the door, I saw Dima with a needle in his hands, about to poke this girl in the crook of her arm. From the waist up, which was all I could see, she was naked. When she saw me, she screamed.

That's when Dima turned and roared, "Get out!"

In my game, Dima lived on the far side of a yellow door and Cropsy roamed the garden, protecting him. To kill Dima, you had to cross the garden and survive Cropsy's attacks. The game-winning move would be to trick Cropsy into cutting off Dima's head, then watch Cropsy die as he bathed in Dima's blood.

One game, two bogeymen.

Janine Murphy and I had crossed paths many times at the dorm, but she was nowhere to be found when DCF dragged me back this time. I wondered where she'd landed or if she'd run away, as I intended to do. But I didn't wonder too much because she wasn't a good person. Neither was I. The truth was that in Janine's beautiful face I saw my ugliest self. That's what DCF did to us: made us into blood bathers and head choppers, each sunk in her own little nightmare. The worst of it? Janine was the only friend I'd ever had, and I missed her.

— • —

A few weeks before Miss Roberts came for me, Nate decided one day to practice his magic outside. We were seated on a bench on the Cambridge Common, just outside Harvard Square. Our first show at The Mystery Lounge was approaching, and he had printed flyers to distribute and to tape in store windows.

I grabbed some flyers, ready to advertise the show.

Nate held me back.

"Watch," he said.

He pointed to a man in a blue jumpsuit pulling gear from a truck. The man wore knee-high rubber boots and rubber gloves that nearly reached his elbows. On the side of his truck I saw a name, "EZ Exterminators," printed beneath cartoon drawings of a long pole and a net that held a raccoon, a squirrel, and two plump rats.

"Watch him work," said Nate. "Cambridge Common dates to the 1700s, and there are tunnels underneath us thick with rats bigger than you."

We watched the man set bags of poison in black boxes, which he placed in quiet, shady spots: between a wall and a utility pole, behind a trash can, in a cluster of bushes. He set eight rat traps, total. Then he did something strange. The common was beautiful, with old oaks, a ball field, and a playground. Maintenance crews had worked hard to keep it in good shape. I thought it odd, then, to watch this man reach into a plastic bag and cover his traps with large handfuls of leaves.

"He's junking it up!" I said.

"No, he isn't. He's thinking like a rat."

Nate explained. "The leaves hide the bait and give the rats a quiet, protected place to eat. They feel safe," he said. "And when they feel safe, they'll take the poison. If they're scared or jumpy, they won't. And if they don't, the rat catcher won't kill them and won't get paid. That's why he uses leaves. It's a trick." He reached into a pocket for a metal comb and worked the hair from his eyes. "It's more or less what I'll be doing at The Mystery Lounge."

I set the flyers aside.

"You're going to kill your audience? I don't think so."

He shrugged. "You'll see. When you step up to the Big Show, you need to kill them. They expect it. In fact, that's what they pay for."

I didn't get it.

"You've got to put them at ease, Grace. Let them eat what you're serving, then *bam*." He made a fist. "Think of it this way. A magic trick is like a cliff, and my job is to walk people to the edge and, with a smile, push them over. People need that edge. They want to be pushed because they want their Tabernacle Moments. We all do. You'll know you're a magician when you perform a trick and see total and complete confusion in the faces of your audience. It only lasts a second, if that long, but I'm telling you it's a beautiful thing."

I hated all this talk of poison and killing, but I had to admit Nate was making a weird kind of sense. I remembered *The Three Roses* and *The Disappearing Coin*—tricks that had left me speechless. With those as with others I watched him practice before his mirror, I had fallen somehow. Each trick killed me just a little in the sense that, in the second or two after, it was as if he'd placed my head in an enormous bell and went *gong*. How to say it? I wasn't *me* for a moment. I was . . . just *there* wondering what had happened.

He pointed to the rat catcher. "Your turn," he said.

I wasn't sure what he meant.

"It's time, and there's no reason you can't do this. You've been practicing, and I know you brought your cards. Go show me you can drop somebody's jaw. Go on, push someone over a cliff."

No way was I ready.

"The first time's the hardest," he said. "I know you can do *The Vanished Card*. What about your patter? Have you come up with a good story?"

"Nate, I'm not going to go *kill* anyone."

"Use your own words if you don't like mine. But one way or another, you've got to kill them—at least for a second or two."

Nearby a young couple was kissing on a bench. I'd been trying not to stare, and I was mortified when Nate pointed to them just as openly and clearly as he'd pointed to the rat catcher. "What do you think? Are they enjoying themselves?"

"You're embarrassing me. Stop it."

"All right, then I'll answer my own question. Yes, they're enjoying themselves! You can't fake love, and you can't fake being amazed by magic. You can read wonder in a person's face every time. If those kids were faking, either one of them, they'd know it in a second and they'd go bust."

He pointed again.

He could have put it a thousand ways, but in the end what he wanted was for me to lie, to set people up and if not kill them for real at least fool them, which is a kind of killing, just to get them to go *Aha!* at the end of a trick. Part of me felt bad for what I was about to do with *The Vanished Card.* I'd gotten good, and I knew I could fool people.

I confessed I was nervous.

"Of course you're nervous. But if you want to be a magician . . ."

"I'd be lying, Nate. Magic tricks are lies."

"Yes, they are. But your audience knows that, so where's the problem? If you're good, they forget you're lying. Do you know how you'll know? By the look on their faces when you amaze them. Come on, do your trick for me and at least one other person on the Common. If you're still upset about lying to people, then you can give up performing. Let's hear your patter for *The Vanished Card.* What did you come up with?"

"It's terrible."

"I'll be the judge of that."

I closed my eyes and blinked them open. I stood before Nate as if he were a complete stranger. "Excuse me, sir. Here's a flyer for a magic show on July 8th. My grandfather's performing, and he's one of the world's greatest living magicians. He's related to Houdini, which makes me related to Houdini. He studied with people who studied with people going all the way back, and he taught me a trick. Can I show you?"

"Good. There's not a soul alive who'd refuse an opening like that. Go on."

"Magic runs in our family, sir. It skips generations. Ever since I can remember I knew I was different. I could tell what people were thinking without their saying a word. It really spooked my parents. They'd be looking for car keys, and without their ever telling me the keys were lost I'd say, '*They're on the floor behind the radiator.*' When I was eight years old, they took me to the Crocker School of Mind Reading to see if I could develop my gift. It's a terrible gift, sir. The teachers taught me to look into people's eyes and learn all their secrets. I couldn't take a bus trip down Mass Ave without knowing what made everyone wake up screaming at night. This gift of mine was *scary*. I finally left the Crocker School last spring. Now I'm studying with my grandfather. I'm his apprentice, and he's performing at The Mystery Lounge. He's amazing, and I learned this trick from him. I'll show you, okay? I'll read your mind."

I performed *The Vanished Card*, gave Nate a flyer, then sat on the bench and crossed my arms. "I was horrible. *Horrible!*"

"No, that was very good."

"I couldn't kill *anyone* with that story. Not a flea."

"The Crocker School—I like it. See that woman over there, on the bench, reading? Walk over to her and give her a Tabernacle Moment with *The Vanished Card*. Use the Crocker School story."

"Nate, *please*."

"Just go and we'll talk."

I owed him at least one public performance. That was our deal, so I walked over to the woman and very politely interrupted her. She was friendly enough. She listened and agreed to watch *The Vanished Card*, all forty seconds of it. Then I handed her a flyer and ran back to Nate, my heart pounding.

"Well?"

"Her face," I said, struggling for the words. "It went blank, Nate. Then she went, '*Oh my!*' Then she smiled. Then she started *laughing*. She loved it. It was crazy! I really did something to her."

He touched my cheek with a knobby finger and handed me a stack of flyers. "No," he said, struggling to his feet. "You did something *for* her."

Nate spun my head that day and didn't care if it ended up pointing backward. I was a little giddy when I asked what story *he'd* be telling at the show to give folks their Tabernacle Moments. He was cagey with his answer: "My patter? It's the story of a young woman from my childhood in Europe, during the war."

"Which war?" I asked.

"The one that ruined me."

THE VANISHED CARD

STEPS:

1. FORM A SIX-CARD MINI-DECK WITH FACE CARDS. USE OVERSIZE CARDS FOR A CROWD.

2. ASK AUDIENCE TO MENTALLY SELECT A SINGLE CARD.

3. REVERSE FAN AND MAKE A SHOW OF PULLING ONE CARD.

WE'RE OUT OF FLYERS!

4. OPTIONAL: CREATE A DIVERSION, USING ACCOMPLICE IF NECESSARY.

5. SWAP OUT THE SIX-CARD DECK FOR A NEW
FIVE-CARD DECK.

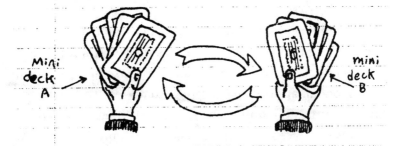

Mini
deck
A

mini
deck
B

6. DISPLAY THE SWITCHED
DECK TO THE AUDIENCE AND
ASK THEM TO FIND THEIR CARD.
THEY CANNOT, SINCE ALL OF
THE CARDS HAVE BEEN
SWAPPED OUT.

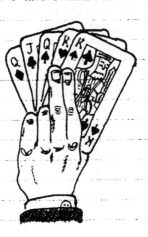

7. SNAP THE FAN SHUT QUICKLY.

Fifteen: Nate Larson

In any language, the name of the anonymous person who filed a DCF complaint against me was spelled M-A-X-I-M P-E-T-R-O-V. I was sure of it, and I vowed to make him pay not in pieces, but all at once and severely. To do that I'd have to get him out of Boston, on the road. But first things first. Within an hour of Grace's abduction—there was no other word for it—I was on the phone with the US attorney's office demanding to speak with Eleanor Hunt. The receptionist put me off, at which point I asked her to tell Miss Hunt I wouldn't testify against my brother.

Somehow they found room in her busy schedule.

Two hours later I was standing before the Moakley Courthouse, a glass and brick wonder far too handsome for the nasty business conducted inside. To my back, across Fort Point Channel, the city and its towers gleamed with the kind of money I would never make. I didn't care. I didn't need my name on the masthead of a law firm or a bank. I didn't need to build office towers. I needed this child, the one I had considered abandoning for my brother's sake. I had reached a crisis. Dima was guilty of tax evasion and far more, though the laws he broke in saving the Rachels meant nothing compared to the good he'd done. If Hunt somehow managed to return Grace to me and I testified, I would condemn my brother to prison. If I ran out on Grace, which was now unthinkable, I'd be condemning her to foster care hell. And if I didn't do something about Petrov, he was going to shoot me.

The receptionist directed me to a conference room, where I found the US attorney at a table overlooking the same skyline that had left me cold. "I heard about your little problem," she said. "I received this a few hours ago from your case manager at DCF." She slid a letter across the table.

> To: The Department of Children and Families, Commonwealth of Massachusetts
>
> Re: Grace Larson
>
> From: A concerned citizen
>
> I have observed a potentially inappropriate physical relationship between Nataniel Larson and Grace Larson. As her foster parent, Mr. Larson has formal custody of his granddaughter. I have seen him touch her bare leg, above the knee, and touch her bottom in the way coaches will sometimes touch players at sporting events—except his hand lingered where it shouldn't have. My conscience requires me to call this potentially serious matter to your attention.

"A lie," I said.

"I'll be the first to lock you up if it isn't. The Department of Children and Families is obligated to investigate. Sexual predation is a nuclear offense, that and physical abuse. It's the absolute worst, and neither DCF nor I can be put in a position of—"

I was in no mood.

"Let me tell you what we're discussing here," I said. "It never happened. Get Grace back by the end of the week, or you can tear up my deal and send me back to prison. Without custody of my granddaughter, I will not testify against Dima."

She took the letter from my hands.

"I have no control over DCF."

"Then lock me up now. I'm sorry we ever met. I would never hurt that child."

I doubted she cared about Grace, and I knew she didn't care about me beyond the testimony I promised: that the grocery ran a hefty profit and Dima buried those profits in losses for equipment he never bought and payments to contractors who didn't exist. Hunt was half right. The grocery had become a front for trafficking Petrov's girls. But to give her that story meant I'd have to explain the Rachel Project, which presented a problem. What Dima did, what I helped him do, broke a dozen laws. He'd risked everything to give girls like Sveta Zelenko a chance the real Rachel never had. I could not break faith with him, not yet. I wouldn't tell that story unless I was out of options.

She asked me to wait.

I returned to the reception area, where a uniformed marshal had parked himself just outside the door. When I went in search of a restroom, he approached. "Mr. Larson, can I help you?"

"I'm sixty-six. Maybe in twenty years. For now I'm good."

"I've got instructions to keep you in the building. I'll stand outside, if you don't mind."

An hour later, Hunt summoned me. "I bought you your summer back," she said. "With allegations of abuse, DCF typically presumes guilt and then investigates. Their first step is to remove the child. I got them to presume innocence this time, mostly because of the good report you got from one of their case officers just a few weeks ago. So you can have Grace for the summer. I don't need to tell you what will happen if the charges turn out to be true."

"I appreciate—"

"Don't thank me. Just testify in August. If I had any sense, you'd be in Danbury until then." In fact, she'd pushed hard for that when we negotiated my release. But I refused to help her if she didn't let me out early, for the summer.

Hunt pointed me out the door. "Stay in touch," she said. "And don't think I don't appreciate how close the Canadian border is to the last stop on your tour. What is it, Canaan, Vermont? My father was a Baptist preacher, Mr. Larson. He taught me that the best way to resist temptation is to keep clear of it, but you've gone ahead and booked a show in Canaan, which is not even ten miles from Canada. I've got some advice: *Don't*. We've already alerted customs agents on both sides of the border about who you are and when you'll be in the neighborhood. They've got your ID and prints, so don't make that mistake. Don't even think about running."

Sixteen: Grace Larson

Jacqueline Roberts came to interview me at the DCF dormitory the day after I arrived. She carried a large canvas bag and in it a loose-leaf binder better suited for interviewing six-year-olds. She turned pages and showed me drawings of all the ways stick figures could touch each other. She never used the word *sex*. It was all very embarrassing, and I answered her like a metronome: No. No. No. No.

"Has he ever offered money or gifts, then tried to touch you?"

"*No*. That's what Mr. Parker did."

Twenty-three pages, twenty-three *Nos*.

"You don't understand," I said. "He was my best foster parent ever. He never hurt me. I'm just sick of foster parents. All of them. Why are you showing me these things?"

At this point, she turned to a checklist devoted to forms of psychological abuse. I should have thanked Miss Roberts for wanting to protect me, but it was all so stupid. Did Nate curse at me or yell, did he make me feel small or scared in any way, did I feel unsafe even if he never hit me? Again, *No, not ever*.

"I understand you need to ask," I said. "Did you see my file? I know *exactly* how people can hurt me. There's been nothing like that with Nate. He's sweet, but I don't care about him anymore. I should never have cared."

She closed her book.

I was six or seven years old when my fellow inmates at DCF told me what I needed to know about foster parents and touching. Even if I had a hard time believing that people bumped those parts together, I trusted these girls because many of them *had* been touched the wrong way. Why hadn't any DCF caseworkers brought their binders with stick figures to Mr. Parker's house? It shouldn't have taken one of my school teachers to call DCF with a by-the-way, Grace has been crying in class for no reason.

Aside from the fact she only appeared when something in my life was broken, I liked Miss Roberts. Or could have outside of DCF. I liked that she was no-nonsense, that she was tough but still took time with her clothes and jewelry. I think she wanted me to like her too. Not in all my life had anyone ever asked if I wanted to wear bangles or talked with me, seriously, about whether to dress in jeans or a skirt for a school dance, or tennis shoes or flats or even heels. I had no mother or girlfriends to go shopping with, no one to tell me how many buttons to leave open on a blouse. I was young when my mother died. Did I miss her? What could that even mean? I barely remembered her. Still I missed someone in my life who could say, *Yes, those earrings are perfect.* Or *Don't think you can get by on your looks, young lady. Study! That means math too!"* My father didn't even know I existed. I didn't miss not having parents, exactly. I missed the voice in my head that gave me confidence to work on computer games even though I was the only girl in school who did. I imagined Miss Roberts could have spoken to me that way. Why, I wondered, had DCF never sent me home with someone like her?

"I have to ask these questions," she said, handing me an envelope. "Your grandfather left money and a note with directions about which bus to take to Portsmouth. That's in New Hampshire. Can you manage traveling yourself, or do you need help? I could send someone down to the bus depot with you."

"You mean I can leave the dorm?"

"You're free to go. Your grandfather had to get to Portsmouth for his show. Otherwise, he would have come today. The bus should be no problem for you."

She held out a hand for me to shake, but I wouldn't take it. She looked so sad for me, but I refused to be sad for myself.

"Take care," she said. "Be safe."

"I *hate* this place."

"I know. I'm sorry for that. But you had to live somewhere. We couldn't have put you on the street."

That was true. They couldn't. But I still could.

— • —

SEVENTY-TWO degrees and sunny: a perfect day for burning all my ties to DCF. I had a little business to take care of before heading to South Station though. Miss Roberts had hired a taxi to take me, but I gave the driver a different address. He took one look at my slip of paper and said, "Somerville? I was told to take you to the bus station."

"The Green Grocer in Somerville, please."

"The lady only paid me for South Station. You'll pay the meter rate?"

I'd already peeked at the envelope and saw enough twenty-dollar bills to take care of my little detour plus a bus ticket. I only needed to go for as long as it took me to snap a picture of Uncle Dima for my game. Monsters need faces, and just as I'd pasted Mr. Parker's photo into my earlier games, I needed a photo of Dima for *Chopped!* because *Chopped!* was going to be a voodoo doll. No matter where I was, as long as I could play that game on my laptop I could remove Dima's head from his shoulders anytime I liked.

The grocery surprised me considering Nate's brother and that creepy man, Maxim, ran it. I expected dirty floors and mouse droppings but instead found display cases filled with fresh meats and cheeses. They used a misting machine to crisp the vegetables. They had an organics section with lettuce that looked like it was still growing right on the shelf. I rummaged around, looking for Dima but found Sveta instead. She saw me first.

"Little Sister!"

She set aside packages of string cheese and gave me a hug as if we were old friends. The fact was we'd met only once, but she seemed so interested in me and I really did feel close to her. At The Mystery Lounge, she'd worn a dress that made her look like a movie star. In the store, she was wearing the same uniform as everyone else: khakis with a shirt, which had a logo of a dancing green pepper. Even wearing that, she was the most beautiful girl I'd ever seen.

Her skin was clear and her long hair was the same color as mine, flipped and tied into a loose bun at her neck. A few strands had escaped but those looked as if she'd placed them, carefully, for a photo shoot. We both had hazel eyes. I *could* have been her sister, and I certainly wanted to be. She wore bangles like Miss Roberts and turned up the collar of her blouse, a small thing that made a big difference. On her, the store's uniform didn't look like a uniform. Sveta would have been beautiful in overalls planting vegetables or, bundled like a mummy, shoveling snow. She could have worn my same clothes and looked a thousand times better than I ever did.

"Grace, you've come to visit!"

I set down my suitcase and backpack.

"Nate wants a new picture of Dima," I said.

"You don't have a picture of me, I bet."

She struck a pose, turning away from me, hands on hips, legs set wide—then whipped her shoulders and head back with a pouty look. We burst out laughing. "Or maybe this?" She took a step toward me, parting her lips and narrowing her eyes. "Maxim pays for me to go to modeling school. He says I'll be a big star one day. Hey. Come on, take our picture."

We leaned our heads together as I pointed my camera back at us. "What did I tell you," she said, pointing at me on the screen. "You're beautiful, Little Sister!"

"Maybe I'll be a model too."

The smile faded. "No, you should be a doctor." She tapped her watch. "*Opivdni.* Ukrainian for twelve o'clock. Noon. No more work today. Ella and I are going to Newbury Street to shop. Maxim's giving us money. You'll come!"

She disappeared up an aisle and returned with Ella Bianchi, who greeted me as warmly as Sveta had. We were so loud, the three of us, laughing and chattering as if we were headed off on the adventure of our lives. The thought of shopping with Sveta and Ella made me happy in a way I couldn't remember being. I had nearly forgotten why I'd come when Maxim Petrov appeared, Dima shuffling at his side. Uncle Dima looked like a broom handle with a skull jammed on top.

"Hello, girls!" Maxim wore the same khakis and shirt as everyone else. His loafers were polished, and his teeth were very white. He looked straight at me, at my jeans and T-shirt, and said: "We can do better than that, young lady! Why don't you go shopping with these two. You're gorgeous, Grace. You definitely have potential. Why don't you come work in the store with these two? I'll take good care of you."

He pulled out his wallet and handed Sveta a credit card.

Dima finally noticed me. He grinned, and it was horrible to see a smile ripped across that craggy face. That's the photo I took for my game. I suppose it wasn't fair using a picture that ugly. But then I only needed it for one thing.

"Ready to shop, girls?"

"We'll spend no more than one thousand, five hundred, Maxim. Was that the number?"

Petrov winked. "Up it to twenty-five hundred. But that *includes* lunch. Somebody's got to set some rules around here."

"A little black dress," said Dima. "Every girl needs a pretty dress!"

"You bet, old man."

Sveta kissed Dima on the cheek and Petrov on the lips. Ella tried thanking Petrov with a handshake, but he held tight then pulled her close and put a hand on her bottom. She giggled. "Come on, Grace. Show us a little love." He opened his arms, and I kept my distance. "Buy something red," he told Sveta.

"A pretty dress," said Dima. "Why don't you all get a pretty dress!"

Pretty dress, pretty dress! Petrov mimicked him like a parakeet. Then he laughed and pointed us out the door. "Go on, get out of here. Have fun!"

Off I went in a taxi to Newbury Street with my new friends. I had a few hours before my bus left, and the thought that I could do exactly what I wanted in the meantime was delicious. We started at the Public Garden and strolled past galleries, restaurants, and stores with clothes on mannequins that I couldn't believe real women would wear. The pants looked too tight to pull on, and the skirts would have gotten me thrown out of dances at school. I didn't see a thing that could go with jeans and a T-shirt.

Ella went into attack mode and began trying on clothes. First she tried a tube top with designer jeans. The top fit her snugly, like a bikini. "What do you think," she asked, stepping from a dressing room. "It's not too tight, is it?"

"It *is* too tight," said Sveta. "I can see your *soskies*. Leave something for the imagination."

"Whose?"

She shrugged. "Maxim's for one."

"Oh, he's seen them."

"*What!*"

"It was no big deal," said Ella, her face turning red. "I was changing and he came in to the dressing room."

"He walked into the *women's* dressing room?"

"I had my blouse off and was putting on a sports bra. He said, *Hi,* and I turned around. He just stood in the doorway looking at me. I mean, you know, them. It's not like he touched me or anything."

"I will hit him for that!"

"No, please don't. I like that he looked. He's nice."

"He's a snake!"

"So I should wear flannel shirts all the time? You're worse than my father."

I pretended not to hear any of this and grabbed for the first thing I saw—the label on the tube top. "Two hundred dollars!" I said, trying to change the subject. "That's *crazy!*"

"Maxim said we could spend around a thousand each, and I'm going after every penny. What do you think, Sveta? Should I get this outfit? I'd need to hide it in my closet behind some old sheets. If my father ever saw this . . . I *have* to get heels for these jeans. Red! Maxim told us to get something red. And then maybe we'll go back to that last shop for those hoop earrings."

Sveta wagged a finger. "You're all mixed up, Little Sister. You're going to wear Band-Aids over your *soskies*? For one thing, it hurts when you pull them off. No. Get a different top. You're too young."

"I'm almost the same age as you."

Ella rejected the dress Sveta picked out for her and settled on a different pair of jeans, which weren't so tight and only cost three hundred dollars. I couldn't believe these prices. At the Goodwill store, Mrs. Alcott would have bought me a year's worth of clothes for that much, including a winter coat. At one point, we walked down a set of stairs to something called the Zebra Shop, which carried clothes in only two colors. In we went, and when Sveta emerged from the dressing room, I could have cried she was so gorgeous. The dress was cut above her knee, but not too high, like the one Ella had tried. Seeing them both amazed me, but only Sveta looked comfortable. Ella was pretending to be someone else in her dress, but Sveta was herself. She was *home*. The silky material followed her body without pinching or pulling. Something in it caught the light and made me want to touch her.

"Black heels," she said, turning this way and that in a three-way mirror. "Not too tall. Red lipstick, not too loud. A leather purse to match the lipstick. And a gold chain, very thin and very light. Maxim will buy it for me." She laughed. "He doesn't know yet!"

They both bought dresses and asked if I wanted to try one on since they had some money left over. There was no way I could move from blue jeans and school uniforms into something like that. Ella told me I'd get over it as we took our seats at a restaurant. "Wait a little longer," she said, "when guys start paying attention."

"They already do."

"Yeah, but boys in school are puppies. Older guys are what you want."

Sveta corrected her. "There's nothing wrong with puppies. I love puppies. Older men want only one thing."

"Well, Maxim's older, and I like him. I hope he likes *my* little black dress. Sveta, let me keep it in your locker at the grocery. *Please.* If my father finds this, he'll kill someone. I'd be grounded, like forever. Remember when he grabbed that kid at the magic show? He was being *nice* that night. What am I going to do?"

"Listen to him," said Sveta.

"He's Italian. You never had an Italian father."

"I had a Ukrainian father, and I should have listened."

We were seated at an outdoor café, and I ordered a hamburger and fries. They ordered salads with dressing on the side, which they hardly used. They picked out the olives and set them on the edges of their plates. They picked out the croutons. They barely ate the lettuce. Mostly they watched me eat.

"At least you have a father," I said, munching a french fry. "So what if he yells and keeps you locked up? That's better than no father."

We went to three more stores, Ella and Sveta determined to buy me something. They decided I needed a scarf and wrapped several around my neck, knotting them every which way then draping them across my shoulders like a shawl, even wrapping them around my head so that I looked like a swami. For an hour I was their mannequin, their pet, and I loved how they fussed over me. We laughed and argued as they matched the colors and materials of the scarves to my hair and face. Finally we settled on something with cashmere and cotton, speckled with turquoise thread that "brought out," the blue-green of my eyes. "It's a great look with jeans," said the sales clerk. "You can upshift or downshift with the right scarf."

I said good-bye to them as they stepped into a cab back to Somerville. I was headed downtown, to the bus station. Thinking I was going north to join Nate, Sveta gave me a big hug. "Go learn some magic from your grandfather," she said. "Then come home and teach me to disappear."

Seventeen: Nate Larson

Before I left for Portsmouth, I drove to the Mount Auburn Cemetery in Cambridge and, after some searching, found the graves of my wife and daughter. The bronze markers were simple, names and a span of years, too brief. They lay beside each other on a hill beneath spruce and poplars, Gabrielle in the plot intended for me. Of all the gifts Nora hoped to give our daughter, the BRCA gene mutation was not among them. What was this tiny hiccup in their DNA that had opened the gates to cancer? I had lost them both to the same disease and didn't believe I could survive.

Yet people survived. I knew this because the evidence lay in every direction I turned as I wandered the cemetery. Here was the family monument of Captain Albert Snow, born 1812 and died 1889. Beneath his name was chiseled the name of his first wife, Mehitable, who died in her twenties. Beneath her name, his second wife, Alice, and her dates. Beneath Alice, his third wife, who outlived him. Abihall. On another face of the monument I read the names of their sons and daughters who didn't survive childhood. Six names. Thomas, age three, one month. Susannah, age fourteen days.

I stopped reading.

What had Captain Snow to teach me of loss? After his first and second wives died, he had heart enough to remarry. He buried children yet had heart enough to want more. Why? Burying Gabrielle had proved a destruction beyond imagining. When she died, I became a shadow haunting my own life. To risk love again? How, when each morning I tore open the sky and grabbed God by the collar and screamed: *You would permit this*? After Nora and Gabby, I was done with love. But apparently Captain Snow had found a way. *Good for him*, I thought. At least one of us had figured how to put one foot in front of the other after getting hammered flat.

I'd come to Mount Auburn to decide, finally, whether to betray Dima or Grace—to cut off my right hand or left. Reason alone couldn't settle the matter because each time I tried I got caught in a vicious loop. Running to Canada to save Dima would doom Grace. Staying in Boston to save Grace would doom Dima. Round and round I went until, disgusted with myself, I opened the trunk of my car and set out a folding chair and table beside the graves. On the table I unrolled my oilcloth checkerboard and vowed that with Nora and Gabrielle as my witnesses, I would decide. If the black discs won, I'd run. If red, I'd stay. Of course, I played to a stalemate, ending with one red and one black chasing each other around the board for an hour. It must have made a peculiar sight, an old man in a cemetery playing both sides of a checkers game.

As I made one last push to choose, a woman and a boy came walking up the path. He was seven or eight years old. I greeted them. To the mother, I assumed it was his mother, I said, "It's a beautiful day for a visit."

The child said, "You came to a cemetery to play checkers?"

He had honey-nut skin and the sweetest smile.

"Yes, I did."

"Hey, Mom, can I play?"

"The man didn't invite you."

A Caribbean lilt. Identical smile.

"We come every week to see my dad. Who do you come for?"

I pointed.

"*Two* of them?"

"I was just packing up," I said. "I don't have time to play, but I do have something you might want to see." I walked over to the car and, with my back to the child, quickly found what I needed.

"I came across a lucky penny the other day. I could show you."

The child looked to his mother. The mother nodded.

"What's your name, son?"

"Ferdinand Beck. I'm seven!"

I held the penny in the flat of my hand. "Ferdinand," I said.

"Ferdy, not Ferdinand!"

"Okay. Ferdy, I was walking in Central Square, and I saw a penny on the curb, by a parking meter. When I reached to pick it up, it flew into my hand. It was the strangest thing. It just leapt right off the ground! So I put it in my pocket, and it's been jumping around in there ever since. Can I show you."

"You said it *flew*?"

I asked him to blow on the penny three times, and the last time to blow like he was blowing out candles on a cake. On the third puff, I floated the penny off my palm and made it spin in midair. The light was perfect, the sun at my back.

Ferdy was jumping and clapping. "Mom, look!"

She was no less amazed.

I closed my hand, passed left over right and presented Ferdy with a different penny. "Now," I said. "Place the penny back on my palm, and when I make a fist, sprinkle magic dust over it."

He told me he didn't have any magic dust.

I lent him some. I took a big handful of nothing from my pocket and offered it to him. The kid caught on and took a few pinches and sprinkled it over my fist. I asked for more. He sprinkled more and told his mother to do the same. When I opened my fist, I presented two neatly folded dollar bills on my palm. "For you," I said.

"Thanks! That was amazing!"

"It certainly was. This coin is strange! Here's what I want you to do. Spend one of these dollars on candy, if it's okay with your mother. The second dollar I want you to tape to a wall by your bed. When you look at it, I want you to remember your powers. Because you've got powers, Ferdinand Beck. I can tell. I'm a magician."

The kid ran off, two dollars richer, as his mother, in her soft lilt, thanked me. But I should have thanked them for the wide wonder in Ferdy's eyes and the sadness in his mother's. Both were real. Of course they were. No one lies in a cemetery.

THE FERDY

1. KID VOLUNTEERS PENNY.

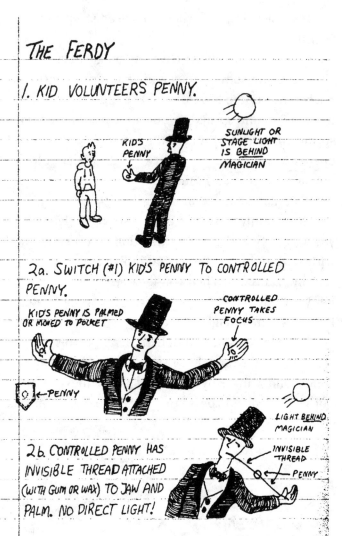

KID'S PENNY

SUNLIGHT OR STAGE LIGHT IS BEHIND MAGICIAN

2a. SWITCH (#1) KID'S PENNY TO CONTROLLED PENNY.

KID'S PENNY IS PALMED OR MOVED TO POCKET

CONTROLLED PENNY TAKES FOCUS

←PENNY

2b. CONTROLLED PENNY HAS INVISIBLE THREAD ATTACHED (WITH GUM OR WAX) TO JAW AND PALM. NO DIRECT LIGHT!

LIGHT BEHIND MAGICIAN

INVISIBLE THREAD

PENNY

3. AS MAGICIAN MOVES HEAD + HAND, PENNY LIFTS, FLOATS, SPINS.

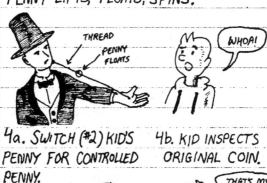

4a. SWITCH (#2) KID'S PENNY FOR CONTROLLED PENNY.

4b. KID INSPECTS ORIGINAL COIN.

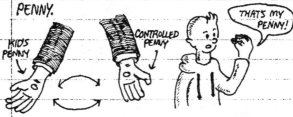

5. SWITCH (#3) KID'S PENNY FOR TWO $1 BILLS.

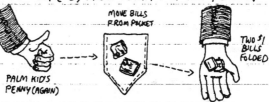

6. RESTORE KID'S PENNY. KID WALKS OFF WITH 2 BUCKS!

Eighteen: Grace Larson

The bus station in Boston was exactly as Nate had described it in the note he left along with the money: the kiosk listing destinations and departure times, the ticket queue, the smell of fresh cookies in the vendor stalls. He had included a schedule and, sure enough, the kiosk listed a bus leaving north for Portsmouth at 3:45, just above the 3:47 to Washington, DC, via New York.

There were three hundred dollars in an envelope, along with instructions for taking the bus and finding him before the performance on Saturday night. He didn't know which day DCF would be releasing me, so he'd also included the name of the motel where he'd booked two rooms and wrote that, should I arrive in the daytime, I'd likely find him in Market Square performing a few magic tricks and drumming up business for the show.

I boarded the bus to Washington.

I didn't feel good about leaving despite how thoroughly I convinced myself he'd given me up to DCF. It was even possible I'd miss him, but I knew that in time Nate would fade from my memory just as all the other rental parents had faded. After a few months, they became ghosts who retained the power to bother me from time to time, but mostly they stayed in their coffins where they belonged. I was more interested in the life I was going to live than in the one that had dragged me down. Besides, I figured, I'd never have an easier chance to escape, so I boarded the southbound bus mostly because I didn't have money enough to head west to Chicago or Los Angeles. I was also thinking that Washington was warmer than Boston and that if I made it on my own until winter, I might need to sleep outside for a while. Who knew how long that would take? The bonus of Washington: I'd be changing buses in New York, and I had decided to stay overnight and visit the Houdini Society.

Except for my mother and grandfather, I didn't know who or where in the world I came from, and a link to the most famous escape artist of all time would have made for a promising start. The more I read about Houdini, the more I recognized in myself a God-given talent for wriggling out of trouble. I was on the bus, after all, inventing my own escape from DCF. Physically, too, I had some talent. I was double-jointed. My thumbs and shoulders could bend backward without hurting me at all. I could arch my back and put my hands flat on the ground. Nate even let me wear the straitjacket once and applauded as I wriggled right out of it—so well, in fact, he promised he'd write me into next summer's show. I was going to be a featured act! Of course, there'd be no next summer with him because I'd be long gone. Still, in my heart, I felt I could be a world-class escape artist one day. I wanted to see that tuft of Houdini's hair in person, even touch it if they'd let me. I hadn't yet received my DNA test results, but I was feeling confident. Those results would be sent to Nate, which was my second reason for staying over in New York: to give the head of the society my e-mail address and phone number so they could contact me directly with information about the scholarship.

The bus station in New York was like an ant colony. When I stepped into the Port Authority, I could scarcely find my way for all the people. I followed a crush out onto Forty-Second Street, turned a full circle, and thought *What now?* Cars zipped past, honking. People bumped into me, and I thought I must be the only person who didn't know where, exactly, to go. Someone tugged at my computer bag, and I jumped and backed against a wall. It was about then I realized I had no place to stay, no one to call to come get me. It had been easier to plan my escape from the safety of the DCF dorm, horrible as that was, than to be a stranger finding her way among eight million New Yorkers, at least half of whom were clogging the same block I was on.

A young woman approached.

She wore jeans and a T-shirt, like I did. She'd also buzz-cut her hair and had a tattoo printed on her scalp that read *No you don't*. Without a word, she handed me a card with the address and phone number for a place called COVENANT HOUSE, on the back of which were a few simple words. IF YOU'RE SCARED OR FEELING ALONE, STAY WITH US.

Finally, she spoke: "A bed and a meal, just in case." She was eighteen or so and looked so tired and beat around the eyes. I must have looked pretty desperate myself for her to have stopped. "Just off a bus?" she asked.

I nodded.

"Covenant House is on West Forty-First Street. That way. Four sixty. You'll be safe."

It hadn't occurred to me I wasn't safe.

"I need to get going," she said. "Just don't sleep on the street tonight or in the subways. And if any men approach you to ask if you're hungry and say they'd be happy to buy you a meal, don't. They'll seem nice, but don't."

What kind of jungle had I wandered into? But then everyone feels nervous in a big new city. The thing was to have a plan. I walked back to the Port Authority and found a taxi. I avoided making eye contact and felt for the Covenant House card in my pocket every few minutes just to be sure I still had it. Then it occurred to me that maybe I shouldn't trust the girl who'd given me the card. What if *that* was a trick?

The one sure thing I knew in all of New York was the Houdini Society, and I had an address. The taxi driver read the scrap of paper I handed him, then turned in his seat so that he was facing me. He had a cigarette tucked behind one ear and a pencil behind the other. He wore thin gold chains with little disks, one of which I could read: Saint Christopher, the patron saint of travelers. He looked at the address again and said, "Kid, if you want to go to Queens, take the F train. This ride'll cost you fifty bucks, easy. Plus tip, if you're feeling generous. You can cover that?"

I reached for my pack and counted out the money in the envelope as he watched. I had already paid for cab fares in Boston, going from the DCF dorm to The Green Grocer, then from Newbury Street to the bus terminal. I'd bought some food. I was already down fifty dollars, and I hadn't bought the ticket from New York to Washington yet. I added everything up. Allowing for the second bus ticket and a few meals, I'd have sixty dollars after paying for the taxi. The Houdini Society was my one anchor and, according to its web page, was going to close at nine p.m. I could make it if we hurried. I handed him the money.

"No," he said. "You pay *after* I take you. You just get off a boat?"

The trip took an hour, and I kept checking the time and the amount on the meter. Already the sun was setting. We arrived with just enough daylight for me to get a good look at a tree-lined street with two- and three-story brick apartment buildings on either side.

"It's a neighborhood," I said. "How come it's a neighborhood?"

"What were you expecting, Buckingham Palace? That'll be fifty-one seventy-five, plus tip. You know how to figure a tip?"

I counted out fifty-two dollars and told him to keep the change. I asked again why this was just a neighborhood, not the sort of a place that looked like it had a museum, but he started grumbling and drove off about a half-second after I closed the door.

It would be dark soon, so I checked the address on the scrap of paper in my hand for the last time and opened the door to a building with six mail boxes in the foyer. I checked the name on each, and none read "Houdini Society." I stepped outside and checked the building number again. I even walked to the corner to make sure I was on 166th Street. No way did I think an apartment in Queens could double as the Houdini Society. For one thing, where would they put all the display cases?

The mail box to Apartment G read Bela and Jodi Kunz.

I was tired and hungry and realized I'd have only ten dollars left if I took another cab back into Manhattan, to Covenant House. But no use thinking about that just yet. I was there, and I had no idea what to expect when I knocked on the door, holding a suitcase in one hand and a backpack in the other.

A woman answered.

"Yes, hon?"

The place smelled like a tobacco factory, except it wasn't a factory. I looked past her to a living room, where a man was seated upright on a coach, sleeping in front of a large TV, his mouth wide open. On the table beside him were two beer bottles. The TV was playing a commercial for deodorant sticks.

"Hi. I'm looking for the Houdini Society of New York. I spoke with somebody here a few weeks ago, and I copied this address off your website. My name is Grace Larson. I'm from Boston, and I want to see Harry Houdini's hair, what's left of it. I'm also interested in the scholarship, if I'm related. I think I am."

The lady asked to see the address I'd used to find her. I did better than that. I had printed out the society's web page and dug it out of my backpack. She looked at the web page, looked at the man sleeping behind her, and looked at me.

"Wait a minute, hon."

She turned and yelled, "Bela, you know anything about a Houdini Society?"

The man snorted and coughed. "Wha—?"

"You mean the magician, hon. Is that right?"

"Yes, Ma'am."

"The magician, Bela. Houdini."

"What?" said the man. "What about Houdini?"

The woman asked me to wait and closed the door, but I could still hear them. "There's a kid outside who looks like she just stepped off a train from Kansas. Something about Houdini. *What* is going on, Bela?"

"Nothing—"

"Nothing? I'm supposed to believe *nothing*?" Their voices got so low I couldn't make out much until I heard the lady shout: "You told me you were done! What, eight years in lockup wasn't enough for you? You *promised*."

"He was a friend from Danbury. You don't turn your back—"

The next thing I knew the man himself was at the door, his hair scrambled every which way, his shirt untucked. The lady stood behind him, still wearing her ID badge from a hospital. They both stank of cigarettes.

"Sorry," said the man. "The Houdini Society went bankrupt. I had to shut it down."

"But I came all the way from *Boston*. I wanted to touch Houdini's hair. Can I still see it?"

The man scratched himself, and the woman poked her head over his shoulder. "Hey, hon. Have you eaten?"

"We had to sell the hair and everything else. Sorry. You were a member?"

I had a membership card in my wallet signed by the president of the Houdini Society, Bela Kunz. "Let me see that," said the woman. She looked from the card, to me, to her husband. "That's your signature. You'd better refund the fee."

Lola and Frank had used their credit card to pay the seventy-five dollars, on top of paying for the DNA test. Mr. Kunz reached into his pocket and pulled out a roll of bills. "Here we go," he said, "A hundred fifty, some extra for your troubles."

The woman gave him a look.

"All right, two-fifty."

"We were just sitting down to dinner, sweetie. Did you—"

"What's going to happen to my DNA test?"

I was feeling nearly frantic. On the bus ride, I'd written my phone number and e-mail address very clearly on a card so that the society could contact me directly with news about my connection to Houdini. Mr. Kunz assured me the DNA test went straight to the lab in Schenectady and that the lab wasn't part of the bankruptcy proceedings. "You'll be hearing from them about whatever it is you're waiting for."

"I'm waiting to find out if I'm related to Houdini."

On that point he was very clear. "Look," he said. "The lab already has a copy of Houdini's DNA—you know, from the hair sample. They'll be making the comparisons and reaching out to you. Absolutely reaching out." He checked the card I'd given him. "I made sure about that when I shut our offices."

"Your *offices*?"

"Quiet, Jodi."

"How about the scholarship?" I asked.

"Houdini's money was . . . yes, I'm sure it was in a separate account. Completely protected. So if you *are* related . . . someone will be contacting you. Good luck. Really, it's a terrific program with the best people running it."

"How did you say you found us?" said the woman.

"Though your website."

"Yeah, well. I had to shut that down too."

"My grandfather told me about it. He's a famous magician. Maybe you heard of him—Nate Larson?"

The woman looked at the man, who was looking at me. "Yes, I know him. I've even seen him do magic."

"You *know* him??"

"Sure I do. We spent some time together."

"That settles it," said the woman. "I don't know what this Houdini business is about, but you're the grandchild of my husband's friend, and you're staying for dinner. Do you like stuffed cabbage, hon? And tell me where you're sleeping tonight."

The smell of cigarettes was hurting my stomach, but it was a long way back to Manhattan and Covenant House. The girl with the tattooed head had told me to trust no one, but the stuffed cabbage smelled good and I was tired. Besides which, Bela Kunz knew Nate. I pointed to the couch and asked if I could sleep there.

That's when I noticed the checkerboard, same as Nate's, painted onto a square of oilcloth. He'd set it up on a table by the couch. Mr. Kunz saw me staring and asked if I wanted a go. He laughed when I told him about playing Nate every night to decide who chose dinner.

"Well, tonight's dinner is already made so you're getting stuffed cabbage whether you win or lose. How long 'til we eat, Jodi?"

"Twenty minutes, give or take."

He motioned to the table.

Mr. Kunz was serious about his checkers. He and his wife ate at the kitchen table, which was already set—now for three. This table was smaller and had two folding chairs facing each other. All the pieces, red and black, were laid out, waiting in place. He turned off the TV.

"There's only one right way to play," he said. "Without mercy. You okay with that?"

Finally, someone to give me a challenge. I told him to bring it on.

Mr. Kunz beat me the first game, the second, and the third—all before dinner. It wasn't even close.

"Have enough?" he said. "Tail between your legs yet?"

Mrs. Kunz was moving food to the table, and I needed a break. I hadn't lost three straight games in months. "How'd you learn to play like that?" I asked.

"I had a good teacher."

"Who?"

"Nate, as a matter of fact. After a while, no one wanted him entering the tournaments because he always won. He was a real warrior."

I sniffed to give myself a second. "Sure," I said. "I knew that."

"Time to eat everyone!"

The cabbage was delicious. We also had salad, potatoes, and stewed pears. After dinner, Mrs. Kunz plumped a few pillows and laid out fresh sheets, which also smelled of tobacco.

They were very nice, the Kunzes. On Saturday morning when she drove me to the Port Authority, Mrs. Kunz offered what she called free advice as I stepped out of the car. "Hon," she said. "I was young and pretty once, like you, and I spent some time on the road, alone. Trust me, it doesn't usually turn out for the best. Why don't you go back to your grandfather. Just listening to you describe him . . . he sounds like a good man."

I agreed Nate was a good man and, in fact, I'd been thinking about him. I also knew DCF was a poisoned well and that people went there to die—inside, anyway. I walked into the Port Authority and bought a ticket to Washington, DC.

Nineteen: Nate Larson

On the Wednesday after my debut at The Mystery Lounge and before my next stop in Portsmouth that Saturday, I stumbled around the apartment as if someone had kicked me senseless. I wiped down the counters and the kitchen table, though I hadn't eaten. I straightened piles of books and magazines I couldn't bear to read. Bobby Bianchi had called again to suggest, this time just shy of screaming, that I quit Grace and run.

I told him, again, to go away.

He asked if I was stupid, if I couldn't read a message when I saw one. "What's the matter with you? I'll have to keep tabs now," he said.

"Meaning what?"

"Meaning I'm also headed north. I've got some business up there—moving product. If you're going to wait until the end of the summer, Maxim wants to know what you're doing in the meantime. He doesn't trust you, and I can't say I blame him. Which means I'll be coming to a few shows, checking in just to know where you are in the event you need to leave in a hurry. You're a boil on my backside, Nate. This could have been simple."

Nothing was simple. I didn't know when or how it happened, but I'd come to depend on games of checkers with my granddaughter and on our arguments about the merits of Chinese versus Mexican carryout. I missed the way she worked for hours on her computer games at the kitchen table as I practiced at my mirror. She never climbed stairs. She vaulted up them. She ran Lucy around the block and came home winded and flushed and so full of life that I felt stronger just being in the same room. Grace was a young life rising and I was a graybeard moving in a different direction. I couldn't accept the fact she was gone.

Hunt's office had called with the news that DCF would restore custody, though they couldn't say precisely when. I had hoped we would drive north together, but I couldn't wait much longer because I needed to check the setup at the Saint James Theater before the show. There were lighting considerations and viewing angles to my sides and back, where I worked the business end of my tricks. Anyone with a 180-degree line of sight to the stage would see my every move.

The doorbell buzzed, and I ignored it. When it buzzed again, Lucy started yapping and I could hear her tearing through Frank and Lola's apartment. I didn't really care who had come, but to keep my landlords from returning home to a disaster, I started down the stairs, shouting: "All right. *All right* already! I'm coming!" At the door I found a middle-aged woman clutching her pocketbook. She carried no Bible or pamphlets. I saw no boxes or cases, nothing on wheels to suggest she sold Tupperware or magazines. She might have been one of the nuns from the Cathedral School visiting to discuss Grace's progress that year. But someone would have called.

"Can I help you?"

"I'm Janice Alcott. I had custody of Grace before you did. You're Mr. Larson?"

"I am."

"Is she home?"

I was pretty sure this visit broke a half-dozen rules. But with Grace gone, I didn't see the harm. "She's not here," I said.

"When will she be back? I could wait."

"Not all summer you can't. We're about to take a trip. How'd you get this address?"

"May I?"

She took a half-step toward me, inviting herself into the apartment.

We went upstairs.

"You don't know who I am," she said as we sat at the kitchen table. "There's really no reason for you to even listen to what I'm about to say, but I want to see her again. We didn't part on especially good terms, Grace and I. Maybe she told you?"

"Mrs. Alcott. I don't think this is a particularly good idea—"

"There are things I wanted to tell her. The fact is . . . I don't have anyone to bake for anymore. I wanted to tell her that. She's such a skinny thing, and some nights I lost sleep hoping she'd eat more. Is she eating? I used to bake her pies and bread. I know she didn't like me much. But I tried. When will she be back?"

The news that we wouldn't return until August visibly upset her. She sat very straight in her chair, her pocketbook in her lap. She closed her eyes and kept them closed for a few seconds, then started glancing around the apartment, looking for signs of her former foster child.

"I miss her," she said.

I felt a stab of sympathy. At fourteen, when other girls were primping themselves in front of mirrors, obsessed with boys, Grace was hanging upside down from a low-hanging branch of the Maloneys' oak to see if the world looked better that way—because it couldn't look any worse, she claimed, than it did right side up. Two weeks before the end of school, she asked me to buy twenty helium balloons so she could float a fork for a science project. She made a little basket, a gondola, attached the balloons, and tied the whole thing off to a post only to have the knot slip. The balloons floated away, carrying the fork to who-knows-where as I drove from Arlington to Cambridge and then across the river to Boston as Grace tracked it with binoculars. A week before that, she ate a piece of cauliflower in one of her carryout dishes and liked it so much she bought a packet of cauliflower seeds for Lola. They planted them and spent an afternoon at Lola's kitchen table discussing recipes. Without intending to, just by being herself, Grace drew us into her world before we had a chance to say *no*.

Apparently she'd had the same effect on Janice Alcott.

I asked if she would like a cup of tea. I had exactly one tea bag left from our emergency raid on the Maloneys' kitchen.

"You were a convict," she said.

"Thanks for stopping by, Mrs. Alcott. I'll tell my granddaughter you visited."

I stood.

She didn't move.

"You must know all about stealing. Isn't that right?"

"You've really got to go," I said.

She was clutching her pocketbook as if I were about to steal that. She was struggling, and she was furious. "Grace stole my rolling pin, and I want it back! It was my great-grandmother's and it got handed down. If Grace were here, I'd do two things. First, I'd demand she return it and apologize. It's outrageous what she did! She'd have to apologize to my face, and I'd expect a card, too, sent in the mail. With a stamp, you know? In good handwriting, a written apology, a proper one!"

She snapped open her pocketbook and produced a scrap of paper.

"And another thing," she said, reading from her notes. "She never thanked me. If she thanked me properly and apologized, then I'd . . . I'd give my rolling pin right back to her. I'd make a present of it, Mr. Larson, because that's what's going to happen anyway when I die. I've already put it in my will. There's no one to leave my rolling pin to! I started baking with my grandmother when I was five, and I've gotten forty-seven good years out of it on my own. Now it's someone else's turn. I had wanted that someone to be Grace. I came here with a question."

Her voice shook. She was reading from her notes.

"I want to come over on one Sunday a month to bake with her—you know, show her how to make a proper crust. Things like that. You don't bake with her, do you? I want her to remember me for *something*. Would you allow me to do that?"

"I'm afraid I don't—"

"She *stole* from me, Mr. Larson! Do you understand how that hurts—someone in your own home! And another thing." She was reading again. "I don't even have a photo. Can you give me a photo of her?"

I owned exactly one, a Xeroxed copy from her DCF case file that Miss Hunt had given me, and it looked like a mug shot. Her eyes were dull and blank, her hair pulled severely off her face. When Grace saw that photo, she told me to rip it up.

I opened my wallet and gave it to the lady so she'd leave.

I couldn't wait any longer. I finished packing my car alone, tidied the apartment, and shut it down alone, and said my good-byes to Lola and Frank—preparing them for difficult questions when the Department of Children and Families conducted its investigation concerning child abuse. Somehow they'd developed a soft spot in their heart for me and an even softer one for Grace. They had played along with the Houdini business so she'd let us take a good sample for the DNA test. They knew me well enough to trust I hadn't laid a wrongful hand on that child. If Frank thought otherwise, he'd have strangled me.

If Hunt could be trusted, Grace would return soon—possibly before the show on Saturday. But nothing was certain, so I left for the first road date on my Tabernacle Tour without her. I felt nearly desperate on the drive north. Child that I was—at sixty-six!— I screamed when I couldn't find my Matryoshkas. I had opened every cupboard, every door, every closet. I had even checked beneath the beds and checked the trash. I remembered Mrs. Alcott and her rolling pin. Could Grace have stolen the Matryoshkas?

Whether I set them dancing or tucked them safely inside Mama Matryoshka for bed, they were all that was left of my childhood. They were the steady hand at my shoulder, a comfort when my wife and daughter died. Now I had only Grace. She'd bent my name, calling *Na-ate* as they carried her off. It was a slender thread, but I grasped at it just the same, praying I had become for her what she had long since become for me: proof that you either have someone to love in this world or you have nothing.

Mrs. Alcott knew that.

I wanted my granddaughter. I wanted my brother. I wanted a home.

Twenty: Grace Larson

As I waited to board my bus to Washington, I watched a man who carried everything he owned in five plastic grocery bags. He sat on a filthy stretch of floor in the Port Authority and propped himself up against a concrete pillar, surrounded by his belongings and checking on them constantly, pulling shirts out just to refold them, pairing mismatched socks. I watched him remove a tennis racquet from one of his bags, inspect its broken strings, and return it very carefully. When I walked over to him and dropped a quarter into his cup, he said, "God bless!" with such gusto he made me smile. Homeless people gathered near my school, by the cathedral, all the time. I'd often talk with them and give away the apple from my lunch bag. If I had no food to share, I'd give them money. This man had only four or five teeth left in his head, and I could smell him from several yards away. I'd never seen anyone in rougher shape, yet here he was blessing me. I thanked him for that and returned to a bench and watched him for a while longer. When he didn't move for another fifteen minutes, I decided to buy us Italian ice. It was hot that day.

"Watermelon or grape," I said, holding the two ices. It seemed to me this man and I were cousins. In my suitcase and backpack, I carried everything I owned too. He looked happy enough reading a leather-bound Bible.

He considered my offer. "Grape. Aren't you kind!"

His bags were filled mostly with protection against the coming winter: thick cushions, seats to a long-discarded couch; a heavy sleeping bag; a blue tarp, the cheap kind people throw over wood piles; flannel shirts and long underwear; and a pair of firemen's boots with big pull-on rings. Wherever he slept that night would be his home, which would pretty much describe my situation on landing in Washington. I had no idea what I'd do there, aside from visiting the Lincoln Memorial. The way I saw it, sleeping in a national park with Abraham Lincoln sitting in that big chair would be a huge improvement over the DCF dorm. Who'd bother me with Honest Abe looking on?

"I study the Bible at school," I said, joining the man on the floor.

"I believe you may be the one," he answered, grinning. "Little Sister, you saved New York City just now. This very second. You did, child!"

"Huh?"

"Says so, right here, Jeremiah 5:1."

I didn't remember Jeremiah.

"I don't think I saved anything today, sir. Not yet."

He had a gray, matted beard with flecks of his breakfast still in it and a tangle of greasy hair. He smelled of toilets and gym lockers and was wearing a flannel shirt on a ninety-degree day. His big toe stuck through a hole in his sneaker. I'd seen men just like him at the shelter near school, where our class served lunch sometimes. His fingernails were rimmed in black, which was awful to see as he slurped his Italian ice. "Says here to 'Go up and down the streets of Jerusalem, look around and consider, search through her squares. If you can find but one person who deals honestly and seeks the truth, I will forgive this city.'"

He grinned and slurped more grape ice, which left his tongue purple. "The Lord scheduled New York for destruction this very morning at 9:56. Why? Because New York Is Babylon! Because no one has dealt honestly or sought truth for a long, long time, not in this city! Are you catching me? Are you? Everything and everyone blasted, gone, except you and me and these Italian ices. Shh. Don't tell, but Jeremiah was my grandpap's grandpap going all the way back to Bible times. I'm telling you, New York was once a shining city but she whored and deceived and my great-great-great grandpap left it to me to find one person who deals honestly. And that, Little Sister, would be you. You have saved the New Jerusalem!"

Maybe I had. No one knows, really, when the next asteroid will hit, and it's always possible that my conversation with that man at precisely that moment changed—I don't know, ions or something in the atmosphere—changed the balance of the whole universe so that the asteroid would miss Earth. Why not? But more important to me at that moment was knowing when and where this man would get his next meal. I opened my pack and grabbed Nate's envelope. "If I give you money," I said, "will you promise to get food tonight and a room where you can take a shower?"

He nodded.

"Will you clean your fingernails?"

He nodded again.

I gave him sixty dollars. That left me with about two hundred fifty, which I thought would be plenty when I arrived in Washington. The man said nothing, didn't thank me even, which was okay. It's embarrassing to give money because there's no good reason some people should have so much while others don't—or at least not enough to eat and sleep in a clean place. I boarded my bus, which was parked a few spaces down from another bus headed to Boston and points north. I watched the man from the window and saw him right out in the open counting and recounting his cash. I hoped no one would take it from him.

Our driver took a circuit around the bus to inspect it. I had a whole seat to myself, so I set my suitcase and computer bag beside me and stretched out. Other than taking a school trip to Old Sturbridge Village, I'd never traveled outside Boston. Now I'd seen the skyscrapers of New York, and soon I'd get to see the capitol building and the monuments in Washington. The bus rumbled to life, and I felt the vibration in the floor and in my seat. I smiled. *No more DCF!* No more rental parents! As the driver checked his mirrors and closed the door, I heard a whoosh of air and my ears popped. I was pressing my nose to the glass, wishing the man with the shopping bags good-bye, watching him turn onto his hands and knees, pushing himself up. When he stumbled and fell, something inside me broke.

I stood and shouted: *"Stop!"*

Everyone stared as I ran to the front of the bus, which was already backing up. I lost my balance and nearly fell. "Stop! Please stop!"

"Hey up there! The kid wants to get off!"

The driver began barking at me through an intercom system: "Sit down! State regulations prohibit stoppage until we reach a scheduled rest break. Our first scheduled break will be in one hour, thirty-eight minutes at the Walt Whitman Service Plaza on the New Jersey Turnpike. You can get off there."

"No," I screamed. "I want to get off *here!*" I had reached the front and started banging on the door. "Let me out! I want to get *out!*"

Someone called, "C'mon, buddy. We haven't left the station."

The driver pushed a button and the door hissed. I leapt off, but instead of running to the man who stumbled, I raced down the row looking for the bus headed to Boston and Portsmouth. It, too, was just leaving. I threw myself at the closed door, banging on it, running alongside as it pulled away from the curb. "Open up!" I yelled. The driver held up his hand to say *NO* and shook his head. But I kept banging until, finally, he stopped and let me on. Strangers stared down the aisle then turned away, not wanting me to sit next to them and disturb their comfort. But there was one lady patting the empty cushion beside her. I stowed my things, and once I was settled she introduced herself.

"That was a close call," she said. "Isn't it just a fact about trains and buses? Boats too. You're late, you're running, racing to catch them, you're out of breath and your heart's pounding *boom boom boom*. You're praying they'll open the doors and it looks like they won't but then they do! It's so sudden, the change. You go from crazy, they won't let me on, to relaxed, just like *that*." She snapped her fingers. "Have you caught your breath yet, dear?"

I barely heard her.

We talked, it was polite, and I don't remember a word we said because something wild in me had broken loose. The horses were out. Mountains were crumbling. I began to shiver and hugged myself, rocking back and forth groaning *Nate. Oh, Nate.* The woman laid a hand on my shoulder. "There now, little darling. Can it be *that* bad?" I feared it was, or could be. I fell into the lap of this stranger, knowing— unsure how I knew—the world was about to collapse on my grandfather.

He needs me, I realized.

And I cried all the harder on realizing I needed him. I'd
broken my one and only rule: never, *ever* care. What was I
going to do? At that moment I hated Nate for needing him. I
didn't want to go back. I had to go back. The woman stroked
my hair and hummed a tune. I missed my mother. I missed
Nate. There *are* good people in the world, I thought as I
drifted away, more exhausted than anyone has a right to be.
I knew this because I had met two of them that afternoon,
along the road.

— • —

THE MANAGER of the Pochet Motel gave me a key for the room
next to Nate's. Jacqueline Roberts had said "two rooms." She
meant it, and my grandfather listened. It was six o'clock, and
I knew the show would begin in two hours. Nate left instructions for me to meet him in the old town square between five
and six thirty, at which point he'd head over to the Saint James
Theater. "You can make it to the square by six thirty, no problem," said the motel manager. He called for a taxi, and while I
waited I asked if he'd gotten any packages from Lola or Frank,
who'd told us they'd be collecting any mail and forwarding it.
It was early yet, but I was expecting the report from the lab
in Schenectady.

"Sorry," he said. "I'll leave a note on your door if anything
arrives."

I didn't see Nate right away, so I took a little tour of Market
Square. I walked past glassblowers and weavers. In a coffee
shop and something called The Cookie Factory, I found flyers
he'd taped to windows. The heat of the day had baked itself
out, and Portsmouth Harbor and the quay were swept clean
by a breeze blowing off the ocean. Ships and ferries cut sharp
waves through the water. I saw parents and their kids feeding
seagulls, timing their throws so the birds would catch bits of

bread and other treats midair. *Look for children,* I thought, *and you'll find him.* Sure enough, not five minutes later, I saw Nate was entertaining a knot of six- and eight-year-olds along with their parents. I approached from behind and watched as he pulled quarters from their ears and turned scarves different colors. Everything anyone needed to know about my grandfather could be learned from the faces of these children. They laughed, their eyes laughed, their jaws dropped. They were young enough to believe he performed miracles. The parents knew better, not that they were any less amazed. From their smiles and sideways glances, I could tell he'd delighted them too.

Once I asked him, "Why magic?"

It was a Sunday. We were helping Lola in the garden before she went to church.

"What's that?"

"Why do you do magic?"

"Oh, you know. There was Uncle Nestor. I loved his tricks and his stories."

"But *why* did you love them? Why do you?"

We were weeding the beds, on our hands and knees. He set aside his rake and reached into Lola's basket for a packet of beans, already opened. He shook one onto his palm. "Watch," he said. He wiggled his finger in the ground to make a hole. He placed the bean in the hole and covered it loosely with dirt. "There. I've made the bean disappear. But that's not magic. The magic happens when the bean grows into a plant that makes more beans. And then those beans grow and we eat. That's why I do what I do."

"*Huh?*"

"Why is a bean plant amazing?"

"I don't know."

"Think. You're missing the mystery of beans."

"A bean's a bean."

"And the universe is the universe. Why should there be beans in it?"

"I don't know."

"Why are you in it?"

"I don't know that either."

"Why *is* there a universe?"

I shook my head.

"Did anyone ever read *Jack and the Beanstalk* to you?"

Certainly not my foster parents. They just ordered me to sleep and checked to make sure I wasn't disturbing the other kids. At school I found the story and began reading aloud to myself because no one else ever did. I was eight. The librarian saw that and pulled me onto her lap and finished.

"If you understand the mystery of beans," he continued, "then it should come as no surprise that a beanstalk could shoot straight into the sky and that you could climb it and discover a whole world. And *that's* because if you allow one mystery, you've got to allow them all."

"Nate—"

"Look, when I float a table or a coin in my show and people believe—even for a half-second—that it's floating, *anything* is possible for them. They're in the mystery, Grace. That's my job: to give people half-seconds. Once they have that, they're safe."

"From what?"

He turned back to the garden. "What am I going to do with you? Just don't ever tell me that when you look at the sky at night all you see are stars. That would be disappointing. Do you understand?"

That day, I didn't. Yet in Portsmouth, as I watched him and watched the children amazed by his magic, I began to think he wasn't so crazy. Yes, a book could explain how beans grew. Nate was talking about something else. About how the moon, when it's full and bright at the horizon, stops people in their tracks. He was talking about how Lola sang to her plants and the way she smiled as she pulled a fresh tray of cookies from the oven. I saw wonder in the eyes of those children. I saw what Nate saw and began to feel it in myself, and when I did I could barely stand to be inside my own skin because *everything* around me suddenly bloomed, began to shimmer and crackle.

Nate was sitting on a bench in Portsmouth Square and I was standing behind him as pigeons cooed and clouds drifted. Out on the ocean whales breeched and sang to each other. Somewhere across the world, a mongoose was eating a snake and wolves were howling and mothers were kissing their babies. Somewhere rain was falling. *Rain.* The *raininess* of rain. Beans were growing and bums were begging quarters in the Port Authority and men were fighting wars as priests in their chapels swung bowls of incense and it was all happening, all of it, right then. Life itself. What *was* this?

"Please?" said the kids. "Can we *please* see the magic show!"

Those parents didn't have a chance. Nate pointed them across the square then up a street toward the Saint James Theater. Always his own best advertisement, he had wrangled six more customers for that evening. His little audience took a few flyers away with them, and he settled onto the bench, reaching into his bag for one of his notebooks. I watched from a near distance as he flipped through it, found his last entry, drew a line, and began scribbling. What now, I wondered. Details on new ways to palm a quarter? A note on how to turn a shy kid, face buried in his father's arms, into a willing partner for a magic trick? He filled his books with observations of every sort, all focused on the same end: how best to claim a full half-second of people's lives. It was a small thing to ask of an audience. In Nate's mind, it was also everything.

I walked up behind him, looking over his shoulder as he scribbled, and waited for him to feel my presence. When he turned, I said, "Hi, Grandpa."

All you need to know about how you stand with someone can be read in a half-second if you catch him by surprise. Nate looked up. He saw me when he didn't expect to see me. Yes, he knew I was coming to Portsmouth, though he didn't know how close I came to leaving for good. He'd been scribbling, and I surprised him. Was he happy to see me? Was I an interruption in his life? A dead weight? In the first half-second of being surprised, no one can lie. Nate had no time to pretend he was overjoyed that I'd made the trip to Portsmouth. Either he welcomed what he saw or he didn't. It was as if I had performed a magic trick myself, appearing out of nowhere, and was waiting to see in his eyes and face if I'd done well. Did I amaze him? Was he *pleased*?

How can I describe what I saw that day?

Eight months earlier, in mid-November during a recess at school, I let myself into a stone chapel adjacent to the cathedral. I would go there sometimes to gather my strength for end-of-day pickups, the very worst part of my day. That's when moms and dads fetched my classmates and drove them home while I walked to the bus stop for the ninety-minute ride, in silence, to Mrs. Alcott's.

Some afternoons, the prospect of that bus ride would choke me, and I'd escape to the little chapel not to pray but to imagine living my life in a mirror. I'd move my right hand and, in the mirror, my left would move. When Mrs. Alcott grunted at the breakfast table with something like, "I hope you took out the trash," I'd think that somewhere in the city, in my mirrored life, my mother was saying: "Good morning, sweetie.

Don't forget—Dad and I are picking you up after school for dinner and a movie." Where I ate dust, my mirrored self ate strawberries. Where I buried my head in the pillow at night to scream, my other self curled into my mother's arms on a couch as we watched *The Sound of Music.*

I remembered that November recess when I let myself into the chapel. Usually the nuns gave us our break at noon. But with state tests taking up so much time, we didn't go outside until three thirty, an hour or two after a soaking rain had ended. The chapel was chilly and damp, the stones and even the pews cold to the touch. I took a seat—third pew from the back, left side, midway down—and settled in, ready to imagine better times in my mirrored life and gather what strength I could for the ride to Mrs. Alcott's.

I tried. But for some reason I couldn't get past the heavy stones and damp, gloomy air. This was my world, I realized: ugly in every way that mattered, and I had better get used to it. I had no right to expect more than Mrs. Alcott and the Del-Reys and the Elliots and, God help me, Mr. Parker. When I stood to leave, there on the flagstones before me were two bars of light, one red and one yellow, as bright and sharp as if someone had just painted them. I turned a circle and looked for anything that could explain these beautiful colors. I looked higher along the stone walls and turned another circle—when there, above the entrance, I saw it: the chapel's rose window. From the playground, I'd seen it a thousand times but never paid much attention because stained glass, seen from the outside—even on a bright day—is dull. At the noon hour, when I usually slipped into the chapel, the sun was overhead and no light would cut through the window. But midafternoon, seen from inside the chapel, the stained glass drew every bit of light from an overcast sky until the window burned with reds and violets and with the orange of volcanoes. The window was *on fire.*

There are moments in life when joy leaps from the heart or does not, when everything you need to know about someone is over in an instant and set forever. Busy scribbling in his notebook, Nate must have forgotten our meeting, so focused was he on his work. Then, feeling my presence, he looked up from his bench, into my eyes—as if *they* were rose windows. His lips parted and quivered. The breath caught in his throat. He said nothing. What I saw in his face was this: the wonder of the children who'd just watched his magic, and the surprise and gratitude I felt that day in the chapel.

Finally, I was loved. Again.

And if Nate could love me, so could others.

Then and there I decided to become a magician. I would live for what I saw in Nate's face that day, hoping that the magic I performed in coming years would move my audiences the way Nate moved his, the way my appearance that afternoon moved him.

"Grace," he said, collecting himself. He touched my cheek. "We're in trouble. There's work to do."

Twenty-One: Nate Larson

When my granddaughter joined me on the bench in Market Square, I set out as much of the problem as I thought she could handle: what Eleanor Hunt was demanding—that I testify against my brother; what I was demanding of myself regarding Dima—that I not send him to prison; and what Bobby Bianchi and Petrov were demanding—that I leave the country and ruin Hunt's chances of winning a trial. What I didn't tell Grace was that if I stayed, Petrov and Bianchi would throw me across the border, or worse. She listened quietly, and when I was done said, "What about me? If you leave, what will happen to me?"

"I'd never give you back, Grace."

If she only knew.

I explained that in the interest of getting Petrov off my back, I needed to ask her to do something that wouldn't, strictly speaking, be legal. "Feel free to say *no*," I added. "But one way or another I need to beat Maxim over the head with a club, and we'll have to go through Bobby because he's as close as we'll get to him. We need to . . . borrow a few of Bobby's things."

"You mean steal?"

"It's not stealing if you give back what you take."

"It *is* stealing, Nate."

"No, it's almost stealing. I stole something once—I told you about that, about what got me sent to prison. I know the difference." I tapped the center of my chest. "Here. It feels different here." We were walking up Market Street, toward the theater, and I asked her about my Matryoshkas, whether or not she'd seen them. "I looked everywhere," I said.

"That's really too bad. Sorry."

"You realize how special they are to me?"

"Why are you saying that? Of course I know. I'm sorry you're hurt."

What hurt worse was knowing she'd taken them and wouldn't say. Worse, still, was that I'd planned to abandon her and wouldn't say. The magician and his apprentice, both of us liars: what a fine pair we made.

— • —

SURE ENOUGH, Bianchi was seated in the first row of the Saint James Theater when I walked onstage, his wide body a reminder that I was supposed to fear for my life. Any other two-hundred-fifty-pound knee breaker would have delivered that message just by showing up. But I knew this man. He cared for Dima and, possibly, he still cared for me. If Petrov ordered him to start turning thumb screws, Bobby would hesitate—and I counted on that. He was my only access to Petrov, and I'd have to use him to advantage. That felt unholy, but then Petrov was a dangerous man.

Before I went onstage, I asked the manager to deliver a message: *I've thought it over*, I wrote. *You and Maxim are right. I'll give you what you want. Even Grace agrees I should run. See me after the show.*

She was peeking around the edge of the curtain as Bobby pulled out his glasses and read the note. "You should see him smiling, Nate!"

Progress.

My performance at the Saint James repeated the show in Cambridge. I opened with *The Three Roses* and followed with Rachel's story, the falsehoods of which left a few members of the audience teary at the thought that someplace in this corrupted world heaven could take root. If a miracle had touched a little village in Ukraine, why not Portsmouth, New Hampshire? Why not Boston or Beijing or sin city itself, Las Vegas? Even I wanted to believe the lies I spun about Rachel and Kortelisy.

But facts are stubborn things, and the facts were these: On September 23, 1942, German soldiers murdered 2,875 Kortelisians, 1,620 of them children. Dima and I would have raised the death toll by two had our father not sent us to a neighboring village to repair an axle. On returning, we met a neighbor who warned us away: "They're dead!" he screamed. "Everyone!" What could he mean? Fyodor was on his hands and knees throwing dust in his hair, weeping, snot running down his face, a madman. "They made us dig trenches. When they started with machine guns, I ran. A few of us reached the forest. The Germans used bayonets to cut the unborn from their mothers! When the dead filled one pit, the soldiers covered it with dirt and moved to the next. They played music on their truck radios as they murdered us! Don't go back. Escape while you can!"

We went back.

Would it have been better had I told my audience in Cambridge and Portsmouth the truth? That the man and woman who raised me, Dima's parents, and Rachel had been murdered along with everyone else? The truth would have ruined an otherwise lovely evening. "It's a *beautiful* story," a woman told me after the show in Portsmouth. She'd stood in line for twenty minutes so I could sign and date one of my flyers for her. "Maybe I'll go to Kortelisy one day."

Everyone loves a pretty picture.

Backstage, I sat heavily into a folding chair and stared at myself in the mirror. A crack ran its length, shifting the top half of my head—cheekbones, up—from the bottom so that the parts didn't fit. For as long as I could remember, Dima insisted I see the world in all its ugliness. "How else can you change anything," he said, "if you don't start with the truth?" Fair enough. But to acknowledge the ugliness meant I'd have to live with the ugliness. I wasn't built like him. I couldn't stare into a pit and see writhing bodies and stay sane. But I had no choice now because Petrov was real, and if I didn't see him in all his vicious detail, he would crush me. He would crush *us*. When Grace arrived earlier that evening in Market Square, I realized *one* was no longer a meaningful number in my life. Every decision I would make from that point on would hold her at its center. We were now partners. Petrov had to go away.

She was still dressed in her ninja suit, which I'd packed hoping she'd arrive in time for the show. Though we hadn't practiced for a week, she performed her part flawlessly, and the audience roared when I jumped from behind the curtain and yelled: "The man you are worried about is right here!"

The manager pronounced *The Kortelisy Escape* a triumph and invited us to perform a second show the following night.

We heard a knock at the door.

"Ready?" I whispered.

Grace peeked over her computer, looking like she might actually enjoy bending all the rules of fine behavior she learned at the Cathedral School.

Bianchi grasped my hand with real affection. "Nate, you're terrific. The audience *loved* it! Great work! Hey there, kid. Good job on the escape tonight. Look at your grandfather. He's still breathing. I'd call that a success after getting wrapped in plastic. I spoke with Ella earlier. She tells me the two of you got lunch the other day. Very nice!"

"It was fun, Mr. Bianchi. She helped me pick out a scarf."

"For once, my daughter has a *girl*friend! Imagine that—it's not just boys all day every day, thank God. She said you went shopping. I'm glad you're hitting it off. Now tell me, Nate, what's this note of yours? Have you come to your senses?"

The dressing room was little more than a closet lit with a few naked bulbs. If I hadn't wheeled a coatrack into the hallway, Bianchi would hardly have been able to fit. Another knock, and the theater manager poked his head in: "So we're good for tomorrow night? I'll get the word out. And on your loop back to Boston in August, give us a few more nights. You killed 'em out there, Nate! You lit it up. That Kort-a-hachy Escape's the real deal."

He waved and closed the door.

"It's like this," I said, turning to Bianchi. "Grace and I talked things over, and we agree I should go to Canada and then to the Caribbean. Who can take these winters anymore, right? She'll wait a few months and join me. It's the best plan. Grace, don't tip your chair backward like that. You could fall."

Bianchi cocked an eye. "You mean I won't have to break a piano leg over your head? You're actually going to leave on your own. For real?"

"I will. If—"

"Here it comes. If what?"

"If Grace and I get to perform the rest of our shows. Grace, I mean it, set that chair up. Bobby, we're having too much fun on the road. You saw the crowd tonight. Who knows if we'll ever get to spend time like this again? She's my only grandkid. Our last show's in Canaan, more than two weeks before the trial opens. That's plenty of time to run. I'll leave that night.

We could even buy the ticket now. Grace will go back to the dorm in South Boston for a few months, and one day on her way to school, she'll hop in a taxi and take a flight to Saint John or Aruba to find me. She'll leave a note. It'll look like she ran because she couldn't stand foster care anymore."

"Which is true, Mr. Bianchi. I can't."

"I don't know," he said. "If something goes wrong, two weeks is not a lot of time to find a Plan B. You should leave earlier. I don't like it, and I *know* Maxim won't like it."

I leaned forward. "I'm meeting you halfway, bud—three-quarters of the way. I'm committed. I'll buy the ticket. I'm with you. Take a step and let's work this out."

I stood and Bianchi stood. I opened my arms to him, looking to close the deal, and just as we were about to embrace Grace fell over backward in her chair with a tremendous crash. I jumped against Bianchi in my rush to reach her. "Are you okay? What did I tell you! You'll scare me to death! Go on. Go outside. Mr. Bianchi and I have a few things to discuss in private. Are you *sure* you're okay?"

When I helped her up, I slipped Bianchi's wallet into her waistband, beneath a jacket she wore for the occasion. "Look," I said, turning to Bobby, once she left. "She's emotionally fragile. I've got to let her down easy, so give me some time to get things settled with her and then I'll leave. It'll be better this way, even if she doesn't end up joining me in the Caribbean. Trust me. I know my granddaughter."

"And I know Maxim. I can't do this. He wants you gone yesterday."

"Then let him come up here and escort me to the plane himself. Come August, I'm running. It's definite. He can hold my hand, then wave good-bye."

"You really mean this. You're serious?"

"I've mapped out four different routes into Canada. I can fly from two different airports. Let Maxim choose which one."

Bianchi considered it.

"So maybe both of us will come to the show in Canaan. We'll get in the car afterward. Maxim will want to do this his way. No games, no more chances. If you don't leave after the last show, I swear I'll wash my hands. I've tried to be on your side, Nate. You know it's true. I've got a daughter to put through college, and she's *going* because I won't let her bounce around like me."

"Sounds totally fair, Bobby. Bring Maxim up here."

"As for sending the kid after you leave, I can't make promises that I'll help. It's better if she gets to the Caribbean herself. You set it up from your end, once you're established."

"That could be tricky."

"You're a magician. Figure it out."

I suggested we sleep on it. "Let's meet for coffee in the morning," I said. "Where are you staying?"

"The Pochet."

"Perfect! So are we."

"The diner next door—best in New England. We'll get coffee after breakfast. Nine o'clock. I got a long day, client meetings all up and down the state. I'll call Maxim tonight and get him on board. Don't misunderstand, buddy. I appreciate that you're offering something here. It just might not be enough. And really, don't worry about the kid. Kids make it through. Who knows, maybe Ella and Grace'll become best friends after all this."

"She'll be gone, Bobby. To the Caribbean with me."

Grace knocked at the door, on cue.

"Grandpa, I'm going across the street to that ice cream store. You want anything?"

"We were just finishing up. I'll go with you."

She bent down to tie a shoelace. When she stood, I pointed. "Bobby, is that yours?" A wallet lay on the dressing room floor. Bianchi patted the breast pockets of his sport coat, then his pants pockets.

"Damned if it isn't. I woulda walked right out of here!"

"Come along for ice cream, Mr. Bianchi. You can treat. You know, a finder's fee."

"I *like* this kid," he said. "She's got pluck. You know what, not even a year ago my Ella was just like her. Tell me what happens when they turn sixteen? Sometimes I think aliens crawled inside Ella and took over. She used to invite me to do all sorts of things. Basketball games at school. Fenway Park. How old are you, Grace?"

"Fourteen."

"Well, watch out for aliens."

"You can still get ice cream with us."

"Nah, I'm watching my weight." He stepped past her. "Nine tomorrow, Nate. I'll be at the diner. Be on time, okay? I've got a long day—got to move some product. I hate working out here in the boonies."

Twenty-Two: Grace Larson

"Just stuff," I said, reporting what I'd found.

"I don't know what that means, *stuff*. What kind of stuff?"

"Credit cards, photos, slips of paper. Wallet stuff."

"You didn't take any money, I hope. He'd notice that."

I set my hands on my hips. "I'm doing research. I'm not a thief!" Then again, I certainly was, having stolen Nate's Matryoshkas and Mrs. Alcott's rolling pin and all the other mementos of my captivities. But I wasn't the sort of thief who stole money.

We had borrowed Bianchi's wallet for ten minutes so that I could take photos of everything. My digital camera had a little screen, and I worked Nate through Bianchi's receipts, lotto tickets, and notes scribbled on matchbook covers and scraps of newspaper. "There's nothing here," he said, frustrated. "Nothing we can use. What else do you have?" I showed him the rest of the photos, and he stopped me when we came to a short-haired woman with beautiful dark eyes. "That's Nadine, his wife—or former wife. And here's his daughter. Why so many photos of her?"

I'd wondered the same thing. Here was Ella playing in a toddler pool, maybe three years old. Here she was in her junior soccer uniform. Ella skiing, Ella suited up for hockey, Ella at

First Communion. I was jealous. Mrs. Alcott kept photos of everyone who meant anything at all to her: nieces and nephews, parents and grandparents, friends from work, even her dogs. She kept no photo of me. It's not that I needed to see my face smiling out from a frame because I was special. It's only that for *once*, it would have felt good to know someone cared enough to want to remember me. I didn't know Bobby Bianchi or Ella, but it was clear he loved her. Or the old her. In none of these photos did she show any curves, not the sort she wanted to advertise with the clothes she bought on Newbury Street. The Ella I'd met wore eye liner and blush on a ninety-degree day, in the afternoon, just because. The Ella in Bobby's wallet still had bangs and wore braces.

Nate scratched his head. "We need something else, something more. When he's at breakfast, we'll search his room."

"Nate!"

"Don't worry. I'll get you the key. Bobby'll be at breakfast, and I'll be standing lookout. Did you notice the cubbies behind the front desk when you signed in? The manager keeps extra keys in each cubby. I checked. Bobby's in Room 207. He'll go to breakfast. I'll distract the manager with a trick, you'll get the key, you'll search the room, then you'll return the key saying you found it in the parking lot. We'll need to take more pictures, Grace. We need *something*. I can't even tell you what to search for because I won't know it until I see it."

Nate's slipping me Bianchi's wallet was scary enough. My heart was pounding when I took it to a stall in the ladies room and took my pictures. But breaking into a motel room? I didn't think I could do it.

"What if he comes back and I'm there? He might kill me!"

"Don't be dramatic. He won't come back because he loves his breakfast. In any event, he'd go after me, not you. But that's not going to happen. He's going to sit down to that buffet and not move for forty minutes except to get seconds and thirds. I'll be watching the diner with my binoculars, and you'll have plenty of warning if we need to get you out. There'll be no problems, guaranteed."

I didn't like it.

"Nate? Living at the DCF dorm is bad enough. Jail would be worse."

He looked genuinely troubled by that. "You're right," he said. "Don't worry. I'd tell everyone I put you up to it—and then I'd deal with Bobby and Petrov myself. Meanwhile, I'm all tired out from the show. Out with you. We'll talk about this in the morning."

At bedtime, Nate always performed a little trick for me. We never hugged or kissed; but he usually sent me away with something to make me smile and I'd nearly come to depend on it. This time, he brushed a few strands of hair from my face and tucked them behind my ear. "You need to wash better. I found something in the scruff of your neck. Hold out your hand." I did, and he dropped a folded bill—twenty dollars— and a slip of paper, also folded: a shopping list. "In case you wake up before I do, here's some breakfast money. And I'll need a few things from the little grocery next to the diner." I read the list: small wicker basket, apples, pears, banana, and orange. "Make sure you get an orange," he said. "A small grapefruit would also do." When I asked him why, he said we needed it to break into Bianchi's room.

"How do you break into a room with an orange?"

He yawned. "You'll understand when you go onstage. When you're out there in front of all those people, you can't afford to have a trick go bad on you. We borrowed his wallet. That didn't work, so I had a backup. Break into his room. You should always have a Plan B because you never know when the bottom's going to drop out. You never want to be left onstage—or anywhere else, for that matter—without a plan."

"What if I *had* found something in his wallet?"

"In that case, you'd have gotten a quarter instead of twenty bucks and a grocery list."

"You knew he'd be at this motel?"

He just shook his head at me. "Hoping for good luck is a bad plan. Of course, I knew. I called the bookkeeper at the grocery—she's worked there forever. Dima and I came up here for years on business, and Marsha negotiated discounts at a whole string of motels. I asked her where Bobby was staying. So, no, it wasn't a coincidence. Satisfied?"

I was, nearly. I still didn't want to add burglary to my list of crimes.

— • —

I woke early and went to the little grocery near the motel and returned with everything on Nate's list, including the orange he'd been so particular about. He was dressed and waiting when I knocked on his door.

"Good work!" he said, unloading the grocery bag. "Time for some surgery!"

He had laid a bath towel across a desk, and on the towel was a pair of tools: an actual scalpel and something I'd never seen. It looked like a thick nail except that it was hollowed out and one end was serrated, like a steak knife or a saw. Instead of a "head" for banging the nail into a piece of wood, there was a knob for turning. He set the orange and a big green apple on the towel, stems pointed up. Using the scalpel, he cut a small, tapered circle around each stem and gently removed it. Then he set the scalpel aside and used his second tool to bore a hole straight down into the core of both pieces of fruit.

He checked his watch. "It's eight o'clock. Go to the balcony and tell me when Bobby leaves for the diner. That's when our clock starts. Breakfast is his favorite meal. In the old days, he'd take an hour sometimes at the buffets in Somerville. To be safe, let's say he's going to eat for thirty minutes today. I'll finish up in here."

The Pochet Motor Lodge was a two-story motel bordered by thick woods on one side and the Tastee Diner on the other. The parking lot in front of the diner was already filled with pickups, and even from a distance I could tell at least half the people heading inside for the all-u-can-eat buffet had potato-sack bellies like Bianchi's. I hadn't watched for long when Bianchi left his room at the far end of the balcony. I reported back to Nate, who greeted me with a fruit basket.

"For the motel's manager," he said. "Come on, let's do some magic."

I followed him to the motel office, the first-floor corner room, which sat more or less directly beneath Bianchi's room. The office itself had vending machines, an ice maker, and a registration desk backed by a cubby-board with compartments for mail and room keys: two keys if the room wasn't rented, one if a single guest had checked in, and none if it was a couple. Bianchi was staying in 207. I saw one key in the cubby.

Nate presented his gift.

"How was your night, sir?"

"Terrific," said Nate. "Here's a little something to express my appreciation. I've been on the road a long time, and this place feels like home."

A lie.

"I'm telling you, this has got to be the cleanest, best-kept motel I've stayed at."

He looked so earnest, sounded so believable.

"And I wanted to thank you for getting a taxi for my grand-daughter last night. Here's a little something for all your trouble." Nate set the fruit basket down on a table between two empty chairs, a good five feet from the registration desk. The man would have to come from behind the desk to get it.

"How'd your show go last night?"

Nate had left a flyer in the motel's office window, and the manager had apologized in advance for not being able to attend.

"Thanks for asking. It went fine," Nate said, pulling a deck from his pocket. "So well, in fact, I don't mind telling you I got a standing ovation. I was fresh and ready, thanks to the nap I took here yesterday afternoon."

Another lie. He'd been in Market Square all afternoon.

"And with you delivering Grace safe and sound, it couldn't have gone better. We met up in plenty of time. Here, I'll give you a little taste of what you missed—you know, as a small thank-you. Mind if I do a little trick?"

There was no one else about, and the manager stepped from behind the counter.

In all his hours of practicing, I'd never seen Nate's trick with an orange. It was so good and I was watching so intently I nearly missed my cue. Nate flashed his cards—a standard deck—then flipped them and fanned them.

"Pick a card, any card."

Good magicians, I'd learned, can force a specific card on just about anyone. The manager figured *he* was choosing his card when, in fact, Nate was steering him to the two or three cards he was controlling as he shuffled. For every single trick, he worked with A, B, and C versions. That way, he'd never embarrass himself on stage if a trick blew up on him. His B and C versions were impressive enough that audiences would clap without ever knowing what they'd missed.

When he said, "Pick a card," the odds were nearly nine in ten the manager would pick either of two cards, both of which Nate had targeted for his "A" trick. Had he chosen any other card, Nate would have performed a simple vanish—in which case I may not have had time enough to grab Bianchi's room key. But sure enough, Nate forced the four of hearts.

"Okay," he said, "You've got your card. Please rip it down the center."

"Really?"

"Go ahead, tear it up."

Rip.

"Excellent. Now square up the two pieces and rip them again, in the other direction."

Rip.

The man continued squaring and ripping until he held sixteen evenly sized pieces, which he then handed to Nate. Nate took them, hesitated, then returned a corner: "Hold onto this for safekeeping," he said. "Do you see the four and the heart clearly?"

The manager inspected the ripped corner and agreed he did.

"Good. Now watch closely."

Nate stuffed the remaining fifteen pieces of the card into his open palm, made a fist, blew on his fist, said *Poof!* and then opened his hand to reveal—nothing. He had vanished the four of hearts, all its pieces, leaving the motel manager with the only evidence that he'd chosen that particular card. He could have ended right there, which was his "C" version of the trick—the vanish—but the manager had selected the four and Nate was maneuvering for the kill.

"You made them disappear," said the man. "Nice!"

I watched and listened, ready to make my move. Nate reached to the table for the fruit basket and grabbed the orange. "I brought these up from Boston. I have this thing about oranges. Can't stand bad ones, even mediocre ones, so I signed up with this fruit-of-the month outfit that ships me oranges and apples all year. You like oranges?"

The manager said, "Sure, why not."

Nate opened the blade of a baby pen knife he kept in his pocket and started cutting around the orange's equator, holding the orange by the poles and hiding the area he'd worked on with his scalpel and hollowed-out nail. "You've got to see the inside of this orange," he told the manager. "Juicy, just perfect." When he completed his cut, he lifted the northern hemisphere of the orange away from the southern and there, sticking straight up from the center of the southern half, was a spindled playing card. The manager leaned close as Nate carefully pulled the card from the center of the orange. He unspindled it and asked, "What do you see?"

A bomb could have gone off in the next room and the manager wouldn't have heard it. Disbelieving his own eyes, he said, "It's the four of hearts! Incredible!"

"But it's not any four of hearts," said Nate. "Look, it's missing a corner. Do you still have the corner of the card you ripped apart?"

The manager reached into his pocket, and when he pieced his corner to the missing corner of the spindled card, it was a perfect match. It fit like a puzzle piece.

"*What!*"

The instant his jaw dropped, I pulled Bianchi's key from the cubby and stepped back around the counter.

"I have *never*—"

"You missed a good show last night, but I'm glad you got a little taste of my magic."

Nate was *perfect*.

Earlier, when he returned the corner of the ripped card to the manager, Nate had made a switch. He actually gave him the corner of a card he'd ripped himself in his room twenty minutes before. He then spindled and set that (earlier) card into the orange, which he'd bored it out with his little nail-like tool. He refitted the orange's plug at the top, then handled the orange in such a way the manager couldn't see the cut. Absolutely perfect. Somehow, the four of hearts had reassembled itself, with no rips, and found its way inside the orange! Had the manager chosen the six of spades, the second card Nate was trying to force on him, the "A" trick would have proceeded with the apple that was waiting patiently in the fruit basket.

Nate reached into the basket and tossed me the apple. "My granddaughter's always skipping breakfast. You don't mind, do you?"

I walked away from the motel office with both a key to Bianchi's room and the only remaining evidence of Nate's *Card in the Fruit* trick. Not five minutes later, I let myself into Bobby Bianchi's room as Nate stood guard on the balcony, pretending to watch birds in the woods and in a nearby field. Every few minutes, he would train his binoculars on the Tastee Diner, watching for Bianchi to make an early exit.

I got to work.

Bianchi had already packed his rolling suitcase, which lay open on the room's second bed. I rummaged through its contents and found nothing useful: Old Spice deodorant, two different kinds of athlete's foot powder. In a separate, zippered case he had packed three different kinds of floss, gum massaging picks, "X-Stream" whitening toothpaste, and an ultrasonic toothbrush. He did have nice teeth. He also wore garters to hold up his socks. He must have worn a second set of shoes to the diner because a polished pair with tassels lay at the foot of the bed. He'd set his reading glasses on the nightstand beside a book titled *The Art of Pruning Bonsai Trees*. Alongside that was a framed photo of Ella when she was twelve or thirteen, holding a basketball. I saw no photos of his former wife.

Nate opened the door. "Come on, let's finish up."

"I don't even know what I'm looking for!"

"Then look *harder*. And be quick."

Bianchi had left his laptop propped open on a rickety desk, beside the bureau and TV. I couldn't steal the computer, though that was the only sure way to search the hard drive. An outright theft would have set off all sorts of alarms and involved the police. Who knew where that would lead. So I tapped the space bar, hoping for a few juicy hits. The good news: his computer hadn't gone to sleep in the time since he'd left for breakfast, so I didn't need to guess at passwords—though *Ella*, spelled forward and backward would have been a good bet. The bad news: after five minutes of scanning his e-mails and files, I found nothing Nate might use against him.

Most of the hard drive was devoted to the grocery business. He kept files for different suppliers, separated into Meat & Poultry, Vegetables & Fruit, Dry Goods, and so on. Another folder was devoted to employees. I opened a few, Ella's and Sveta's included, and found their work logs for the previous six months, nothing unusual. Bianchi's computer files were as orderly as his suitcase—and boring, which was not good for us. His e-mails looked to be limited to people connected with the grocery. I searched on "Maxim Petrov" and found nothing. That was odd. But I didn't have time to look more closely. Nate wanted me out of there, and I wanted to leave too. To finish up, I rummaged around his computer bag and discovered a zippered case. Inside were five DVDs, each titled with a woman's name written in black magic marker: Anichka, Katerina, Sveta, Sofiya, and Nataliya. Bianchi had packed a box of twenty blank DVDs as well.

I didn't dare risk playing them, so I helped myself to one of his blanks and started burning a copy of the DVD marked Sveta. I backed up my computer games all the time and knew that burning DVDs takes more or less time depending on the amount of information it holds and on a computer's processing speed. Video takes longer than audio, and audio takes longer than text. I crossed my arms and waited. The burn would take at least three minutes and, possibly, as many as eight.

When Nate opened the door again, he had actual news. "He left his table by the window in the diner. He was making motions like he might leave for a minute. Bathroom break, likely. Let's be safe. Get out now."

I was not getting out, not yet.

Forty seconds later, he opened the door in a panic. "He didn't go to the bathroom in the diner. He left and he's heading this way. Leave *now!*"

I told Nate what I'd found.

"I don't care. It's not worth it."

I didn't move.

Hurrying a file transfer is like coaxing a pot of water to boil. The job's done when it's done, and there's nothing to do except watch and, in my case, get nervous. Nate turned into the room, frantic. "You've got twenty seconds. Once he reaches the balcony, there's no way out. This is *not* smart."

But it wasn't stupid either. Without even looking, I knew where I would hide because Bianchi's room was laid out the same as Nate's and mine: in the case of the Pochet that meant all three rooms had the same ugly burnt orange curtains, the same sagging beds, the same smelly shag carpets. His bed, as mine, was set on a fixed wooden platform so there was no crawling beneath. His room had the same open closet for hanging clothes, so there was no hiding there. And though I hadn't seen his bathroom, I knew the tub would have a curtain, like mine did, for people who wanted to shower.

The file transfer meter read 95 percent.

Outside, I could hear Nate greeting Bianchi. "We were going to meet here, right Bobby? Eight-twenty? No, you said the diner at nine? Oh, that's right. My memory. I scare myself sometimes."

Finished.

I popped the DVD out, hit the power button, returned the original Sveta DVD to the computer bag, and had nearly reached the bathroom door when I sprinted back to the room door and pushed the button on the handle to lock it. As I did that, the handle began to turn as Bianchi fit the key into its lock. I just reached the bathroom when the door opened. I stepped into the moldy tub behind the curtain and just about screamed when I saw a gun on the tile floor, poking out of a paper bag.

"Hey, Nate!" Bianchi called from the room. "If you're losing your memory, I'm losing my eyesight. I couldn't even read the newspaper at the diner without my cheaters. Here they are, by the bed. Give me a minute. I need to hit the can. We'll walk over to the diner together, okay? They got a special on blueberry pancakes—a twelve-stack for three bucks. Can't beat it with a stick!"

He jostled his belt, and I had to listen to him unzip his pants and sit on the toilet, not three feet away. He strained, then cursed. I heard sounds I didn't want to hear and fought gagging. It occurred to me I could pick up the gun, point it at him, and run. But the sliver of my brain that was still working told me that would be a mistake. Things only got worse when he started singing. I bit my finger, hard, praying he couldn't hear the pounding in my chest. If he decided to check on his gun—why did he need a gun?—I supposed he'd kill Nate and me and ask questions later. What a way to die.

He flushed and zipped.

As he opened the motel door and closed it behind him, he called: "Come on, buddy! Let me buy you the best buffet in New England. Where's the kid? Maybe she'll join us?"

The kid was curled into a ball, hugging her knees, promising God that, if she survived, this would be the very last time she broke into anyone's room to steal anything. I didn't have the nerves to make a decent thief. As for the gun, I tried not staring. But the more I tried, the more difficult that became. I gave them ten minutes to get to the diner so that I could leave safely. Panicked, I was expecting state troopers in their tall boots and puffy pants to be waiting for me on the balcony. But no one was waiting. I started for my room but then turned back. Bianchi was threatening Nate. Bianchi had a gun. Bianchi was not a good man. I concluded my grandfather was in danger.

Still shaking, I inched my way back to the bathroom and grabbed the paper bag, making sure the barrel of the gun inside was pointed at the ground. I thought of one of my rental parents, Mr. Elliot, who once gave me a test I was sure to fail. He had filled a pitcher to the very top and told me to set it on the table, across the kitchen, for dinner. We both knew I was going to slosh lemonade onto the floor, and we both knew he was going to yell at me and slap me when I did. I walked very slowly, very carefully. That's how I walked holding the bag with Bianchi's gun. Back at my room, I set the bag in my suitcase and stuffed clothes all around it. I snapped the lid shut, hoping that when I opened it next—presto!—the gun would be gone.

Twenty-Three: Nate Larson

My nerves were shot after Grace's close call in Bianchi's motel room. Somehow I managed to make it through breakfast with him, and when he left to drive north and tend to business, I took a nap—which didn't last long because Sveta called. I'd been dreaming once more of the German soldier. Again, I shot him. Again, I listened to his life leak away. When the phone rang, I was struggling to breathe under his weight. It was a kindness she woke me.

"Nataniel!"

She slurred my name.

"Everything is bad. I have a day off from the store. I want to visit."

I explained that we were on the road.

"How far?"

Portsmouth is only sixty miles north of Boston, an easy drive. "Grace and I would love to see you," I said. "But why come all the way to Portsmouth?"

"I need my good friends, Nataniel. You said *no* that day in the car. I trust you. It's bad now. Very bad."

Given how casually Petrov had ordered her to bed me down, I could imagine. I told her how to find us, and she said she'd borrow a friend's car and come that afternoon because she didn't know when she'd get another chance. The visit would be brief because she had to work for Maxim that night at a party.

I was left staring at my phone, wondering how—after meeting me twice—she could count me as a "good" friend.

I hadn't slept more than five or ten minutes at a stretch all night, and I was unsure I could make it out of bed. Grace took one look at me and ordered me to stay put. Fifteen minutes later, she returned with a shopping bag. We never made our own meals aside from an occasional bowl of cereal or a bologna and mayo sandwich. But now Grace looked to be mounting a feast. She'd bought Velveeta cheese, something called Bimbo Bread, and a small tub of margarine. I reminded her that our rooms had no refrigerator or microwave.

"I *know* that," she said, shushing me. "I can still make you a home-cooked meal!" She lined up her ingredients on the bureau. "The key," she explained, "is that none of this needs a refrigerator. I don't know, maybe it's not even food, but it'll fill you up. We all kept crackers in our bureaus at the DCF dorm. Sometimes we'd have Velveeta parties after lights out." She set out the ironing board. "I don't remember much about my mom," she continued, plugging in an iron, "but I think when I was sick she let me stay in bed all day and brought food to me. I remember she . . . I think I remember someone sitting on the side of the bed, smoothing my hair. Then I'd feel better! You're going to get better just as soon as I make you a grilled cheese sandwich."

She tore off a long sheet of aluminum foil.

She couldn't have known that six decades earlier, another woman —actually two women—sat with me through my fevers, dabbing my forehead and chest until I regained my strength. Like Grace, I didn't remember much except that there'd been a time when the world and its troubles could be made right by a sponge, a basin of water, and caring hands.

"You have to use the linen setting," she said as the iron heated up. "You want it hot." She smeared margarine on two slices of bread, placing the smeared sides down, against the foil, then piled on slices of Velveeta and wrapped it all, tightly. "Here goes!" She began ironing the sandwich through the aluminum foil as if she'd laid a shirt across the board. "Two minutes each side once the iron's up to temperature. There's an art to melting the cheese but not burning the bread."

I hardly knew what to say when she sat beside me and presented a perfectly grilled sandwich. She'd cut it in half, set it on a paper plate, and cut up an apple as a little garnish. I took a bite and smiled. I was tired. I knew it was going to be a rough day, and I didn't want her to see me struggle. "Let's skip rehearsal," I said. "Why don't you go to the park down by the store or into town if you like. I believe there's a bus."

On her way out, she asked me to play her new computer game, which she was calling *Chopped!* She said it was her best yet, even if she'd finished it in a hurry. "Sometimes faster is better. But watch out. It's bloody."

Back at our apartment in Arlington, she'd taught me to advance through her games by using a mouse. As I played them, admiring her skill, I realized she worked as hard on her computer games as I worked on my magic. It was a thing to behold, watching someone that young so committed.

She left me with her laptop, cued and ready to go.

My granddaughter was certainly right: *Chopped!* was a dark excursion into a violent world, and I was glad she'd left because I didn't want her seeing the rawest of my reactions. The game opened with an image of a garden and a path, all of it very pretty. I heard birds singing. Leaves fluttered in sunlight. As I cursored up the path, I knew enough to click on rocks and trees, looking for the special powers Grace was fond of salting throughout her games. If I guessed correctly, I'd be able to fly or breathe fire later, when I was in danger. If I made the wrong choice, and I must have made every one of them, I died, which in *Chopped!* meant watching the swing of a hatchet held by an arm that floated across the screen, making chopping motions. Demented organ music played when the hatchet appeared. Grace had even taken the trouble to steal the sound of a woman screaming from some horror movie she'd found on the Internet. As the woman screamed, blood spattered, and a skull and cross bones appeared over the words: YOU'RE CHOPPED! GAME OVER!

I played for two hours, trying to reach a series of milestones that placed me farther along the garden path before getting chopped. Had the violence not worried me for her sake—about what was going on in her head to inspire such a bloody show—I would have complimented Grace on her killing me off in such creative ways. One time I fell into a pit after venturing too far along the path without using any of the powers I'd collected. I knew I was in trouble when the only tools I had to escape were the bones of people who'd fallen into the pit before me.

When I finally managed to navigate to the yellow door at the shed, I discovered a man seated with his back to me. A syringe lay on the table to his left. To his right sat a young woman, terrified, and though she didn't move—this was a photo-based game, not video—she was crying: "Don't, please don't. It hurts! *Stop!*" When I clicked on the man's back, a new image appeared: of Dima, old and sick, the Dima I'd seen just a week earlier. "*Get Out!*" he roared. Somehow Grace had slowed and distorted her own voice until it had a man's depth. It was a frightful voice, filled with hatred.

Twelve more times I returned to that screen and its inescapable conclusion that my brother was a monster. What could he have done to deserve such treatment? Each time I clicked on him, I took a hatchet stroke to the neck and got sent back to start the game over. Finally I chose the correct sequence of moves and used the necessary powers. Instead of the bloody hatchet lopping off my head, it lopped off Dima's.

Click: the girl at the table smiled.

Click: the syringe disappeared.

Click: Trumpets blared, and the words YOU WIN! flashed across the screen.

I showered and changed, and not long after answered a knock at my door. Sveta Zelenko stood before me, and she'd been drinking.

"That was fast," I said.

"Good roads in America, Nataniel."

I sat her on the corner of the bed, guessing what happened. But I needed to hear it from her. "It's good to see you, Sveta."

"It's good to see you too."

Her eyes were rolling.

"I was wondering . . . When Dima found you in Kiev, you wanted to come to America?"

She nodded.

"What did he promise?"

"He promised good work. He told me I could start my life again. That I'd learn English at the store, then he'd help me move on. But he got sick, Nataniel, and now there's only Maxim. Maxim says, 'There's no free lunch in America. You have to earn your freedom. All Americans do. It's what makes the country great!' Five years, he says I owe him. *Five*! I am to pay with these." She cupped her breasts with her hands. "Here, he told me to give you this."

She handed me a note.

"You *told* him you were visiting me?"

"I said I might. It's my day off. I can do what I want."

I opened the note.

> No more freebies, Nate. If you so much as touch her,
> it's $700—the going rate for prime beef. And believe
> me, I'll check when she gets back.

I tore the note in half and walked it to the trashcan.

"What if you said *no* to him?"

She made a spitting sound. "He would burn my papers and give me to immigration."

"Fine. Go back to Ukraine. In fact, go to the police yourself."

She checked her watch and laughed. "I almost needed to leave before I got here. I have to work at one of Maxim's parties tonight. No more Ukraine for me, Nataniel. I won't go back. I'm in America now. Land of big opportunity."

"Run," I told her. "Tell the police about Petrov and run."

"He knows I came here."

"I'll deny it."

"I saved six hundred dollars. How far will that take me?"

"Not very. I'll give you money."

"Where would I *go*?"

"Sveta, just get on a bus and leave. It doesn't matter where."

"And do what? When my money runs out, there's only one thing I know."

"Try something else."

"I want to be doctor! In Ukraine, my grandmother was a doctor. Dima told me I could be a doctor in America. Maxim? He beats me, then he's sweet and nice. He wants me to be a model. I have to make movies with men for him. I *hate* my life." She checked her watch. "If I miss his party, he'll beat me."

Her head fell back to the pillow, and she passed out. I hoisted her legs onto the bed and started pacing—after I dumped what was left of the vodka I found in her purse and replaced it with water. Dima had brought her to Boston with the best of intentions. It wasn't his fault that his mind collapsed and she was the first casualty. Sveta was at least partly his problem, which made her partly mine. When Grace returned from her trip to town, she took one look at our visitor and ran across the room.

Sveta woke.

"Little Sister!"

How much time could they have spent together? No more than a few hours over a few visits. Yet here they were embracing as if they'd each crossed continents for this reunion.

"See? I'm wearing my scarf!"

Sveta adjusted it across Grace's shoulders and straightened the knot.

"Very beautiful!"

"Why did you come?"

"I missed my American sister . . . and father."

"Wait! I got something yesterday from Bobby Bianchi's computer bag—" Grace put a hand to her lips and gave me a quick look. "Uh-oh."

"It's okay," I said.

She dashed to her room and reappeared with the DVD she'd copied.

"We didn't watch yet. It had your name, so I copied it. Let's watch!"

Sveta grabbed the disk. "Where did you find this?"

"In Bobby Bianchi's bag. He had a few disks with names on them."

"What names?"

"They sounded like yours, a little. Sofia maybe. Katarina."

"Where's my name?"

"I copied only yours, so I didn't need to write a name. Let's play it!"

Sveta snapped the disk and it splintered, an edge catching her finger. "I've seen this movie. It's no good. And look at the time! I have a big party in Boston tonight. I'm wearing the little black dress we bought. Remember?" She sucked at the cut.

"It's *so* beautiful on you, Sveta. But why did you break—"

"Someone will take my picture at the party. I promise to send you a copy."

Grace asked her to stay. I asked her to stay. Sveta thanked us for our time, and I followed her onto the balcony, where I could speak freely. "We can fix this," I said. "You don't have to work for Petrov. I'll help you make a plan."

She was too overwhelmed to plan.

"Maxim tells us he finds girls who run. Anywhere in the world, he finds them, no matter how long it takes. Then he cuts them. He would find me, Nataniel. I know he would. Five years is not such a long time."

Client by client, three times a night, every night of every year. I did the math. Sveta could earn Petrov up to sixty-three thousand a month, even allowing for a discount as she wore out. I called after her: "People like Maxim won't let you walk away. Ever. You've got to run or go to the police." She was already down the stairs and onto the parking lot when I called to her a last time, *Don't go back*. Maybe she believed Petrov's promises, maybe she couldn't imagine living more than five years in any event. She swigged back her pint of Stolichnaya, spit out the water, and slammed the bottle on the asphalt.

Grace meanwhile had retreated to her room. When she joined me an hour or so later, she was fighting tears. "Nate, to come all this way only to turn around? She looks so sad! And she broke the disk. What do you think was on it?"

I gave her a version of the truth, and let her draw from that what she needed. "A story," I said. "Everybody's got one. If she didn't want us watching hers, that's her business. Our business is here." I pointed to her laptop. "I played *Chopped!* while you were gone."

She perked up.

"Did you make it to the end? Did you chop off his head?"

"You mean my brother's?"

"Dima's. Yes."

"You forced me to chop off my brother's head?"

If I had to explain why Dima was a good man, I'd already lost the battle. But I couldn't keep silent, either, given the violence she'd done. "You made him into a monster. I don't even recognize the man you put in your game. Look what you've done to him, a decent and kind man! He doesn't deserve this."

It took an hour before I untangled what had happened, an interrogation that left us both exhausted. After I went to prison, Gabby and Grace attended a July Fourth party at Dima's farm—a few acres he leased in Lincoln where he grew vegetables for the store. She'd forgotten the whole thing until she saw Dima again, after ten years. Someone had typed up a scavenger hunt for the children, and Grace found herself walking up a garden path, looking for a buttercup. Gabby was feeling weak from her treatments and had found a chair in the shade. She told Grace to go searching with a friend she'd just made, a ten-year-old, but that child got distracted and left Grace alone. She wandered up the path toward the yellow door. She opened the door and found Dima seated before a partially naked woman, preparing to inject her with drugs. It wasn't pretty, and the worst of it came flooding back when she saw him at The Mystery Lounge.

"You didn't ask what he was doing?"

"He screamed at me! The woman was crying. She said it *hurt*! I ran, Nate. I was four."

She's too young, I thought. But young or not, this was her world and I was the only one who could help her make sense of it. Dima wanted me to see things as they were. For once, I agreed. I told Grace all that she needed to hear, probably too much.

"I'd hoped you'd forget."

"About the shed? You *knew*?"

Dima visited the jail the following week and confessed to feeling terrible about what had happened. Grace had interrupted him in the middle of an emergency that called him away from the party. "You were so young," I said. "All he could think to do was yell so you wouldn't see more. He didn't have the time to explain. It was a delicate situation, Grace. You were a child. You shouldn't have been there at all, especially alone."

"What was he doing?"

"The young woman, she was one of Dima's Rachels."

"His *Rachels*?"

To tell her or not tell her?

I told her.

"Like Rachel in the story," I said. "The young woman you saw was pregnant, and she chose that moment, at the party of all places, to have her baby. Dima couldn't take her to a hospital because she had no immigration papers, and he hadn't brought the fake passport he'd forged for her. The doctors would have delivered the baby, and the child would have been born a US citizen. But the hospital would have called the immigration police. The child could have stayed, but the mother they'd send back to Ukraine. Dima was delivering a baby, Grace. During the war, he was a doctor as well as a fighter. He removed bullets and stitched people up. He'd been good at working on animals on our farm. He'd set bones, he helped deliver calves and baby goats. It's true, the young woman you saw in the shed was in pain. Childbirth is painful. Women scream. They can be scared, especially the first time. There's blood and it's messy. If you had arrived a few hours later, though, you would have seen a newborn at her mother's breast. This Dima in your game, this monster—" I pointed to her laptop. "I don't know him. It's not right what you've done. He was a good man. He *is* a good man, what's left of him."

We fell silent.

She picked up the TV remote and flipped through a few channels, then shut it off again. She sat at the end of my bed, then stood, agitated. "Rachel," she said at last. "Who was she? What really happened in Kortelisy? And why do you call it the *Kortelisy* escape? No one wants to escape from heaven!"

I was exhausted. I couldn't speak without cards in my hands. It happened from time to time, when talk cut so close to my heart and I needed to hide as I spoke. I squared and presented a deck. "Tap the top card," I told her. "Then flip it."

She did as I asked

"The queen of hearts."

"So then. Do you remember my story from the show?"

"Of course I do."

"I'm going to tell it again, this time with cards. And I'm going to tell you exactly what happened, what really happened, all of it. Let's call the queen, Rachel. She arrived at the farm pregnant and alone, half dead. She was fourteen, just like you. A solider had raped her, and her parents were so ashamed they threw her out of their home. They said she must have seduced the man. Do you know that word, *rape*?"

She nodded.

"Rachel wandered from village to village, barely finding enough to eat. Finally she collapsed in a ditch. She just fell where she stood, by a barley field that Dima's parents owned."

"Dima's parents? You mean your parents. Dima's too."

"No, Grace. Rachel was my mother. Her child—I—lived. She never jumped into a lake because there was no lake. There was no big fish. She was just a child herself, in trouble, who had the good fortune of collapsing where Dima and his parents found her. I figured out a long time ago that she was my mother. Dima still doesn't think I know we're not really brothers. His parents, the Lazarenkos, adopted us. Rachel, after all, was young enough to be their daughter—she was only two years younger than Dima. Overnight, they went from a family of three to five. There was no paperwork in those days. They just took us in and gave us their name. The one true part of the story is that I had two mothers who loved me. I called them Mama Anastasia and Mama Rachel. Dima changed the family name to Larson when we came to America after the war.

I instructed her to take the queen and slip it back into the deck, anywhere.

I shuffled, then cut the deck twice. "The world is so broken," I said. "You already know this. When I was a child, there were many Rachels wandering about. Times were hard. If you had daughters in those days, you hid them. Stalin's soldiers were bandits in uniform who were told they could do anything they pleased, as long as they killed when the generals ordered them to kill. Stalin wanted Ukrainians gone. He wanted the fields, not the farmers. Hitler wanted the Ukrainians gone for the same reason. Between them, they killed millions. Almost every year a new Rachel would wander into our village, pregnant and half-starved. Sometimes people helped them, sometimes not. Tap the top card and flip it."

The queen of hearts.

"See what I mean? Another Rachel."

"Nate . . . how did the queen get to the top after you shuffled her *into* the deck?"

"Because there are too many Rachels, too many ruined girls. They turn up everywhere." I fanned the deck again, but she stopped me to inspect the cards to make certain they weren't *all* queens. I was working a real deck, telling her a real story about the real world in all its brutality. She took the queen and slipped it into a new spot in the deck. I shuffled, then asked her to cut. Again I squared the deck and presented it. She tapped the top card. When the queen showed the third time, she put a hand to her head and laughed.

"How are you doing this?"

"Watch closely. To live in those years was craziness. Everyone suffered. Many people died. When farmers went to the authorities to protest the rape of their children, who should come to investigate but a lieutenant in the same army, a rapist himself! The people of Kortelisy began dressing their daughters in boys' clothes, trying to hide them."

I dumped the cards on the table, scramble-shuffling like a child whose hands are too small to hold a full deck. "Not even disguising their daughters worked!" I gathered the cards, squared them, then presented the deck.

"Go ahead," I instructed my granddaughter.

Another Rachel.

"That's not *possible*, Nate! That card was way at the bottom. I was watching it!"

"Yes, it was possible. Crimes like this are always possible. Dima and his parents saved Rachel and me, and Dima fell in love with her. From the way he tells it, she loved him too. They planned to wait a few more years and marry. Then the war came, and she died."

I paused.

"How did she die?"

"It was wartime. People died in all sorts of ways."

"How?"

"Soldiers. That's enough for now."

My hands began to shake.

"How come you didn't die?"

"Because Dima took me to another village to repair a wagon. A broken wagon saved my life. I was eight years old. When we returned . . . the German soldiers had already come and gone."

"And your . . . Dima's parents?"

"Dead."

"Rachel?"

"Dead. But she was beautiful, so she suffered first."

"She was my age?

"Twenty or twenty-two at that point. Dima took me and we ran to the forests. Somehow, he kept me alive. The war ended, but something in him had changed. He couldn't forget Rachel. When we came to America, he decided to save as many girls like her as he could, girls like Sveta who were dumped onto the streets. There's no hiding the fact that some of them became prostitutes after they were raped. No one wanted them, and they had no hope of doing anything but selling their bodies. Dima couldn't stand it. He traveled back and forth many times and returned with thrown-away girls. He brought them to Boston and arranged for false papers so they could start over."

"You were eight?"

"When the soldiers came? Yes. I don't remember my mother much aside from Dima's stories. But what stories! Because he loved her, he told me only the good things and the funny things—like how she sang to the cows as she milked them, the same tunes she used when nursing me. How she let me stick my finger in the sugar bowl when she made bread. How she taught me Russian and German. How she played Matryoshkas with me. Maybe that's the only thing I remember myself—how one winter night Dima's father gave me the Matryoshkas. It was Rachel who taught me to dance the dolls on the table top, then set them in a line. How I loved my Matryoshkas! When I dance with them, I think of my mother."

I fell silent, and Grace looked away.

"It all happened," I said. "It's not just a story. It *happened*, and you're going to meet one of the Rachels very soon. While Dima was in Eastern Europe looking for throwaways, I ran the grocery. When he returned, I helped find them homes and jobs. Eleanor Hunt couldn't be more wrong about my brother! Yes, he brought throwaways through the store, but he never hurt them! Who cares that he didn't pay taxes? Petrov's the animal. He's hijacked the Rachels to sell them, and now Dima's too sick to do anything about it."

A spigot had opened. I fell back against the chair, drained.

"Is she a prostitute? Sveta?"

Grace choked on the words.

"What she is is Dima's last Rachel. My brother's sick, and Petrov's sunk his claws into her. Here, tap the deck one last time."

She pulled an ace of hearts.

"You're busted! But it's still a great trick."

"Not so fast. You're going to use that ace to buy one more card, and then I'm done. You think the problem is solved? You think there's only one Maxim Petrov dragging people down? Rachels and the Petrovs who feed on them are *every-where*. Do you have any idea how easily someone can become a throwaway!"

I knew exactly when Jacqueline Roberts released Grace from the dormitory in South Boston. I had called, and I was sick that Grace didn't come to Portsmouth that same night. Had her night alone turned to two nights or seven or more, my own granddaughter could have become Sveta: alone, pretty, vulnerable.

"Where you least expect to find a Rachel," I said, "there she is. It can shock you sometimes. Go open the bureau drawer across the room. Top drawer, left. See what you find."

"Why?"

"Go on, open it."

In an otherwise empty drawer lay a card, facedown. I planted it there so that I'd have the option of presenting *The Persistent Queen* at an appropriate moment. What surprised me was the patter that had tumbled out. Somewhere Dima must have been smiling because for once in my life I looked ugliness head on and didn't flinch. "Flip the card," I said.

She reached into the drawer, hesitating.

"Come on now! You're so eager to know what happened? German soldiers murdered the Rachel Dima loved, yet he continued seeing her everywhere. He went mad a little. He returned to Europe again and again and saved girl after girl but that was never enough because he could never bring back the Rachel he lost in Kortelisy. He could never bring back my mother. But he tried, Grace! And it's a crime what you did to him in that game of yours, *Chopped!* It's a crime what I did to you by going to jail and leaving you alone in the world. Flip the damned card, Grace. Flip it!"

She did. When the queen of hearts showed, she looked up—eyes brimming.

"Come on, out with it! Why the tears?"

She turned to leave, then paused at the door. "You didn't know your father either," she said, fighting for the words. "And you don't really remember your mother. Just like me. Why didn't you say so, Nate? I wasted so much time hating you."

THE PERSISTENT QUEEN 👑

STEPS:

1. FIRST REVEAL: BEGIN WITH QUEEN OF HEARTS ON TOP OF DECK, FACE DOWN. TAP TO REVEAL QUEEN.

2a. SECOND REVEAL: FORCE RETURN OF QUEEN TO CONTROLLED POSITION WITHIN FANNED DECK.

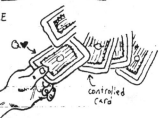

controlled card

2b. CONTROL-CUT DECK TO CREATE IMPRESSION OF THOROUGH MIXING, MOVING QUEEN TO TOP WITH FINAL CUT. TAP AND REVEAL QUEEN.

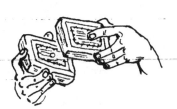

3. THIRD REVEAL: FORCE RETURN OF QUEEN TO CONTROLLED POSITION WITHIN FANNED DECK. SEE 2a. CONTROL A QUADRUPLE SHUFFLE TO RETURN QUEEN TO TOP. TAP AND REVEAL QUEEN.

4a. FOURTH REVEAL: FLIP THE QUEEN FACE DOWN ON TOP OF DECK AND PALM IT, USING PUTTY IN PALM IF NEEDED.

4b. SCRAMBLE CARDS ON TABLE TOP, WITH PALMED QUEEN SHIELDED BY AND STUCK TO UNDERSIDE OF COVERING HAND.

4c. COLLECT CARDS, SQUARE DECK, AND RELEASE QUEEN FROM HAND, DELIVERING TO TOP OF DECK. TAP AND REVEAL QUEEN.

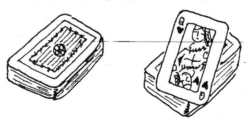

5a. FINAL REVEAL: TAKE CONTROL OF
QUEEN AND VANISH IT IN POCKET.

5b. THIRTY MINUTES BEFORE TRICK BEGINS,
TAKE QUEEN OF HEARTS FROM SECOND, IDENTICAL DECK
AND PLACE BENEATH SOME OBJECT, OR IN A DRAWER,
AWAY FROM TABLE, ACROSS ROOM.

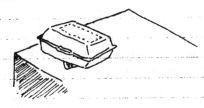

5c. HAVE AUDIENCE MEMBER LIFT OBJECT
TO REVEAL QUEEN.

Twenty-Four: Grace Larson

The Greyhound bus rides to New York and north again to Boston and Portsmouth had been the first I'd traveled alone. The warm air and rolling motion of the buses made me drowsy, and I missed most of the sights. I had no intention of sleeping through this next trip to Concord. Nate took Route 4, the old two-lane road from the coast to the state capital. I could scarcely believe all the cows and pastures. Every fifteen or twenty minutes we'd see a farmhouse and a barn, maybe a grain silo. New Hampshire was like the green, prickly hump of some enormous animal. From time to time I made Nate stop just so I could get out and feel the ground beneath me. I needed to know we were there, not caught in some movie playing outside the windows.

"People really live on farms?" I asked.

"Sure," said Nate. "You could if you wanted."

"With you?"

"Nah. You'll have a husband and kids by that point. See those Guernseys? You could run a dairy, be your own boss. It requires a lot of schooling these days to be a good farmer . . . All right, so maybe you could build me a little room in the barn. You could bring me oatmeal when you milk the cows each morning."

"And llamas. I want llamas."

Married, with kids? I doubted very much if I wanted to inflict the world on more children, given that I'd never seen a family that wasn't broken. On the other hand, owning a farm with a herd of dairy cows sounded like a worthwhile life. Around noon we pulled into a cutout along the road for a lunch break, by a pasture. We ate our sandwiches, and Nate and I were leaning against fence posts, staring at the cows. I tore off a long piece of grass and put it in my mouth the way I'd seen cowboys do in Westerns. A few feet behind us, the car ticked and clicked as the engine cooled. A breeze blew across the pasture, and I smelled fresh-mowed grass and cow patties. I closed my eyes, and when I opened them, the cows and the fields and the mountains hadn't moved. I was there and so was Nate and it was real, a long way from the asphalt playground of the Cathedral School.

"Thank you," I said.

"Sure. For what?"

"Nate?"

It was just like us to watch a herd of cows as we talked. At home, our eyes would have been glued to the checkerboard. Out here, same difference. "Nate," I said, "you never told me it would be so pretty."

"You never asked."

One of the cows was peeing like someone tipped over a gallon jug. I giggled.

"You know what I read once?"

"What's that?"

"That if you laid all the stone walls in New England end to end, you'd reach the moon."

"No way."

"That's what I read."

"Doesn't make it true."

"I'm the adult. That's what *I'm* supposed to say."

We didn't talk for a while, and I chewed my blade of grass.

"Nate?"

"Um-hmmm."

"Why did you go to jail? Really. You told me once, how you stole money. But what made you do it? I know my mom was sick and that you took something that wasn't yours to help her. Why did you do that? Are you a bad person if you steal for a good reason?"

A Guernsey mooed and swished her tail at some flies.

"I made a mistake," he said. "Actually, three mistakes. Your grandmother was sick. I tried to help and couldn't. Then I was helping a friend and something stupid happened. It doesn't even matter what anymore. When your mother's cancer hit, I tried to help her and couldn't. I was so frustrated, Grace. So helpless. To get money for her treatments, I lied to an insurance company. They caught me. I *deserved* to get caught. But your mother didn't deserve to die, not so young. And not with a four-year-old."

I inhaled the scent of hay and cows.

"You took something that wasn't yours, something you had no right to take."

"I did. I got sent to prison—for too long. I broke the law and was punished."

I waited. I closed my eyes and let the breeze play with my hair.

"I couldn't save Rachel either. That was my real crime. I couldn't save my own mother, and I don't think I ever left Kortelisy. I've tried, Grace. My whole life I've tried, but I can't manage to put it behind me. Every day I'm fighting for my life, and I'm tired."

"But you escape at every show!"

I had to look at him. He was resting his head on his arms and resting his arms on the fence post. He spoke into the hollow he made with his body as if he'd entered a cave. "I try," he said again, more to himself.

Then he was up again, pointing. "Do you see those? Look! Red-tailed hawks. They can spot a mouse in a field from a quarter-mile up. Watch the way they hold steady, riding the air currents. Right now they're wondering if we're too big for dinner. I'm too big, anyway. You? You're just about the right size."

Other than the occasional car or pickup, we were alone on the road and had the fields and mountains to ourselves. We watched the hawks for a while, and Nate said he wanted to tell me a story, if I could stand it. After learning about the real Rachel, I wasn't sure. "If it's scary," I said, "no. Or bloody. Does anyone die? Because if there are more soldiers and guns I don't want to listen."

"It's nothing like that. It's a sweet little thing. After the war, Dima and I wandered through what was left of Ukraine and ended up at a displaced person's camp in Germany. DP camps were where people went who didn't have a home anymore. We had no family or money or papers. Our village was gone. The camp was run by the Red Cross. They gave us beds, three hot meals each day, and if Dima and I had gone no farther than that camp, life would have been very good compared to what we'd lived through. The people in the DP camp put on shows, set up committees to build barracks and cook. It was a regular little town.

"So Dima and I are there, doing well enough, waiting for papers to get us into Canada or America, when one day he says to me, 'They're running a camp for kids your age. This will be good for you.' And it was! We played soccer, we made fires at night, we slept in tents. One night, our leader, who couldn't have been more than seventeen or eighteen herself, woke us up and said, 'Shhh.' She gathered ten of us away from the camp lights. She gave us caps to pull down over our heads. 'We're on a secret mission,' she said. 'We're going to raid the kitchen!' The word *raid* made me nervous. I expected guns and shooting. But it sounded fun and we followed her like little commandos, single file, crouching, to the mess tent. For some reason, the door was unlocked. We opened it just enough to slip through—and there, on a nearby table, sat a plate of cookies and two bottles of—"

He pointed across the pasture.

"Milk!"

"Do you know how long it had been since I'd had milk and cookies? We tiptoed up to the table, each kid stuffed two cookies into his pocket, and just as we were sneaking out, someone started clanging pots and making a big ruckus. 'What's this? Thieves! Who stole my cookies! Catch them! Thieves! Call the guards!'

"We ran back to our tents, and through some miracle our leader managed to run without spilling any of the milk. We made a fire and, well into the early morning, told and retold the story of how we outfoxed the mean old cook. Do you know what's funny, Grace? Truly sweet—what I never realized until a few minutes ago?"

That camp sounded better than any of my foster homes.

"What's funny?"

"Our leader and the cook had arranged the whole thing." He began to chuckle. "Even the clanging pots."

"They must have wanted to scare you away from stealing."

"No, they wanted us to laugh. It had been years since any of us laughed." He turned to me, brushing something from his eyes. "I am *so* sorry."

He just stared and stared.

"For what?"

"For . . ." He waited a few moments. "For loving your mother too much. I couldn't see what everyone else did, that there was no saving her. I should have let her go so that I could care for you. Instead I took a stupid risk. I got sent to prison, and you got sent to hell. It was my fault, Grace, all those rotten foster homes. I couldn't save your mother or grandmother. I couldn't save my own mother, and I didn't save you."

The farmer who built the fence had set his posts six feet apart, connected with three rows of barbed wire. Nate stood at his post and I stood at mine, and I couldn't close the distance by taking a few steps and putting my arms around him. Something was wrong with me, I realized. We just stood there, and I let the moment pass.

He had confessed to stealing cookies. It was my turn.

"I stole something," I said. "Worse than cookies."

He waited.

"From Bobby Bianchi."

"You mean the disk? I wouldn't worry. You copied Bobby's DVD to a blank disk that cost pennies. That was borrowing. I doubt you're in trouble with God just yet."

"I stole something else too." I went to the car for my suitcase and returned with the brown paper bag. Nate frowned when he felt its weight.

"Careful," I said.

He looked in the bag but didn't remove the gun. Instead, he set the bag on the ground, away from us, then opened his arms. This time I didn't hesitate. In three steps, I buried my face in his chest. He smelled of sweat and shoe polish. He smelled powdery and old, and I didn't want him to die. Ever. I cried so hard my shoulders shook. "I'm scared," I finally managed, too frightened to add, *of everything.* "I'm so scared."

He held me.

"You were right to take the gun."

"But I'm *scared*, Nate."

He pulled me closer. "Dear heart," he said. "So am I."

— • —

As Nate rummaged through the car to find the present he'd brought from Boston, I watched a woman through an upholstery shop window working a thin layer of padding around the leg of an old sofa. She must have been good at her job if the matching wingback chairs in the bay windows of her store were any sign. To the right of the main door was a cat-clawed wreck with half of its stuffing ripped out. Opposite sat a restored beauty: a matching chair but in perfect shape, plumped with filling and looking brand new. Gustavo Carle & Sons Upholstery spanned three storefronts, each with its own set of bay windows through which I saw men working band saws, maneuvering supports into broken frames, and packing fill into seat cushions. Nate walked up behind me. "When I turn seventy," he said, "which is not that long from now, I'm coming back up here for a complete rebuild. New bones, new padding. The works. You sure you want to wait out here?"

I waved him ahead.

When she saw Nate, Mrs. Carle dropped her tools and rushed across the room, dodging bolts of cloth and shimmying sideways between pieces of furniture. I could hear her shouting through an open window: "Gustavo! He's here!" She threw her arms wide and they hugged and laughed. They brushed cheeks, then hugged some more, nearly doing a dance they looked so happy. A tall, thin man with strong arms followed and there came more hugs and laughter. At that point, Mrs. Carle turned toward the street and motioned in my direction. She wasn't waiting for me to decide if I was joining them. She flung the door wide and called, "You are Nora's granddaughter? You come right here, young lady, for a proper greeting!"

Who can resist such people? She reminded me of Sveta, who made me feel that just by being alive I had improved her day. She even looked a little like Sveta, but much older. Heavier, too, and wrinkled around the eyes from a lifetime of laughing. Mrs. Carle had the calluses of someone who worked with her hands for a living. Whether I was ready or not, she buried me in a heavy-bosomed embrace, holding me so close I could smell and even taste the dust from the shop. She rocked me back and forth, and said: "I knew your grandmother. We came over the same year. What a beauty she was! What a fine woman! You look *just* like her." She held me at arm's length. "Grace, Grace, *Grace*! How happy I am to meet you!" She picked me up and set me down and gave me no chance to doubt Nate's story. If she was real and she was one of the Rachels, then Nate was who he said he was and so was Dima.

Nate had managed to find a large jar of Ukrainian borscht in a specialty shop in Boston and presented it with great seriousness. Mrs. Carle was impressed. They lived in an apartment around the corner from the shop, and we joined them for lunch—featuring Nate's borscht. They all got a good laugh when I made a face and pushed away my bowl after one spoonful.

"Shame on you, Nataniel, for allowing a Ukrainian child to hate borscht!"

He answered her in Russian.

When I asked, Mrs. Carle said, "Not for young ears!"

She ordered my grandfather and Gustavo to clean the dishes as she walked me around the corner to a park, which had a playground for kids and a playground of sorts for adults: several exercise stations along with an adult-sized swing set.

"My favorite," she said. She walked directly to the swings and pointed me to the one beside it.

She was younger than Nate, perhaps by ten years, and while we were on the swings she looked younger still. In the shop she had wound her hair into a tight bun, which she'd kept all through lunch. In the park, she unpinned her hair and let it fly as we pumped the swings up and back. For a long time we made no noise save for the zooming sounds all kids make at the swings, except she wasn't a kid, and I wondered how some adults were able to keep a piece of themselves young forever. Sveta was like that: quick to laugh, and quick to call you her friend.

At long last, winded and breathing hard from so much laughter and zooming, we let gravity slow us down. "I should never close my eyes when I do this," she said. "I'm dizzy! But I can't help it. The world's spinning, sweetie. And you know what? Sometimes, it makes more sense that way!"

I never met anyone who seemed so much herself when she laughed. Finally she sat me down at one of the picnic tables. "Ask anything at all. Your grandfather's not here. I'll tell you the truth, whatever you want to know. You must have questions. It's not an easy or usual thing Dima did. And Nataniel? He never takes credit. But he helped in a big way, and he changed my life. So ask."

I asked how she got to America.

She held my hands. "Stop me when you need to. I'm going to speak as I lived it, not very pretty sometimes. Dima and your grandfather saved me from living on the streets of Kiev, and they gave me all this." She motioned to the park, but she meant much, much more.

"Can you imagine? I'm an American now—amazing for a girl so close to ruining her life! Dima found me on the same trip to Ukraine he found your grandmother. She was living in an orphanage near Donetsk, just as the authorities were set to turn her out onto the streets because she was sixteen. They taught her no skills, though she was superb with languages and math."

"My grandmother was a Rachel?"

"Just like me. Yes."

"After I'd got into some trouble in Kiev, my parents kicked me out of the house. I was eighteen years old. There were drugs involved, nothing I'm proud of. I'm lucky to have survived. When Dima asked if I wanted to come to America for a chance to start over, I figured he wanted me to become his whore. I started swearing at him and he shushed me and bought me a hot meal and explained it all very clearly. He told me about Rachel and the war, and he admitted it all probably sounded crazy but that this was how he had decided to live his life, by helping girls like me. 'Think of it as a church mission to America, except there's no church and it's not legal,' he said. He was a little crazy, I think. But then so's anyone with a big heart in a world as ugly as ours. He arranged for false travel papers, he gave me a job in his store in Boston for a few months, and then when I was ready he helped me find work.

"Finding me work was Nataniel's job. He was very thorough. He took pictures of me, he asked questions, he filled out sheets and sheets of paper. He made a file—who I was, how hard a worker I'd be, my skills. I could always work like an ox! Everything about me he put into his file. Then he drove all over New England, looking for someone who needed good, strong help and who wouldn't ask too many questions about my papers. Each girl had a file. For several years, this was Nataniel's job. Eventually he found Gustavo's father, who started our shop almost fifty years ago. He'd come from Spain, penniless. He understood what it meant to give a newcomer a chance. The old man agreed, and I started working here when

I was nineteen. I met Gustavo, Junior—Little Gus—and we fell in love. Same story for your grandmother, except Nataniel never tried to find her a job outside of Boston because he didn't want her to go far. How he loved her!"

"Nate married a Rachel," I said, trying to grasp it.

Mrs. Carle—she asked me to call her Oksana—smiled. "She was a remarkable woman, your grandmother. Then the cancer took her. She was strong. She even died with strength. People don't often do that, you know. They howl and they curse God. She was smiling as she passed, grateful for the time she had. I will always count Dima and Nate among the righteous. The real Rachel must have been an extraordinary woman for Dima to have done all this in her name. He gave his life to her, even though she had died many years before."

Nate had married a Rachel and was the son of Rachel, the first one. I told her about Sveta and showed her my scarf. Oksana agreed it was very handsome.

"Yes, I knew Dima kept up the work even after they sent Nataniel to jail. Your Sveta sounds just like the sort of young woman he would find. But all this is behind us now. I understand Dima's not well and Nataniel's got into a new business. Magic! We're coming to your show on Saturday. What good fun! Your grandfather will give us front-row seats!"

Unless she was a world-class liar, Oksana Carle had filled in a picture that was now complete, or nearly so. That evening, at our motel—another forty-nine dollar per night special on a truck route outside Concord—I sat Nate down by my computer and made him watch as I deleted every file connected to *Chopped!* Then broke all my DVD backups, just as Sveta had done with her movie. "*Chopped!* is gone," I said. "I was wrong about Uncle Dima. I'm sorry. No more chopping off his head."

As we played checkers that evening, I told him I'd stopped by the front desk to ask if they'd received any large envelopes from Lola. "You gave her the address of all the places we're staying, right?" He had, but I needed to double and triple check. "The DNA report should have been done and sent already. What's holding it up?"

"Relax," he said. "It'll come when it does."

"And if it doesn't?"

"Then I'll call."

"Don't you care if I'm related to Houdini? If I am, you are."

He looked at me. "You should pay more attention to the board. I'm about to triple jump you, and I've got my eye on that diner down the road. I hope you like meatloaf."

Twenty-Five: Nate Larson

So a kid walks out the front door of her home and finds every fire hydrant, street sign, and mailbox hovering three feet off the ground. She shakes her head to make sure she's not hallucinating, then runs inside and yells, "Mom, come here! You gotta see something!" Out they go only to find the hydrants, signs, and mailboxes all planted in the ground as they usually are. The mother says, "Why are we here?" The kid says, "*Huh?* I swear I just saw—" And the moment is gone. That's what happened at my shows. I led audiences over a series of cliffs, and after the biggest one, when their jaws dropped and they did double and triple takes, they found the world as it usually is, with everything in order. Or perhaps not, if they trusted what they'd just seen.

I was happy for our success. The show in Concord went so well that the manager booked another performance for Sunday evening in addition to a matinee—minus *The Kortelisy Escape*, to spare traumatizing children. A sister theater in Lebanon, New Hampshire, did the same. More work meant more money, and more money meant Grace and I could eat steak once in a while instead of fried chicken specials at roadside diners. Motels got upgraded to hotels and inns. We were, as they say, on a roll.

Bobby Bianchi kept his word and attended several perfor-
mances to keep tabs on me. After the Saturday show in Lebanon, he let himself into the backstage dressing room, without
knocking, and started in on the shame of it all.

"What shame?" I asked.

"The crying shame that you can't be performing magic
shows once you run. I've come to what, four shows now? Each
one's been great, and I've seen all your tricks. They *still* get
me each time. You're good, Nate. But you'll never be famous
because you can't perform in public. Not after you go to
Canada, because you'll be gone, bud. Disappeared, vanished,
like one of your cards. Too bad. You'll have to give up magic,
at least performing."

Grace had changed into a T-shirt and was pressing the
grip-end of a screwdriver into her leotard, trying to flatten a
piece of metal on a zipper. She opened a little kit for a needle
and thread.

"Unbelievable," said Bianchi, "to find a kid these days who
sews. You know what I got? A sixteen-year-old who hides vodka
empties and skimpy underwear. Ella's mother was cleaning
her room and found a dress that'd be tight on a pencil. And a
bathing suit, one of those string things, with three triangles
no bigger than this."

He made a fist and held it up.

"Grace, do me a favor. Spend some time with her when you
get home. You'd be a good influence. Teach her to sew."

"Sure, Mr. Bianchi. I like Ella."

"Everybody likes her, especially the boys. You know what
I like? Your Kort-a-hooly Escape! It just kills me, the way you
sneak out there."

Grace looked my way.

"Bobby, you know magicians don't—"

"Give me a little credit, bud! She sneaks up, gets the plastic
wrap off somehow, and then unbuckles you. Maxim says he

saw it in Cambridge. In Portsmouth, I sat off to the side and could just manage to see her. But no one who wasn't looking could have seen. Just tell me if I'm warm. Am I warm?"

"You're warm."

"I knew it!"

I opened the door to show him out. "I don't know about Ella and Grace. After I cross into Canada and head to the Caribbean, DCF will send Grace back to the dorm. They'll bus her over to school every day, so there won't be much time for visiting during the week. And it won't be too long before she joins me."

"You got a point," he said. "Too bad, because Ella could use a friend. But Grace could still sleep over on weekends . . . for a little while, which would be good because weekends are the worst: parties, sleepovers, boys sneaking around, booze, and weed. Ella needs a big sister, except Grace is younger. Go figure. My kid has all the advantages, and here's Grace living at the bottom of the DCF barrel. Look who turned into a screwup."

He stepped into the hallway. "I like being on the same team again, Nate. We're not pulling against each other. We always got along, right?"

"You bet, Bobby."

"And Dima and me? I feel like I'm a Lazarenko, an honorary Larson. I'm doing my best with Maxim. He can be . . . difficult."

When we embraced, Bobby said he wouldn't be making the Lake Willoughby show. He needed to be in Maine for some promising leads. "Lumberjacks," he said. "They got big appetites. But I'll be back for the grand finale. Maxim, too. Count on it."

I was.

— • —

I WAITED until Grace went to her room before I called Eleanor Hunt's assistant. I told him I needed to speak with his boss that night about the Dima Larson trial. It was ten thirty on a Saturday. I heard music and people laughing. Thirty minutes later, Hunt herself was on the phone.

"I hope this is good, Mr. Larson."

"It could be. Have you had any contact with my brother recently?"

"After the arraignment? No. I expect my staff has corresponded with his attorney. The usual."

"He's no longer fit to stand trial. Get him evaluated."

"Good-bye, Mr. Larson."

"He has dementia."

"I don't care if he has hemorrhoids."

"And if I said I'll give you your prostitution ring?"

A pause on the line.

"What's that?"

I had made up my mind to trust her. I needed help, and there was no one else.

"Have a doctor check Dima. He's too far gone to defend himself. Do it, kill the trial, and I'll give you the prostitution ring that a man named Maxim Petrov runs out of the store." I explained it all: the Rachel Project and the trips to Eastern Europe, Petrov's hijacking of Dima's pipeline, Bianchi's involvement. "They're funneling girls through the grocery."

"So was your brother, as I'm hearing you."

"Not for the same reason. Ever."

Another pause, then this: "We'll get to your brother and this so-called Rachel Project. You just gave me a name, Maxim Petrov. Any connection to the Petrovs out of New York? Brighton Beach, I believe."

"You know him?"

"Exactly what are you proposing, Mr. Larson?"

Either I would jump off the high dive or not, and there'd be no changing my mind after the first step. "I'm preparing to play a game of chicken," I said.

"Chicken."

"My brother has nothing to do with sex trafficking. I don't expect you to give him a pass because he *did* break laws. But he had good reasons. Drop the tax charge—or postpone the trial, at least. He doesn't have long. Do that and I'll give you Petrov three different ways. I want this guy to go away forever."

"And I wish Christmas came every second Monday. We can't just drive up there and arrest someone because he's a bad guy. We need an actionable offense, Mr. Larson, proof of a crime. Short of your bundling evidence and handing me a folder all nice and neat, you've got nothing. Building a case will take months— unless he does something drastic like trying to kill someone. Or if, as a known felon, he's in serious violation of the law. That I can work with."

"Then you can work with me—on both counts."

"Meaning what? Do you have advance knowledge of an attempted murder?"

"I do."

"Whose?"

"Mine."

Twenty-Six: Grace Larson

Nate thought I'd be pleased to give up moldy motels for hotels and little inns. I was, but I also worried that Lola wouldn't know where to send the envelope from the DNA lab once it arrived. Nate had booked all our rooms in advance and had given her a list of addresses. I made him call and stood six inches away from the telephone, listening as he read off the names and addresses of the new places we'd be staying. Then I got on the phone and asked Lola to repeat it all back to me.

"Stop worrying," she said. "The moment your letter arrives, I'll send it."

"You're sure? I mean, you're positive you will. Right?"

"Grace, even if you aren't related to Houdini—"

"But I *am*. I'll be on the lookout. Thanks."

The next morning, Nate knocked on my door and said he wanted to show me a "curiosity." He asked me to bring my camera into his room, which was nearly as dark as a movie theater because he'd drawn the shades and turned off the lights. When he shut the door behind us, he said, "Show me a picture. Make the screen on your camera glow."

I turned it on and the display showed the last photo I'd taken, outside a diner the day before. In the plate-glass window I saw my reflection, bright but kind of gauzy with pickups behind me and the state road behind that. Sometimes I took pictures for my games and sometimes just because I liked what I saw.

When I handed Nate the camera, things got strange quickly. He unrolled a pair of black socks and slipped one over his right hand and one over his left, pulling them halfway up his arm. He removed his suit jacket—black, the only one he owned—and put it on again, backward, so that his shirt didn't show. Then he set me just outside the coat closet while he stepped *inside* with my camera.

"Nate?"

His instructions were very clear: "Turn away. When I tell you, turn back to the closet."

He counted down from five. At zero, I turned and saw the photo of myself in the parking lot floating in total blackness. Nate's hand, arm, and chest had *disappeared*. They were there, they had to be, but I couldn't see them.

He started speaking in his stagey voice. "I summon the spirit of Grace Larson. Grace, if you can hear me, rise. Rise!"

The image of me drifted . . . up.

"Grace, if you can hear me, stand on your head!"

Slowly the image turned upside down.

He switched on the closet light, and there he stood in his weird, backward suit jacket with socks for gloves, holding my camera.

"What do you think?"

I didn't have the words.

"Black Art Magic. Simplicity itself. It's easy and it works."

The illusion, he explained, is based on a human weakness. Our eyes can't see bright objects and dark objects in the same dark space. They see only the bright ones. But creatures that hunted by night—owls, for instance—can see everything because that's how they evolved. The bright light on the camera display had dazzled my eyes, leaving Nate's hand—covered in black—invisible. It was there, but my brain couldn't process it. He turned off the light again, standing not two feet away. I tried but couldn't see him. More astonishing, when I took a turn and put on his jacket and the sock, I couldn't see *my own* hand.

"This is how we're going to get Petrov," he announced.

He wanted to build something called a Black Art Studio, creating this same effect onstage by using a curtain made of black velvet strips. If I wore my ninja outfit, no one would see my hands or arms poking through the curtain. He claimed the illusion would work even better onstage because he'd be able to control the lighting. With the right setup, he assured me the possibilities were endless. I could hide a canary in my hands, stick my hands through the curtain, and *Presto!* The audience would see a bird appear from nowhere and nothing. He would tell a story, and I would make objects appear and disappear at his command.

"We're going hunting," he said.

"For what?"

"The correct question would be *who*. We've got three weeks to build this thing and practice before the show in Canaan. We're going to trick Maxim Petrov or Bobby or both into doing something stupid. They'll get caught. Eleanor Hunt is sending federal marshals." Nate opened the curtains with his suit jacket still on, backward. He looked like a demented surgeon.

"We've got strong magic in the Black Art Studio," he said. "Now we need to decide what objects to float and what story to tell that will get Bianchi and Petrov *very* angry at me. The angrier, the better."

I wondered if he'd slept at all that night. He looked awful. I still had my Velveeta and tub of margarine, and I considered making him another sandwich.

"Why do you want them angry, Nate?"

"Petrov needs to hurt me—at least try. The moment he makes a move, Eleanor Hunt's marshals will arrest him."

No one was going to prison for throwing a punch. Nate must have meant more than that. Bobby had a gun in his shower, and I was betting he and Petrov had others. Did Nate want them to *shoot* him? He wouldn't answer when I asked.

I told him he was crazy.

"I'm not. He needs to at least think about shooting me. It's the only way I can think to save Dima and stay with you. When I accepted Eleanor Hunt's deal to leave jail, I lied. I was going to run for my brother's sake. But if I did that, I couldn't be with you."

I wasn't sure I heard him right.

"You were planning to run away? Leave me?"

"Before the trial. My plan was to spend a few months together. We'd get to know each other, have some fun. Then I'd go."

I flew at him, hitting his face and chest. "You took me knowing you'd give me back? You *planned* it? I was right all along—you're just renting me for your own enjoyment, like the others. *You!*" I couldn't stand it anymore. Was *every* adult in my life going to betray me?

"I didn't know you yet, Grace. Now that I do—"

I slapped him across the face as hard as I could. His eyes watered, and a welt bloomed on his cheek. I slapped him again, and he didn't raise a hand to block me. I believe he would have sat there and let me hit him until he fainted. "I *hate* this!" I screamed.

He stared at the carpet. "I was afraid of you," he mumbled.

"What did you say?"

"You scared me."

I stepped away.

"*I* scared *you*?"

He peeled the socks from his arms, then removed his jacket and looked at me. Finally. "I was afraid . . . after your mother and Nora died. I thought if I ran, it *couldn't* happen again."

"What couldn't?"

"I can't."

"You can't *what*?"

He mumbled something.

"*What*?!"

"Grace . . . I didn't want to care. I didn't want to love again and hurt. But I ended up loving my granddaughter . . . and now I have a big problem because Petrov thinks he can make me run whether I want to or not. And I won't. Which means I have to get him before he gets me. He's coming to the show in Canaan to walk me across the border. Or worse. Just before I go onstage that night, I'll tell him I changed my mind—that I'm staying because I couldn't imagine leaving you. Which is true, Grace. He'll want to kill me. There's no other way to say it. If the marshals stop him, they'll have him on assault with intent to murder. It's a chance I'm willing to take. At this point, it's the only chance I *can* take if I want to be with both you and Dima."

"You could die."

"That's true. A car could also hit me tomorrow."

"Let's run. Both of us."

"An old guy and a teenager doing magic tricks in Canada? Why don't we just hang a neon sign over our heads? Eleanor Hunt's people would catch us in a week. And if Petrov found us, it would be worse. I've thought it through, and we've got to get Maxim out of our lives. He'll come for me, but I'll control how and when—which is what I do all the time onstage."

"I know what he does," I said.

It took all my courage to tell him how I knew. I'd never told anyone everything that happened at Mr. Parker's because I'd never found anyone I could trust to hold it. I thought of Sveta, who had smiled so brightly and who looked so unhappy standing beside Petrov at The Mystery Lounge. And here was Nate, an adult who was *finally* being honest even if he'd said things I didn't want to hear. The world was bent. Whether we were ready or not, the show in Canaan was coming and with it Petrov and Bianchi. What happened to Nate would now happen to us both. That meant I could trust him to hold my secrets. Since Mr. Parker's, I'd been exploding inside every single day. I had to tell someone.

I told Nate.

We were standing apart as I spoke. He said nothing. When I was done, he looked as if I'd stuck little knives all over his body. He looked like I felt many nights at three in the morning, alone, screaming inside. He opened his arms. But I didn't want to be touched.

"Maxim Petrov is Sveta's pimp."

"That's right."

"He wanted me to come work at the store. I said *no*."

"That was the right answer."

"And Sveta . . . she wanted me to learn from you how to disappear so that I could teach her. She doesn't want to be with him, Nate. I'm fourteen in my body, but I'm a lot older in my head. I see things."

He couldn't speak for a moment, then sunk his head into his hands.

"Dima really found her in Ukraine?"

"Sveta? He did."

"There really was a Rachel?"

"There was. My mother."

"You're not lying? It's not a story?"

"I'm not lying."

"And Mrs. Carle is for real. She's not just some friend of yours?"

"She's a friend, but she was a Rachel too."

"You said you need the right story to catch Petrov?"

"For the Black Art Studio? I do. We do."

"And you're positive they'll be at the show? Both of them?"

"They'll be there. Yes."

"Then I have a story, Nate. A good one, but it's also terrible because something very bad could happen. I'll work it out, then I'll tell you." I went to the bathroom and ran cold water over a washcloth. I wrung it out and folded it, then returned to my grandfather. I pressed it to his cheek, where I'd hit him.

"One more thing," I said.

"What's that?"

"Is it really possible to love someone too much?"

— • —

WE WERE staying at an inn by Lake Bomoseen, west of Rutland, Vermont, where we'd be performing at a Knights of Columbus Hall. We spent most of our time practicing. Nate reserved three hours for tricks connected to Rachel's Story and another hour for the escape. Beyond that, we devoted our time to the Black Art Studio and the trick we were preparing for Bianchi and Petrov. We had no time to order a premade studio, so we made our own. In Lebanon, we stopped at a fabric store and bought every bolt of black velvet in the place. Then we headed over to a plumbing supply house for the pipe Nate used to screw together a portable, stand-alone frame for his curtain.

Our studio was six feet tall and eight feet wide with broad sturdy legs and feet that made it very stable. We wrapped the steel tubes in black velvet and then cut up the remaining bolts of velvet into overlapping strips that hung from a rod at the top of the frame. The project took about six hours in all, and from the moment we set it up we knew that with the right lighting the studio would work at least as well onstage as it did in the hotel room. We closed the room curtains, angled a desk lamp before the Black Art curtain just so, and found it nearly impossible to see my ninja-gloved hand reaching through the strips, holding my camera. The effect was brilliant. We high fived and low fived. Our trick would be the cherry on Nate's Tabernacle Tour, a real triumph.

We weren't going to float a little digital camera onstage. The image was too small for the audience to see, and Nate had begun pressing me for details. What props would we use? What story would he tell?

I'd been working it out and, finally, I was ready. "Promise you won't be mad," I said.

He would not promise.

"Well, just keep an open mind."

I went to my room and returned with my backpack. Inside the pack was a pillowcase. And inside the pillowcase was a rolling pin and the other things I'd stolen from my foster homes. I emptied the contents on the bed.

Nate didn't speak for a few moments.

"Is that Mrs. Alcott's?"

"How did you know?"

"She came to the house looking for it. She told me it meant a lot to her."

Beside the rolling pin I laid lipstick, a belt, a family Bible, a TV remote, a fancy pen, a pair of glasses . . . and Nate's

Matryoshka dolls. He stared at my little collection, which could not possibly mean anything to anyone but me.

"The dolls were yours anyway," he said. "Sooner or later."

"I wanted to hurt you."

"Congratulations. You did."

"I'm sorry."

"Sorry doesn't help. May I?"

He reached for the dolls and unpacked them, setting them in a row on a table, largest to smallest, Mama and her children—a large family. He began to dance his Matryoshkas. I'd always found it strange to see an old man playing with dollies, singing songs in Russian. At this particular moment, it didn't seem so strange. He was happy.

"So the Matryoshkas took a little trip with you," he said, interrupting himself. "That's okay, as long as you took them out every now and then and danced them around. As long as you kept them company. Did you?"

"I kinda did. . . . Nate, I want to use them in the show. You're going to tell the audience all about them."

"It'll get Petrov and Bianchi mad?"

"I'm aiming at Bianchi. He'll aim at Petrov."

I explained my plan, and when I finished he said it was a wicked idea but a very good one. We set to practicing at once. We were hours at it, and when it was time for a break, he stretched and told me we were bound to have a full house in Canaan. "Even Miss Roberts will be there," he said. "When I called the other day to check in, she reminded me she'd be coming. Remember? She wants to see what life on the road is like for a teenager. To see if it's *appropriate*. Her word." He began packing away the Matryoshkas.

What would I tell Miss Roberts when she asked what life was like with Nate? Strange as it was driving from one hotel to the next, the road had become the best home I ever had because I was with Nate and it was an adventure, even the dangerous parts. He laid the Matryoshkas in his suitcase, then thought better of it.

"They're yours," he said, setting the dolls by the rolling pin. "But do me a favor and keep them with your magic coins, not with this stuff. The Matryoshkas are no longer stolen. I'm giving them to you. Officially."

"Nate, you don't have to . . ."

"Try saying, *Thank you.*"

My grandfather was about to be doubly tested: tested once by Petrov and Bianchi, who expected him to run to Canada and maybe to the Caribbean without me; tested twice in his eagerness to convince Jacqueline Roberts he should continue as my foster parent. Either of these efforts would have taxed a fit man to his limit. But Nate was not fit, and the stakes were high. Lose to Petrov and Bianchi, and he might get shot through the head. Lose to Miss Roberts and he'd get shot through the heart.

Twenty-Seven: Nate Larson

After checking into our hotel in Montpelier, I was drifting off for a nap when I was startled by three sharp knocks at the door. My pulse rocketed. Ever since getting trapped in the root cellar with the German soldier, I'd been nervous about entering and especially sleeping in places with only one exit. Prison was a daily nightmare on that account. Once outside, though, I seriously considered traveling with a hundred-foot rope in the event I needed to make a hasty exit out a motel window. But it was too late now. Through the peep hole I saw two men wearing dark blue suits.

"Grace is fine," I said, opening the door. "If this is another inspection, you're supposed to give me at least a thirty-minute warning."

But something was off. They each wore an earpiece connected to a plastic coil that disappeared at their shirt collars.

"United States marshals," one of them said, flashing a badge.

The one with a high, tight crew cut stepped forward. "Gerald Emmers, sir. The Assistant US Attorney for Massachusetts Ezra Richards is in the restaurant on the lobby level and would like a word. Can you be ready in, say, ten minutes? We'll wait here. It's not a problem."

"What's this about? I thought the state sent out folks to check on her. You're federal. What's going on?"

"Ten minutes, sir."

Grace opened her door.

"Nate?"

"It's nothing. I've just got to go with these men for a bit."

"Can I come?"

"Sorry. It's for a chat with someone who works for Eleanor Hunt."

"What if you don't come back?"

I looked at them. "Am I coming back?"

"Yes, sir. It's just a conversation, sir."

If that was so, they only needed to call and ask and I would have met with Hunt or anyone else, no problem. I didn't need two agents walking me to the elevator as if I were headed to the electric chair. Grace looked stricken. She waved as the door closed. When we reached the lobby, the agents walked me around a corner to a small restaurant with a brick oven and a chalkboard listing the various pizzas I could order. The assistant US attorney rose to greet me.

"Montpelier isn't exactly your neighborhood," I said.

"It's close enough to make a day trip, Mr. Larson. Eleanor Hunt asked me to visit."

"How'd you know where to find me?"

Silly question.

"The situation's changed," he said. "We could have faxed this news to the Marshal's Service in Vermont, and they could have handled things. But Miss Hunt asked that I come. Her schedule doesn't permit—"

"It's Dima. Is he ill?"

"Your brother's fine, that I know. Would you like some coffee?"

"Get on with it."

He had prepared a folder, which he set on the checkerboard tablecloth before me. Midafternoon, there were only a few other diners, none seated nearby. "I warn you," he said. "These photos don't leave anything to the imagination. But everyone needs to understand what we're dealing with."

On opening the folder, I needed a moment to register what I was seeing. The angles were off, the legs and arms bent in ways they shouldn't have been.

I closed the folder.

"There are ten more, Mr. Larson. Take your time."

There was no need.

"She was nineteen. We have nearly certain knowledge that Sveta Zelenko was being run as a prostitute from The Green Grocer, your brother's store. She went on a client call this past weekend, and someone slammed a brick into her head. Joggers found the body along the Charles River on Sunday. The theory is she was murdered elsewhere and then dumped. You can see from what she was wearing—black dress, heels—that she had worked that night. We're running a semen analysis to see if we can identify her last customer. It's complicated. Early indications are she had seven clients in two days. It's a mess."

I began to tremble.

"Do you have anything to say?"

"Arrest him and bury him."

"Who?"

"Maxim Petrov."

"She was an earner. The Russians tend to beat or cut their golden gooses—that is, unless they run. Then they might have killed her on general principle. But our thinking is that this was a client. In fact, Petrov might even go after the client himself—if he can figure out who did it—to extort him for what she would have earned. He wouldn't care that she's dead if he could still collect on her future income."

"Petrov's the one who forced her into the business. He's the one you want."

"No doubt. We checked on your brother and had him evaluated. You're right, though we're not dropping the charges just yet. The trial's still on."

"He had *nothing* to do with pimping Sveta."

"We believe you, Mr. Larson."

He called a waiter and ordered coffee.

I felt sick. Sveta's eye, the one that wasn't crushed into the bloody devastation of her face, was open and staring at nothing at all. Seven clients in two days?

"We'll be sending two marshals to your show, in Canaan. That is, if you're still willing to work with us. Petrov's dangerous."

I should have taken Sveta to a bus station myself.

"Zelenko wasn't her real name, by the way. Which is too bad because now there's no one in Ukraine we can call. After the autopsy, the commonwealth will pay a funeral home to bury her remains. She'll get a marker, at least."

She was five years older than my granddaughter.

How would I tell her?

"We'll be tracking his movements. We'll know where he and Bianchi are, relative to you, minute by minute."

"It doesn't take very long to fire a bullet."

"They won't try to kill you in the church. Too many potential witnesses. Either before or after the show, they'll try putting you in their car. Don't let that happen. If they're armed and they've threatened you, that's enough for us. Understood?"

The coffee arrived.

"I've brought a Kevlar vest. When the time comes, I suggest you wear it."

— • —

THAT NIGHT, for once, I woke with a different dream. It was autumn, and Dima and I were picking apples. We had come to Vermont by way of Canada. What a talented young man, my brother! He fixed tools, even tractors, proving himself so valuable that the farmers we stayed with to earn our way to Boston offered permanent jobs. Why waste such skills in the city, they asked. But Boston was our goal because Dima had circled it on a map one day, having read how America fought for freedom there. "Boston will be our beginning too," he announced. "Pay close attention, Little Brother." He reached for the pouch he wore beneath his shirt, on a string around his neck. Waving our papers, he said, "We are in America, Nataniel. We made it! We'll be citizens soon. You need to know something very important about this country. Americans don't cry. What they do is stand and work. You will not see me cry ever, not once after tonight."

Even in my dreams I wondered why a man would cripple himself so. Without tears for Nora and Gabby and the mistakes I made, I would have long since died. Tears had saved me. A man who remakes himself begins with tears.

I woke, staring at the hotel ceiling. The ice machine in the hallway alcove was banging out some kind of Latin beat. Light from a street lamp leaked into the room at the curtain edges, and I said to myself, *Go to him*. I drifted off again and back I went to the night Dima sat me on a hay bale and spoke those awful words. I stared at the ceiling until it began to heave, until I saw rafters and heard cows lowing. Mice scampered and barn cats prowled as Dima reached through the darkness, through decades, his voice ripped and raw: "After tonight, I will never cry. Hold me, Nataniel. Tonight I will cry and be done!"

A boy who understood little of the world opened his arms to his brother that night. A half-century later, prepared to give him so much more, I reached through thin air to that magnificent, suffering soul but he was fading beyond my grasp, a ghost. I couldn't reach him.

Dima? Are you there?

Hold me came the voice. *Hold me for what we lost. Weep for Kortelisy, Nataniel. Weep for Papa and Mama. Weep for the men I killed in war. Weep for Rachel.* My brother sent up a wail that shook the moon as he sobbed and swore an oath that as he lived, as this was America, the land of new beginnings where people *do*, they don't cry; as he lived he swore our agonies were behind us. "We loved our family, Little Brother, didn't we? But they're gone, so cry with me and be done with tears."

This was Dima, the man who now shuffled across linoleum floors staring at his shoelaces. If I died in Canaan, who would stand as witness to his life, to all the good he'd done? Nursing home attendants would wipe his bottom and curse his human smell, they'd weigh him in a hoist like a sack of bones. I had to survive the coming fight with Petrov so that I could walk my brother down the long road and kiss him goodbye. Blood or no blood, tears or no tears, I owed him that. I owed him everything.

THERE WAS AN OLD LADY

Twenty-Eight: Nate Larson

Thank you, Montpelier! Dozens waited in line for my autograph on Saturday night after a solid performance. Promising they'd bring their kids the next afternoon if I were booked, folks pressed the manager into scheduling a Sunday matinee. He even upped my guarantee. By this point, Grace and I had begun earning real money. Not get-rich money, but money enough to give up counting nickels. We were professionals. That evening, we drove north to Lake Willoughby, Vermont, devoting all ninety minutes to practicing my patter for our new Black Art trick, which Grace had invented. She called it *There Was an Old Lady*.

My granddaughter was a tough coach. As I rehearsed my patter, she corrected my word choices, emphasis, and timing—every bit as hard on me as I'd been on her as she learned *The Vanished Card*. The drive to Lake Willoughby flew by as we practiced, and when I pulled into the parking lot of the Willoughby Inn, we sat in the car twenty more minutes until she was satisfied I'd learned my part. When we finally made it to the registration desk, the innkeeper had a UPS delivery waiting for me—return address, Arlington, Massachusetts. Grace lit up. She reached for the package but then hesitated, realizing, I supposed, that she might not receive the news she wanted. I had my own reasons to be nervous.

I opened the box and handed her a tin with an index card taped to the top, which read F O R G R A C E. "We both know what's in there," I said. "Save me a snickerdoodle and give me a minute alone, would you?"

The innkeeper had someone take our bags to our rooms, and I headed to the library with a letter in my hand—return address, Schenectady, New York. I had gone to a fair amount of trouble calling on an old cellmate and friend, Bela Kunz, to set up a website and create a fake Houdini Society. He was a scammer from way back, a very dependable fellow. After I explained the need for a sample of Grace's DNA, Lola and Frank pitched in, too, talking up what a good idea it was for Grace to apply for the Houdini scholarship and even fronting the money for the test. I had paid them a few hundred dollars earlier in the day for the analysis, suspecting Grace wouldn't take my money.

Now the news.

As I opened the letter from the lab, I felt more than heard her creeping up behind me to learn if the blood of The Great One flowed in her veins. I scanned the letter until I found the sentences that mattered:

> We ran three separate analyses of the DNA sample submitted under your name in June of this year. We can say with 99.9% certainty that the DNA donor does not carry a BRCA1 or BRCA2 gene mutation.

"Nate?"

She was at my shoulder.

"I don't see anything about Houdini. What does the letter mean?" She rounded the chair and stood before me as

I blinked away tears. What did it mean? I nearly uttered a prayer in thanks before realizing it was dumb luck, not God's benevolent hand, that had spared my granddaughter. For if I thanked God for *that*, was I to blame God for taking Nora and Gabrielle? What did the letter mean? It meant that it would take something other than metastatic ovarian cancer to kill this child. It meant that if she had children of her own, she might, unlike her mother, live to see them grow. It meant she had a chance like the rest of us: to make or unmake our lives while we're here, to love or not, to do good, to fail, to *live*.

I set the letter aside.

"What about Houdini, Nate?"

"Houdini . . . It says nothing here about Houdini. I'm sorry."

"Are you sure?"

"I am. We knew this was possible."

"I really thought . . . I mean, I can *feel* him in my bones. I'm so good at wriggling out of things."

I assured her she could still be a great escape artist and magician and that the news was likely for the best because no one needed people making comparisons with Houdini at the beginning of a career. "You'll just have to build your own greatness," I said. "Like everyone else."

I was not surprised when she put my advice to work straight off. Seated in the library with us was a man in a wing-back chair, reading a copy of the *Vermont Guardian*. Grace fortified herself with a last bite of cookie and approached him, leading with Lola's tin of snickerdoodles and chocolate chips. He took one, and she produced a deck.

"While you're eating, could I tell you about my family?"

She was skinny as a pole, all arms and legs, clear-eyed and impossible to resist. And she was going to live. The man set aside his paper. I watched from across the room.

"Sure, you can tell me. Can I have another cookie first?"

She placed the tin on the table beside him and fanned her deck. "There are ten of us in my family," she began, "eight brothers and sisters, plus a mom and pop. You wouldn't believe the craziness at dinner time. And imagine getting ready for bed! We have one sink, one bathroom. It's *crowded* at home! Here, pick a card."

He touched one, then its neighbor, and finally pulled a third.

"The ten of hearts!"

Grace snapped the fan shut to control the deck for the next presentation, just as I'd taught her. "Isn't that a coincidence?" she said. "There are ten of us in my family, and you picked a ten. Nice work! My oldest brother is named John, though we call him Jack." She fanned the cards again, and the man chose the jack of spades. "Hey!" she said. "You're very good. Let's keep going." She snapped the fan shut a third time, then offered it again. "My brother Billy is an ace of a carpenter. Come on and pick a card. What do you think it'll be?"

"How are you doing this, young lady?"

"You mean, how are *you* doing it. You're the one with the special powers. You should be on TV! Now if you want to see a *great* magician, my grandfather's performing at the VFW hall on Saturday. He's sitting right over there."

The man looked up. I waved.

"Come on, pick another card. Will it be an ace? I bet it's an ace."

It was an ace. He pulled a two for her twin sisters and ended by pulling a joker as she explained that she was studying to be a comedian. "That's me," she beamed. "The joker. I'm going to be a magician comedian!"

The man, I think, believed her. I certainly did.

— • —

I DECIDED to take a necessary but painful precaution. On our second day at Lake Willoughby, I arranged for box lunches and drove with Grace to a state forest. The innkeeper had circled a green area on my map, marked *Scenic Overlook*. "That's where you want to go," he said, "if you're looking for twelve thousand acres of forest and nothing else. You asked for out-of-the-way? That's out-of-the-way."

"It's the middle of nowhere," said Grace, hunched over the map with us.

"Exactly," said the man. "If you haven't visited *nowhere* in a while, I highly recommend it. Vermont's got a lot of nowhere. People come from all over to see it."

I took a circuitous route through farm country, past homes and barns so isolated they looked like wilderness outposts. Every so often clusters of paint-blistered buildings would appear, which Vermonters called villages. One road marker read *Marshfield, Pop. 272*; another, *Cabot, Pop. 238*. I had always been drawn to rural New England because the people who lived there loved their elbow room. They cleared forests, piled boulders to make fence lines, grew corn, raised cows, built homes and barns that lasted—and, even if only a few gathered on Sundays to pray, they built churches. Every village, even tiny Cabot and Marshfield, had its steeple, and every steeple reminded me that, after Ukraine, New England was my home.

Grace followed our progress on the map.

"You notice anything different about me?" she said.

I looked. "A new T-shirt?"

"Look harder."

"Sorry. I give up."

"Come on, Nate. *Look*. I worked my hair to be more like Sveta's. See how I flipped it in the back?"

And see what that got Sveta? I hadn't told her. I didn't know how or when I should. "Very handsome," I said. "Nice. Am I allowed to use the *p* word yet—*pretty?*"

"No, you're not. Thanks for nothing."

We found the state forest and the trailhead marked on our map. We started walking, and roughly a quarter-mile off the parking lot, an easy walk, the Forest Service had set picnic tables by a ledge that overlooked hills stretching west to the horizon. There was not a building in sight, no roads or electric lines, no fields, no cows, just trees and huge granite humps.

"We made it," I said. "We're officially *nowhere.*"

The innkeeper hadn't lied. The view was magnificent, and it reminded me of the forests I'd fled to as a child and what I'd learned at too young an age: that hills and trees are beautiful from a distance but harsh and indifferent up close. This, too, was God's creation: freezing winters and stinging ants in summer and cliffs that would just as soon see a man dead as a squirrel or a crow. Forests didn't care, didn't take sides. To survive you needed skills. Dima had taught me mine, and I had come to teach Grace.

"I have a new trick to show you," I said.

"We came all the way out here for that?"

"It's a noisy one. A classic."

I reached inside my pack for the brown, crumpled bag, setting it on the picnic table with an audible *clunk.* "I've been thinking about our tour next year because people are already asking about it. Every year we've got to give them something new—it's the first law of show business, right? This year we had the Rachel story and *The Kortelisy Escape.* Next year, I'm thinking about *The Bullet Catch.* You ever hear of it?"

She hadn't. She knew what was in the bag.

"It's famous. All the great ones have performed it. Here's how it works. You are going to shoot a gun, and I'm going to snatch the bullet before it hits me."

"Nate, that's Bobby Bianchi's gun."

"Yes, it is."

"Nate?"

"What?"

"I'm not going to shoot you."

"You weren't going to wrap me in plastic either. If we use blanks, it's all very safe—though it doesn't look that way to an audience." I reached into my pocket to show her a bullet, absent its casing. "Make a gun with your hand," I said.

She pointed a finger at me, thumb raised.

"Shoot."

"I don't like this."

"Go ahead."

When she bent her cocked thumb, firing a shot, I swept my hand across my chest and produced the bullet. "See. I caught it."

"Because I didn't fire a real gun."

"Exactly. The first bullet you'd fire, for the benefit of the audience, would explode an apple onstage, and everyone would believe the next one, the one you aimed at me, was real. In fact, the first bullet would be a blank too—because you can't shoot real guns in a theater. I'd explode the apple another way. Compressed air, maybe. I'll get into that later."

I unrolled the bag and set Bianchi's gun on the table. "Hold it," I said.

She held it.

"It's heavy."

"You're right. First lesson: use two hands."

I opened the cylinder. "The bullets go in here, one into each hole. See, it's not loaded. Here's how you load it." I reached into the paper bag for six bullets. I loaded them. I pointed the gun to the valley and fired one round.

Grace shuddered.

"It's *loud*."

"Guns are loud. That's right."

I opened the cylinder and reversed the process. I set the bullets and the gun on the table before her.

She loaded and unloaded. After double-checking the cylinder was empty, I taught her to aim. "You point the barrel directly at my chest. But first you have to pull back the hammer. Pull it back, point, and squeeze the trigger. The gun will kick on you . . . it'll jump in your hands. Hold it with two hands, pull back, point, and squeeze. You point at the chest, shoot, and I catch the bullet."

She pulled the hammer, aimed at the valley, then squeezed. *Click*.

"Did you ever kill anyone, Nate?"

"That's quite a question."

"You're teaching me to shoot a gun, aren't you?"

"This is for a magic trick. And the answer is no, I never killed anyone."

"Shoot anyone? Not even in the war?"

I checked the cylinder again, beating back memories of the German soldier. Dima wanted me to believe that the war had killed him, but even as an eight-year-old I knew it wasn't so. In either case, the soldier was just as dead, and I was the one who pulled the trigger. Now I was teaching Grace to use a gun. It was wrong, but then not to teach her would have been the greater crime with Petrov on the loose.

She aimed at a tree and fired, *Click*, then at my chest. *Click*.

"Shall I put in a bullet, a blank?"

"Don't make me do this."

"Grace you're always telling me you want to get to the Big Show, to do magic on a big stage. Well, you need skills in order to do that. You need to prepare! So practice. . . . Let's use fake bullets now—blanks."

"I'm going back," she said, not waiting for an answer before starting down the path. Our little lesson in the woods was over, and it broke my heart. She was fourteen, and I was glad no one from DCF was watching because I had just taught my granddaughter to kill. *This* was child abuse. But then the world abuses us all.

Twenty-Nine: Grace Larson

After a packed house at the Lake Willoughby VFW Hall and yet another unplanned matinee on Sunday, we had five days to finish rehearsals for our last show in Canaan and our new trick, *There Was an Old Lady*. Nate assembled the Black Art Studio in his room, and we practiced until we were certain we'd deliver a neatly wrapped present to Bianchi and Petrov. Early Saturday morning we drove to Canaan and confirmed the good news Nate had discovered some weeks before, when he was booking the tour. The Methodist Church in Canaan had just invested in a rollaway, portable stage with a built-in panel of lights and sound system.

It was the best stage we'd seen all summer.

The caretaker, a cousin to the minister, met us at the church door and showed us around. He was a pleasant man, so completely bald that ceiling lights and sunlight reflected off his head as if it were waxed. With his khaki shirt and pants and brown boots and suntan, he looked like a hard-working potato. By the time we arrived, he'd rolled out and secured the stage and set out one hundred chairs in neat rows. He also showed us the "Green Room," not much more than a large closet in the basement where Nate and I could change and rest up. But it had a couch and its own bathroom. I felt like a real performer.

When the caretaker left, I clapped and nearly laughed. The Methodist Church had updated its electrical and plumbing systems, just as the DCF dorm had. The entire basement, including the Green Room had a drop ceiling with removable panels that hid all the new wires and pipes. I half expected Janine Murphy to poke her head down from the crawl space above and say, "It's a highway. Get up here!"

Nate and I set to work laying out our props. One of the keys to success would be to keep the Black Art Studio onstage for the entire show, not wheel it on at the end—which would have called attention. It blended so well with the black of the stage curtains and stage itself that, from where the audience sat, the studio may as well have been invisible. We set out our frame with its velvet curtain and adjusted the lights. When the time came for me to produce the Matryoshkas, I would simply reach my hands through the velvet strips and work them as Nate spun his story. He would dress in white for the performance, we decided, to make for the sharpest possible contrast with the black of the curtains and my gloved hands. Between the stage lights and his vanilla ice-cream suit, the eyes of the audience would be drawn to him. They wouldn't— they *couldn't*—see my gloved hands just as my eyes and brain couldn't register Nate's hands, hidden in socks, as he danced my camera around the hotel closet.

— • —

AT THREE O'CLOCK, we were done setting up. Nate said he needed to rest, and I decided to poke around Canaan. It was plenty hot. Even with my shorts and flip flops and T-shirt, I got no relief. What I wanted most was to go down to the

Connecticut River, which ran through town, for a little swim.
But Nate said he'd worry and wouldn't be able to nap if I did,
so there'd be no swimming, not even toe dipping for me.
The next best thing was to find a cold drink, and not from a
machine either. I wanted ice that I could crunch and swallow.

Canaan was busier than I expected. After walking around
for a bit, I saw two men who must have been cousins of the
men who visited Nate back in Montpelier. It was about one
thousand degrees that day, and steamy, but they wore suits
and ties and didn't even unbutton their shirt collars. Nate said
Miss Hunt would be sending US marshals, and these were so
obviously some sort of police that they might as well have
dressed in regular uniforms. Then, at least, they wouldn't have
had to suffer the heat in those suits. I said *hello* as we passed
on the sidewalk. I supposed they knew who I was, but they
said nothing and didn't even nod. They wore sunglasses, and
I couldn't see their eyes.

Then I spotted Miss Roberts across the street, which was
surprising until I remembered she'd told Nate she'd be coming
to check on me. I put on a cheery face because I still needed to
prove to her how happy I was. I called and waved. She brightened when she saw me.

"Hello there!" she said. "You look good, all tan and sunny!"

"It's been a great tour, Miss Roberts. Nate's been getting
standing ovations, and we're already talking about a tour next
summer. You're coming to the Methodist Church tonight, I
hope?"

"Wouldn't miss it. Got a minute?"

I knew what was coming. I walked her to her car, and she
pulled a big canvas bag from the trunk. I couldn't keep from
groaning when I saw her loose-leaf binders.

"Let's find someplace to sit," she said. "Out of the heat."

I pointed to the Northland restaurant. "I was just going to get a Coke. Nate's taking a nap, so he doesn't need me right now."

No sooner had I said that than a car pulled up and stopped beside us. Perfect timing. *There Was an Old Lady* required that we go to work on Bobby Bianchi and Petrov *before* the show, which I figured would mean finding them at the church a few minutes before eight o'clock. All I needed was thirty seconds. Yet they'd come to me. Petrov was driving.

Bianchi lowered his window.

"Hey there, Grace! Big show tonight! You remember Maxim, don't you?"

"Sure. Hi, Mr. Petrov!"

He lifted two fingers off the steering wheel, a big effort.

"Roll up the window," he said. "It's hot."

"Mr. Petrov . . . It was really fun shopping that day with the money you gave us for Newbury Street. Sveta and Ella and I loved it! Ella couldn't stop talking about the parties she went to with you. And that dress! Did you *see* it on her? The way it hugs her? Really, she's movie-star gorgeous. She says she wants to study modeling, like Sveta. Oh—excuse me. This is Miss Roberts. She came all the way from Boston for the show. Just like you."

Bianchi bit hard.

I didn't lie and didn't need to lie. Petrov had bought Ella clothes and taken her to parties. She genuinely loved the excitement and danger of being with an older man. I just needed to let Bianchi in on the secret.

"What's this, Maxim? You're the one who bought my kid those jeans? My ex said they cost three or four hundred bucks!"

Bianchi rolled up the window and off they went, arguing. Perfect.

"Who were they, Grace?"

"Oh, they work at the grocery with Uncle Dima."

We were standing outside an outfitter's store with a big window, and inside I saw the two plainclothes marshals watching Petrov drive away. One was making a note in a little book, and I made careful notes in my head because I wanted to tell Nate everything.

Once Miss Roberts and I were seated in the Northland's main dining room, she began flipping pages in her binders and asking stupid questions again. "I know it's upsetting to be doing this," she said, midway through. "But I've got to, given the accusation against your grandfather." She flipped pages and showed me the stick figures fornicating until I just about screamed because I couldn't stop seeing Sveta on every page. Finally Miss Roberts left after telling me about the campsite she'd rented in a nearby RV park. It was by a lake, a little piece of heaven, she said. I was happy to see her go—but not before calling to her across the dining room. She paused at the door.

"He's really good to me," I said. "We have two rooms. I'm sleeping and eating. We laugh. We do magic." Was she beginning to see, finally, who Nate was? Her smile looked so honest and nearly encouraging I felt a surge of hope.

Thirty: Nate Larson

The path to the Green Room in the church basement snaked around old AV equipment, folding tables, busted chairs, wrecked stage sets, and discarded religious objects including a waist-high plaster angel who looked as if she wanted to be upstairs with a better class of sinners. But she was stuck with me, attempting to nap on an old couch and gather a little strength before my evening's ordeal. I slept with one eye open, however. Sure enough, fifteen minutes into my tossing and turning, I startled to find Petrov and Bianchi standing at the door. Bobby looked as if he were making a condolence call.

It's no pleasant thing, greeting men intent on murdering you. Still, without the two of them standing in the basement of that church hall, I had no possible way to keep Grace and Dima safe. I'd drawn Petrov to me with the hope of setting off a bomb in his face, albeit with a delayed fuse.

"You snore like a bastard," he said.

"I heard the same thing at Danbury, Maxim. If they hadn't sent you to the max lockup at Lewisburg, we could have been cellmates."

"That's not even funny."

"Change of plans," Bianchi announced. "We're driving you back to Portsmouth after the show and putting you on a ship.

The Canadian border's way too obvious. You'll come with us in the car. The kid stays here."

So this was the play: find a sleepy exit off the interstate, choose some random ditch, and shoot me in the back of the head. Bobby dabbed a handkerchief at his neck. To hide his bulk, he wore an oversize Hawaiian shirt with friendly looking palm trees and pineapples. Sweat ringed the armpits. "Good news, bud! You're going to the British Virgin Islands. We've got your working papers all set. You're now Mr. Ellis Knight, able-bodied seaman. By tomorrow this time, you'll be leaning over a rail puking your guts out. It'll be great."

"Ellis Knight? Terrific. Show me the papers."

"Sorry. They're in the car."

Petrov stood behind him, looking bored, and started plunking out a few notes on an old piano just outside the Green Room. "This is seriously out of tune," he said. "Look, Bobby. This thing's older than Nate. It takes scrolls!"

I pushed myself off the couch after shooting a quick glance to my knapsack, making sure Petrov noticed. I met his eyes first, then looked. In truth, I could have grabbed Bianchi's gun, shot Petrov in the chest, and been happy to spend the rest of my days in prison if only to rid the world of a thug. It wasn't a subtle solution, but at least Grace would be safe and I wouldn't have to testify against my brother. The backpack, which I'd unzipped, lay within an arm's reach propped against the couch.

"Maxim, that was a dirty trick you played."

"The child abuse thing? I thought it was clever."

"You're not the only one with a sense of humor. How's this for a joke: I'm not running anymore. Thanks for the trouble of getting me fake papers, but I won't be needing them. I won't need that ride either. But hey—I'm glad you came for the show. Why not take your seats early and sit up front?"

There was no unwinding this now.

I turned to Bianchi. "What can I say? You were right. Turns out I love the kid. She needs me, so I'm staying. Dima's mind's shot. He won't know what's happening when I testify against him. It's better than fifty-fifty he won't even realize he's on trial. So I'm going to court to testify, and I'm keeping Grace. We've got to get on with our lives."

Petrov stepped around Bianchi and planted a fist in my gut that dropped me to the couch. He grabbed his hand and shook it, then ripped open my shirt. "Kevlar? You are *so* dead, Larson. Plastic's not going to stop the bullet I put in your brain. Bobby, you *vouched* for him!" I lunged for the backpack, just slowly enough to let Petrov beat me. He removed the gun from the paper bag.

"Whoa, Nate! I didn't know you had it in you."

He cocked the hammer, pushed me back against the couch, and shoved the barrel of Bianchi's gun into my mouth. I pinned my eyes on his. If Petrov was going to kill me, let him at least *see* me. Bianchi said what I would have were I not gagging on steel. "You idiot. Think of those people upstairs who saw us come down here. The ones who gave us directions. You ready to deal with that?"

I pushed Petrov's hand and the gun away. "He's right, Maxim. Kill me now and you're ID'd."

He released the hammer and stuffed the gun in his waistband at the small of his back, pulling his shirt over it. "See you after the show," he said. After he left, Bianchi stayed long enough to read me my obituary. "You're a stupid, stupid man, Nate. I protected you. I *trusted* you. Now I don't even know if I can protect myself—or Ella."

I felt sorrier for him than for me.

Thirty-One: Grace Larson

Showtime.

Bobby sat in the front row along the center aisle. I couldn't find Petrov. From behind the stage curtain, I counted 136 people—so many that the caretaker set out extra folding chairs. On any other night of the summer, Nate and I would have danced a little jig backstage for that kind of turnout. But we had other business on our minds.

The meeting hall of the Methodist Church was one large room with a pitched roof above and a basement below that ran beneath its entire length. From what I could gather in town from advertisements in storefront windows and stapled to utility poles, the church was Canaan's largest hall and was busy most evenings each week with groups as varied as prayer clubs, Rotary International, Huntsmen Guild, and Girl Scouts of America. When we arrived that afternoon, the caretaker was rolling away the minister's podium and Bible stand.

"You're sure you saw the marshals?" Nate asked.

I'd already told him. Twice. "I *saw* them," I said. "You know, with my eyes. Why don't you ask me again?"

"They'll keep out of sight. They're trained to do that."

The marshals. The crowd. Petrov. Bianchi. The new trick. I felt the weight of it all and finally said, "Nate . . . my stomach hurts."

He took me by the shoulders and leveled his you-can't-look-away magician's stare. "This is the Big Show," he said. "All summer we've wanted a big audience, and now we've got one. This is no time to go wobbly. We've practiced. We have a plan, and we have backup plans. It doesn't really matter *how* you feel because you're a professional. Professionals do their jobs. Right? Do you understand?"

"What if somebody gets hurt. For real, Nate. Not pretend."

He didn't answer.

He changed into his new vanilla suit, and I laughed when he stepped from the Green Room looking like he scooped ice cream for a living. On any other night of the summer I would have teased him.

"Grace. If by some chance—"

"Don't," I said, covering my ears. "*Don't!*"

I ran up the stairs to the stage. A few minutes later, he joined me at the curtain, waiting for eight o'clock and the show to begin. "Close your eyes," he whispered. "Here's what I do just before I go on. I never told you. I close my eyes and think of every step I'll be taking, every move—everything I've practiced. I skip nothing. When I'm done, I stay in that place. Then I go onstage and perform what I've just seen in my head. C'mon. Try it with me."

I saw nothing when I closed my eyes. I heard the audience scraping chairs and chattering. My heart was pounding in my ears and my leotard was hot and was making me itch. Yet Nate stood there looking serene with his eyes closed, swaying a little, the same carbuncled old man who'd claimed me from DCF: still baggy-eyed and blotchy-skinned, still the same mop of gray hair that kept falling across his eyes. These days, he stooped a little as he walked and wheezed a bit with every breath. He was the man I thoroughly hated when Mrs. Alcott drove me to the courthouse. But something had changed, and

I didn't hate him anymore. He took the deepest breath he could, then opened his eyes, and winked. "Ready? Let's do some magic."

He stepped around the curtain to applause.

— • —

BEFORE HE uttered a word, I knew Nate would be brilliant that evening. I could tell from the way he set his legs for *The Three Roses*. He reminded me of a statue I'd seen in a book at school: of a discus thrower coiled and ready to spin. He didn't merely cover his right hand with his left to produce the first flower. He moved the way seagrass moves underwater, each bend easing into the next so that I couldn't tell where one motion ended and the next began.

Then he spoke.

How to say it? His words hadn't changed. He began the same way: *We learn from the Apostle Peter that life is a pilgrimage. We come from God, walk this world of storm and stress, and return to God.* He spoke the same lines I'd heard all summer and had all-but memorized, yet this time the words were something more than just a wrapping for his tricks. All summer long I had thought any words would do. Not this time.

When he launched into Rachel's story, trick followed trick until he had the room clapping and stomping—until my insides churned because I knew what had really happened in Ukraine. Once again, he told the sweetened version of Kortelisy. The lie. Who wanted to hear stories of Nate being ripped from his village and his mother? Was it the right moment for a history lesson? Did anyone really care to know how Ukraine was wrecked by one army after the next and the next? Why should that matter when all anyone had to do to get bad news was pick up the morning paper? Why should bad news from fifty years ago matter now? I'd looked it all up online when Nate stopped talking about it and could barely believe what I read. Before 1939, Stalin killed ten thousand Ukrainians a week. Then Hitler invaded and killed millions. After two years, Stalin drove Hitler out and started his own killing again. At least seven million Ukrainians died in those years, not including the two million Stalin sent to prisons in Siberia. Nothing about that war and those times came close to explaining how Nate could have found heaven on earth in Kortelisy.

Maybe this time I would understand. I listened. I tried.

I couldn't.

None of this moved Bobby Bianchi. He sat with his arms crossed over that big belly of his, yawning and scratching himself. He'd seen the show four or five times. If he was bored, I was certain *There Was an Old Lady* would wake him up. I was desperate to begin and, finally, Nate paused, opened his arms, and, in his big fancy stage voice, bellowed: "Ladies and gentlemen, you've paid good money to be deceived tonight. You've dared me to fool you. I *have* fooled you, and it's been my pleasure to do so!"

Applause.

"We'll end with a little story and an escape. First, the story: When I was a child in Ukraine, children played with a special doll called a Matryoshka. Matryoshkas are still popular, and they're still made from the linden tree, which has straight white wood and very few knots. Every Matryoshka is actually seven dolls in one, each painted identically with the face of a rosy-cheeked girl. I've brought my Matryoshkas tonight. Each is cut around the waist so that you can separate her top and bottom halves to reveal a hollow inside—and in this hollow lives another Matryoshka, only smaller. She, too, is cut around the middle. Inside this one is another doll and inside that one, another, and so on until you get to the smallest, a solid little doll only an inch tall. In my village, farmers made Matryoshkas during the long winters. A good one took a few weeks to hand carve and paint, and if you had one you treasured it. These days, they're made by machines, by the thousands, and you find them everywhere.

"Here, take a look."

Nate made wavy magician moves before the Black Art Studio. When I thrust my gloved hands through the velvet strips, holding the doll, a gasp shot through the room. From where the audience sat, he had called his doll into existence from nothing, from thin air! As he lifted and rotated his hands, I lifted and rotated the doll. He and his Matryoshka danced in a fashion—or so it seemed to the audience.

The Black Art Studio stunned them.

He continued with the words I'd written: "As a child I played with my Matryoshkas all the time, separating the smaller dolls inside one by one, then lining them in a row as I'll do for you tonight. I imagined this must be very painful, breaking each Matryoshka in half around her belly, so I invented a little story to distract them as I pulled each apart. I called my story *There Was an Old Lady*.

"For some reason I imagined that Mother Matryoshka lived in a shoe. Very strange! But why not? For a child, Matryoshkas can live anywhere.

"Mother Matryoshka," he continued: "Why do you live in a shoe? Is it because shoes take you places and Matryoshka loves to travel?" I separated the first doll and Nate took the halves and reassembled them. "No, I don't think so. Our feet take us places all by themselves! Matryoshka doesn't need shoes for walking. So I ask again: Why live in a shoe?

"I know. Because shoes are smelly? Silliness! Mother Matryoshka loves the open air and sea, yet she chooses to live in a shoe. Very strange!"

Another doll floated apart, another joined.

"Matryoshka dear, do you live in a shoe because old shoes are like old friends—so comfortable and easy? No. Matryoshka has many friends. Her shoe is her home, not a friend. She knows the difference. So why a shoe? Perhaps Mother Matryoshka is poor and can't afford to live anywhere else. Never! Mother is a sensible Matryoshka who's saved all her life. If she chose, she could live in a proper house with a thatched roof and a fireplace."

The dolls drifted and floated as if by themselves. By this point, people were whistling and clapping. We neared the end. "I know!" said Nate. "Is Mother Matryoshka hiding? No one would think to look for her in a shoe. Never! She's an honest lady who's done nothing wrong.

"Then there can be only one reason: Mother is hiding something herself. What could it be?"

We had come to the smallest doll.

The levitation was over, and Nate delivered the words I'd gift-wrapped for Bianchi. First he addressed the doll. "So Mother keeps secrets. Whose? I'll give you a hint." He whispered to the doll—nothing anyone could hear—and placed it inside the next larger doll, assembling it, and placed that inside the next larger until all the dolls were assembled, each neatly nested so that he once again held a single doll, the largest. He turned to the room: "Matryoshkas are the best keepers of secrets in the world because they bury their secrets deep. As a child, I somehow understood they were a fortress for secrets. I played with this very doll and trusted her with all the things I could never tell my parents. What could a child possibly have to keep from the world? My secrets seemed so large! I'd seen horses mating in a field but didn't want anyone to know. Once I hid behind a tree and watched my friend's sister bathing in a stream. I took an apple from a farmer's orchard without asking.

"Oh, I had secrets!

"My real question, ladies and gentlemen, is this: How does a child learn there are some things we tell and others we hide? As a three-year-old, I knew enough to close the cupboard door behind me as I licked my finger and stuck it in the sugar bowl. How, at three years old? Children never tell all. I never told my parents every secret. They never told theirs. Our children never tell us. I don't know much, but I know this: we keep secrets. And if a secret's bursting inside you, one that's not fit and proper to tell the world, then tell it to a Matryoshka—the littlest one—and reassemble the dolls, all of them. Set that Matryoshka on a shelf, in plain view of the world. Let her hide in plain sight. I guarantee your secret will be safe."

He positioned the single Matryoshka—Mother along with all her children inside—before the Black Art Studio. No one could see me reach through the curtain and take firm hold of the doll. Nate released his hands, again with a magician's wave. I held the Matryoshka—making her appear to float for a three count, then snatched it through the curtain. The vanish was so total and sudden that the audience leapt to its feet.

Nate bowed and thanked everyone, then excused himself, announcing he would return in ten minutes for the evening's finale, his grand escape. Backstage, he was sweating and fanning himself with a newspaper. "Tell me," he said, bent at the waist, catching his breath. "Did he bite, Grace? Did Bianchi *bite*?"

I was sure he hadn't, but I peeked around the curtain to make certain. At least Bianchi didn't look bored anymore, but beyond that he didn't move like someone twisted with rage. He reached into his pocket for a cell phone. Nothing about him was hurried or frantic.

Nate was pacing. "I've got to rest," he said, gulping a bottle of water. "See you downstairs."

He leaned close. "This next piece isn't going to be easy," he said. "Remember. We've practiced. We're ready."

I tried to look confident.

"Say the words, Grace. 'We're ready.'"

I couldn't.

"You've practiced. We've practiced. I want to hear the words."

If only to get rid of him I said what he wanted to hear, still unsure of myself. I peeked around the curtain again, wondering what had gone wrong. We'd put so much work into the Black Art Studio and *There Was an Old Lady*. On one level, as a trick, it worked. The audience loved it. But not Bianchi. He wasn't moved, and I had written that trick to go straight after his weakness. Ella. I could see the ending as clearly as if it were one of my computer games: *Click*. Before the show, Bobby hears—from me—that Petrov is buying expensive clothes for Ella. Three hundred dollar jeans. Little black dresses. *Click*. Bobby learns—from me—that Petrov is taking Ella to parties with men three times her age. *Click*. Bobby suspects what Petrov's doing. He's seen it before, with Sveta. *Click*. He's heating up. *Click*. He watches *There Was an Old Lady* and thinks: kids keep secrets. Of course they do! What's Ella keeping from me? *Click*. He's scalding hot. He has to hit someone, smash something. *Click*. What are you doing to her? *Click*. Petrov laughs. She doesn't need Daddy anymore, that's for sure. *Click*. Say it. Tell me! *Click*. All right, if you're that thick in the head. Ella's got talent, and she's doing exactly what she wants. *Click*. What kind of talent? *Click*. Use your imagination. *Click*. You've turned her. *Click*. Wrong. She's sixteen. Age of consent. She turned herself. It's a free country. *Click*. You're whoring my kid. Say it! *Click*. She's not a kid anymore, and the sooner you get used to—. *Click*. He's boiling now. He reaches into a pocket. *Click*. He pulls a gun. *Click*. Put it away. You're out of your depth, Bianchi. *Click*. She's only *sixteen*! *Click*. Remember who you're talking to. *Click*. Like I need reminding? *Click*. Bobby shoots Petrov in the head.

Game over. Our Petrov problem solved.

Only it wasn't. I had so clearly imagined this ending that I was surprised to see that Bianchi, in fact, held no gun as he spoke with Petrov, quietly, in a corner of the hall. *There Was an Old Lady*, our Plan A, had failed. Downstairs in the Green Room I was practically screaming at Nate as if it were all his fault: "Why didn't it work? It was supposed to work. They're upstairs *talking*, not killing each other. What happened?"

"Stop it, Grace. This isn't helping."

"I mean it. What *happened*?"

"It doesn't matter now. Tricks bust for all sorts of reasons. What matters is how we recover. We've got our Plan B. Remember?"

"It should have worked!"

He sighed. "The hardest part is coming, Grace, and I can't do this alone. You're more than my assistant now. So pull yourself together and behave like a professional." He adjusted his bow tie. "How do I look?"

"Ridiculous."

"Wait here seven minutes. If they don't come for you, they'll grab you when you're at the curtain. Remember: they're after me, not you. Cooperate. Do everything they say. Are you ready?"

He could see I wasn't.

"Come on now. Close your eyes. Imagine every step."

I tried, I really did. I tried again. I felt like beating my head with my fists. Nate left, and I waited. And then, just as he had predicted, I heard them on the stairs. Bianchi and

Petrov made their way through all the junk in the basement. Petrov was smiling.

"Hi," I said. "I was just going upstairs to help with the escape. It's the best part of the night. You want to watch backstage this time—to see how I free Nate from the plastic wrap and the straitjacket?"

"Let's just step into the Green Room," said Petrov. "If you don't mind."

As he approached, I backed away. God, how I hated this man.

"Bobby, close the door."

Petrov held up a roll of duct tape in one hand and a rope in the other. "If you're quiet, we won't need these. But if you make a sound, even a small one, we will."

"That's not funny. I've got to get upstairs and help Nate with the plastic and straitjacket. You know that."

"Actually, it *is* funny. Sort of."

"If I don't cut a hole in the plastic, he'll suffocate. I need to go now."

Petrov held up the tape and rope.

"Did you hear me?" I said. "He'll *die!*"

"And I'll be upstairs, watching. Bobby'll be just outside the door. Remember, no noise." He put a finger to his lips. "Shhh. When we're done tonight, I'll give you and that nice lady from DCF a ride back to Boston."

The moment they shut the door, I closed my laptop, which I'd left open just a crack. When I could no longer hear Petrov on the stairs, as quietly as I could I set a filing cabinet on the couch—I'd removed the files that afternoon and stacked them in a corner. I set a chair on top of the cabinet and a cinder block on top of that. Then, wishing Janine Murphy could have seen me, I climbed up my makeshift ladder and removed a panel from the false ceiling. When I pushed off the cinder block into the crawl space above, grabbing onto a pipe, the whole business came crashing down—which left me hanging on for dear life because if I fell back into the room, Bianchi, who'd already come rushing in, was going to tie me up. The pipes held. I swung myself up just as he jumped onto the couch and reached into the crawl space. I thought I'd backed away enough, but he got a hand on my ankle. I held onto the pipes and kicked with my free foot, planting the heel of my shoe in his face.

He let go.

"You *can't* go up there!"

I heard him moving the cabinet onto the couch so he could climb into the crawl space himself. No way was he going to fit. Just as he poked his head through the opening, I kicked him in the face again, this time drawing blood. Down he went, cursing at me. I turned and shimmied inside the air duct I'd checked out that afternoon—just like the old days at the dorm, though because I was taller and heavier it was a tighter fit. But I made it. The duct was an express lane that ran the length of the church. At the very end, I could see a square of light where the duct let into the room above. Just above me, I could hear chairs scraping as people took their seats for *The Kortelisy Escape*. I'd heard Bianchi racing up the stairs and knew he'd be in the hall—but he wouldn't know which vent I'd pop through, which was key. If he guessed right and caught me before I got to the stage, I'd have problems.

THERE WAS AN OLD LADY

1. BUILD BLACK ARTS FRAME AND CURTAIN.

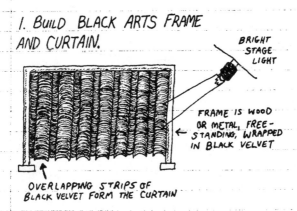

BRIGHT STAGE LIGHT

FRAME IS WOOD OR METAL, FREE-STANDING, WRAPPED IN BLACK VELVET

OVERLAPPING STRIPS OF BLACK VELVET FORM THE CURTAIN

2. HELPER DRESSED ALL IN BLACK STANDS BEHIND BLACK VELVET CURTAIN.

MAGICIAN, DRESSED IN WHITE, COMMANDS OBJECTS TO APPEAR AND DISAPPEAR

3. HELPER (INVISIBLY) MAKES OBJECTS APPEAR AND DISAPPEAR.

NOTES:

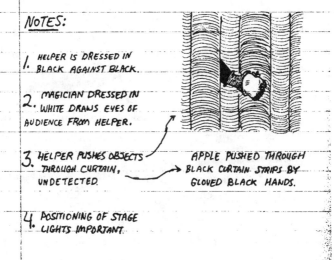

1. HELPER IS DRESSED IN BLACK AGAINST BLACK.

2. MAGICIAN DRESSED IN WHITE DRAWS EYES OF AUDIENCE FROM HELPER.

3. HELPER PUSHES OBJECTS THROUGH CURTAIN, UNDETECTED.

APPLE PUSHED THROUGH BLACK CURTAIN STRIPS BY GLOVED BLACK HANDS.

4. POSITIONING OF STAGE LIGHTS IMPORTANT.

Thirty-Two: Nate Larson

I counted more than one hundred approving faces as I stepped back onstage after the break. I couldn't hear Grace behind me, by the curtain, which meant Petrov had detained her downstairs. So far, so good. I reviewed for the audience the whole nasty setup of escaping the straitjacket and plastic wrap. "No sane man would attempt such madness," I said. "You'd think I *wanted* to die! That's the question, ladies and gentlemen: Why would someone *flirt* with death?"

Like audiences earlier on the tour, these good people were looking pretty unsettled about the prospect of anyone getting his head wrapped in plastic. I played up the danger, invoking Houdini. "It comes down to this," I explained. "Strong magic puts you at risk. If you don't risk, if you're *afraid* to risk, then you fail as a magician." I called for volunteers. I instructed the young man who'd be buckling the straitjacket to wrap me tight. I told the second and third volunteers to hold the curtain high and under no circumstances drop it, no matter how desperate the commotion on the far side. I explained myself clearly: "There's no denying that a dying man fights for his life. If I don't make it, at least I'll have the comfort of dying in a church—that much closer to God!"

I spotted Petrov entering the hall from the rear, alone. He crossed his arms.

"Ladies and gentlemen, Miss Julia Turnhill, our EMT tonight, tells me she grew up right here in Canaan. You all know her as a standout athlete in high school and an excellent first responder. Please forgive me if I make sure she's current with her certificates. Miss Turnhill?"

"Yes, sir! All up to date."

"Okay, then. First step, straitjacket. Second, plastic. Third, curtain! Are we ready?"

I made a show of taking a big breath. I nodded to my volunteers and allowed myself to be strapped and wrapped— holding my arms as I always did, without anyone's notice, slightly away from my torso. Once the volunteer buckled the straitjacket and wrapped me, I relaxed my arms and created just enough room to maneuver. I wasn't about to take chances and play by the rules I'd set out for the audience: summoning the EMT to the stage by kicking over the pedestal with its paper clips. Not with my head wrapped in plastic. All summer long Grace had been my Plan A for the escape. The pedestal was actually Plan C, which was awkward and relied on someone other than Grace taking action. Not a smart risk. I opted for Plan B—which still required a good twenty seconds of holding my breath, close to my limit.

The instant the curtain went up, I reached my right forefinger through a hole in the arm of the straitjacket and felt for a hidden ring. I found it, hooked it with my finger, pulled a zipper, and the straitjacket released. I was free and cut a hole through the plastic with my own serrated knife, which I kept in a hidden side pocket should Grace lose hers. I slipped halfway out of the jacket and partially unwrapped the plastic, looking like I'd made a botch of the job. But I could breathe. I began to flop on the floor, violently, like a—like a man fighting for air. I was fine. The audience didn't know that.

When Miss Turnhill called "Fifteen seconds!" I inchwormed my way to the pedestal and gave it a little shove—just enough for it to slide some, not enough to tip it over. I wanted Petrov to think I'd panicked and was suffering. I wanted him to celebrate. That way when he realized he was in a freefall (I'd already pushed him over a cliff, he just didn't know it yet), his destruction would be complete. My only regret was that I wouldn't be around to see his jaw drop.

"Thirty seconds!"

Again, a little shove.

At sixty seconds, breathing freely, I rose to my knees and dropped to the stage floor with a sickening thump.

At seventy-five seconds, with a last thump, I fell silent.

At eighty seconds, people in the audience were yelling. At ninety, the curtain came down and Miss Turnhill leapt onto the stage to find my one arm free and the plastic gouged, permitting just a bit of air. I rolled and fluttered my eyes and trembled enough to suggest convulsions. I made choking sounds. Poor Miss Turnhill! I'd assured her everything would be fine, and here I was putting all her training to the test. I had no choice. Despite Grace's assurances, I still hadn't seen the marshals. From what I could tell the cavalry wasn't coming, which left me with only one way out of that church hall: stuffed into the trunk of Petrov's car. I chose a safer route, which I hadn't even mentioned to Grace, figuring the marshals would have taken over at that point. As I looked toward the church's double doors at the end of the long hall, there it came, my exit and deliverance: Plan D, on wheels.

Thirty-Three: Grace Larson

My practice run through the air duct earlier that day had taken sixty seconds from the moment I entered the crawl space in the Green Room until I reached the back of the hall, where the duct connected to a vent cut into the floor. The vent plate moved easily, and I could just wiggle through. But now when I reached the vent and pushed with my arms, it wouldn't budge. I shimmied past the opening and kicked at it. Still, no movement—and I saw why: One leg of a chair sat on a corner of the vent plate, and someone was sitting in that chair. There were other vents I could have tried, but Nate and I decided I should surface at the rear of the hall and begin hollering. It made for a better show because I'd have the full length of the church to run and scream, "Save him! Save him! He's dying up there!"

But first I had to get out of the duct. I kicked again and shouted, "Let me out! GET UP!"

The chair moved.

"LET ME OUT!"

The EMT called, "Seventy-five seconds!" My timing was off. Someone above me stood, moved the chair, and pulled the vent free. A hand reached into the duct to help as I turned sideways and blew out all my breath. I pushed against the sheet metal, which buckled, as one hand and then another grabbed hold of my arms and pulled. Someone shouted, "Hey, what's going on? What's all this about?"

I was out.

When I started screaming, people didn't know whether to stare at me, some kid in a black leotard who'd climbed into the hall through the floor (the floor!), or watch the EMT attempting to save Nate. When I saw Bianchi and Petrov headed my way, I raced to the stage. "My grandfather's dying. Let me through! He's dying! They held me downstairs and didn't let me out to save him. He's dying! They killed him!"

No one knew who I was talking about, but I needed only four people to hear me and understand: Bianchi, Petrov, and the marshals—wherever they were. When I reached the stage, Nate looked half dead for real. He groaned. His lips quivered, and his body shook. It took all my strength not to turn and search for Petrov to see how hard he'd bitten.

"Nate?"

We'd rehearsed every step of this little show. For a moment, bending over him on the stage seemed no different than in practice. But it *was* different. This time my performance mattered. The marshals were there. Finally I saw them. Petrov and Bianchi were there. Miss Roberts was there, and I needed to convince them all that Nate might actually die. I cried. I put my heart into those tears, and it didn't take much to make them real because something had burst inside me again, the way it had at the bus station as I realized he was old and I was not and one day I'd be bending over him for real. What was wrong with the world that it would take the people I loved from me?

Nate moved his lips. I leaned close. I was acting. I wasn't acting. *"Don't go,"* I told him. *"Don't leave me."* He mumbled a few words.

I leaned closer.

With my ear at his lips, he said, "I'm fine. Finish this."

I took a deep breath and thought, *With pleasure.*

The marshals ran to the stage from one direction. Petrov and Bianchi approached from another and Miss Roberts, from a third. The first marshal vaulted the three steps onto the stage and flashed a badge to the EMT.

"How do I help?"

The woman didn't take her eyes off Nate. "Get the gurney from the ambulance."

When he returned, the two of them maneuvered Nate onto the stretcher and wheeled him from the hall. The old buzzard—he never told me! Once I saw him disappear through the open doors, safely beyond Petrov's reach, I summoned all my rage to help make what came next real. Oh, how I hated! I could have boiled away oceans and ripped down mountains. I summoned all my loathing of DCF and of every rental parent who ever collected checks from the state and called that love. I summoned every insult, every blow, every effort to *fix* me: *Try smiling, Grace. Talk! Why don't you ever talk? And stop with the moping. What's wrong with you? Do you want to go back to DCF? Is that it?* Ten years of ugliness exploded. I howled and flew at Petrov, biting and kicking him, pounding with my fists.

Was I convincing?

I was convincing.

He was Mr. Parker. He was Mrs. Del-Rey. He was Mr. Elliot snapping his belt, scaring me to death. "You killed my grandfather! You didn't let me help him and you killed him!" I hit Petrov as hard as I could. He covered up and took it until the second marshal grabbed my wrist and held me off.

"What's all this?"

"He has a gun!" I screamed. "He has a gun!"

When the marshal showed his badge, Bobby Bianchi, his nose still bleeding from the kick I gave him, backed away and left the building. Petrov made a *Who, me?* face. "Officer," he said. "I don't know what this kid's talking about. She's obviously out of control. Somebody better take charge of her."

Miss Roberts stepped forward. "I'm in charge."

"Your ID, sir. Let's see it."

As Petrov reached for his wallet, Miss Roberts pointed and screamed: "There! In his pants—in back! A gun!"

The marshal stepped up to Petrov and shook hands as if this were a business meeting. He placed his left hand at Petrov's elbow, then leaned close: "Folks are pretty upset. Are you carrying?"

"I have a license, officer."

"We'll sort that out later. Right now I'm going to reach around you and remove the gun. Then we'll step off to the side and talk. You're good with this?"

"He kidnapped me! He kept me from helping Nate. He wanted to *kill* my grandfather. He knew he could if I didn't help!"

"Officer, I know this girl—but it's the first time I've seen her today."

The marshal reached around him.

"He's lying! I recorded him saying he *knew* he was going to kill him. I got it on my computer. Don't let him hurt me!"

The marshal was now holding Petrov's gun.

Petrov said: "I can explain."

But he couldn't.

THE KORTELISY ESCAPE

Thirty-Four: Grace Larson

That afternoon, Nate had wiped three sets of fingerprints off the gun: his own, Bianchi's, and mine—which meant the only remaining prints (aside from the marshal's) belonged to Petrov, a problem for someone who'd been convicted twice of felonies as a younger man. Felons, Nate well knew, couldn't possess firearms or live ammunition. Petrov had no license. He swore the gun wasn't his, but who cared? Bianchi wasn't claiming ownership because Bianchi was long gone. Which meant that Nate busted Petrov on the same Three Strikes Law that had busted him.

How do you spell TWENTY-FIVE YEARS TO LIFE?

It must have been a Tabernacle Moment for the ages when Petrov realized he'd walked straight into a trap, multiple traps, and saw none of it coming. He possessed an illegal firearm, he kidnapped me, and he attempted to kill Nate. The last charge would have been impossible to prove had I not recorded Petrov on my computer. That was my idea, and it delighted Eleanor Hunt, who produced it as evidence in court when Petrov denied having any designs on Nate's life or even seeing me earlier that day in Canaan. Just to make sure he'd go away for a long time, Nate set him up on a fourth charge: human trafficking. Once Nate knew Petrov and Bianchi were coming north for the final show, he got his revenge for what had happened to Sveta. He arranged for her coworkers to give themselves up to Eleanor Hunt and name Petrov as the one who'd lured them from Ukraine and prostituted them in Boston. Hunt, in turn, gave them visas and green cards. Apparently, the Department of Justice in Washington was cracking down on trafficking nationwide, and Hunt was only too happy to hang a long sentence around Petrov's neck.

Petrov was gone.

And no one heard from Bobby Bianchi again, not even Ella.

— • —

THE EVENTS at the Canaan Methodist Church were all Miss Roberts needed to strip custody from Nate. Apparently guns, whores, and tax evasion didn't quite fit with her vision of a happy family. Had she bothered to ask, I would have told her I felt safer that summer with Nate than with any of my previous foster parents. She wasn't interested in my opinions. She sent me back to the DCF dormitory in South Boston and out of sheer spite wouldn't let me see Nate for a month. The paperwork mentioned something about weaning me from bad influences.

My world turned gray once more as I settled into the dreadful, familiar routine of life in the DCF dorm. Living there was like living behind the Iron Curtain, or at least the place I imagined after reading my homework for social studies. I honestly thought people in East Germany and Poland and Ukraine and all the rest of those countries lived their lives in a black and white world. With its gray walls, gray food, and gray towels and sheets, the dorm was awful that same way. It made me physically ill to be there. I continued taking the bus back and forth to school, but I found pleasure in nothing.

Not even the computer club could save me. I stopped playing games on my laptop.

In October, on a Saturday, I was lying on my bed, reading, when a house matron in her muddy-looking smock leaned into the room: "Larson, pack your things," she said. "You got a new placement."

Impossible. No one had interviewed me. Rental parents couldn't just point to a picture in a book and say *that one,* like I was some mutt in a kennel. "Who is it?" I demanded. "Tell me!"

"I know as much as you do. Just pack and be quick about it."

I was determined to stuff this surprise back into its miserable box: I would pull a crazy. I could act up or flip out, generally scream my way back to the status quo. I could bang my head against the bed rail, bloody myself, then show up at the administrator's office counting off daisies only I could see. That would give anyone a good scare.

I packed my suitcase and followed the matron downstairs to the offices off the main hall. She left when I took a seat, and I waited alone. What a depressing little room, with its fake plants and cracked linoleum. I plotted a quick escape through the drop-ceiling but realized I'd had enough of that.

To be given away *again*? I wasn't sure I could take it.

A door opened and Miss Roberts appeared.

"Grace."

"How come no one tells me anything! I'm supposed to at least meet foster parents before they take me. Isn't there a rule or something?"

"Grace, I thought this time—"

"I'm almost fifteen, and I should have a say in who takes me. I want to stay here. I'm not going. I don't care what you think I should do. I want to—"

She leaned into the next room. Whoever was there had heard it all, which made no difference to me. Let them get a good dose of the monster they were taking home. I was really winding myself up this time. I couldn't help it: "Those people should give me back before they ever take me because I'm going to be the meanest, toughest kid they ever—"

Miss Roberts motioned to someone. I held my breath, waiting to see if they were hunchbacked or Scripture-quoting Bible thumpers or creepy like Mr. Parker, in which case I was going to get violent.

Lola Maloney stepped into the room, followed by Frank. Lola's mascara was running. She took a deep breath and tried to steady her voice. "Dear, dear Grace," she said, opening her arms to me. "The paperwork dragged on forever. I didn't want to say anything until we were sure. But it's all arranged now, if you'll have us. Frank and I want to be your foster parents. We want you to come live with us. Come home, Grace. Please come home."

Thirty-Five: Nate Larson

When the hospital released me, I returned to my old apartment in the house on Marathon Street. DCF had taken custody of my granddaughter, as well it should have. What even half-reputable foster parent would teach a kid to shoot a handgun and tangle her in the ugliness of Petrov's world? But with the Maloneys taking formal custody, DCF was satisfied she'd have a reasonably stable life even if I was a part of it, living upstairs. Grace and I still played checkers, though no longer to decide who ordered carryout each evening because Lola and Frank were good cooks and had instituted a new policy: each of us prepared at least one meal a week. After Grace moved in with them, they welcomed Dima into my apartment. Frank removed the doors inside the front vestibule so that we could all come and go as we pleased. We had to keep the front and rear doors locked, though, because Dima was fond of wandering the neighborhood and inviting strangers for dinner.

I wish I could report that my brother and I spent his remaining months recalling the triumphs and challenges of old days or even recent ones. Dima's mind was shot. His life had become an unending present moment, which has its advantages, I suppose. For one, the loss of his beloved Rachel ceased tormenting him. And while he forgot my name, he continued to recognize Grace. After walking the dog, she would come upstairs to do homework at the kitchen table, and she'd sit him beside her. She might have been reading and writing Sanskrit for all he understood. That didn't keep her from patting an empty chair and saying, "Here, Uncle Dima, help me with my assignments." And it didn't keep him from pointing to her and her books, on occasion, and saying, "Good! Very good. She's a smart one!"

Indeed, she was.

Dima lived out his days among people who knew the man he'd been and loved the gentle, shuffling man he'd become. He died in his sleep, peacefully. When we buried him, every Rachel who still lived in New England attended the service. Leave it to Grace to have found his list of Rachels as we cleaned out the grocery to sell it for back taxes. She wrote to all thirty-seven of them. They brought their husbands and children and grandchildren. Oksana Carle came with Gus. Grace ran to her, and they laughed and hugged like old friends. Even Eleanor Hunt came and listened as each Rachel laid a flower on Dima's grave and said, in her own way: "God bless this man. I was lost, and he gave me America."

So it is that joy may come of grief.

I have always believed that hard times produce great men. Dima was a great man, though he never asked for it. Given the choice, he would have saved his beloved and lived a quiet life on a farm somewhere. As for me, I was happy to have any life at all after the war. It took nearly sixty years, but I was finally able to escape Kortelisy for good—to live and, eventually, to sleep. The German soldier and I had a long talk one evening, and he agreed to let me go provided I joined him sometime soon.

Four years passed. On her eighteenth birthday, the day she swore she'd quit anything and everything to do with the

Department of Children and Families, Grace asked Lola and Frank if she could continue living with them even though the commonwealth would be ending its monthly stipends for her maintenance. "I'll work after school," she promised, hardly giving them a chance to answer. "I'll pay you the same as the state did. You won't have to spend an extra penny on me." The Maloneys agreed she should get a job but advised her to save her earnings. They asked instead if they could adopt her.

I knew what was coming because they'd approached me as if Grace were my daughter and were asking for her hand in marriage. I told them that nothing could make me happier and that, in any event, she wasn't mine to give. So they opened their arms to an orphan and took her in. But not before she stole a long look at me. "I want to keep my last name," she said. "I still want to be called Grace Larson."

— • —

MY GRANDDAUGHTER was not nearly done with magic. She practiced daily and was getting good enough to book birthday parties and library shows. Notebook by notebook, she worked through all my tricks and could manage passable versions of each. Grace was finally growing into her hands. She was also getting ambitious, wanting to invent tricks and record them in her own notebooks. "But first I'll start with *The Kortelisy Escape*," she said. "You never wrote that one up, did you?"

I hadn't.

She rummaged through a box in the closet, emerging with a fresh notebook, its spine unbroken. She opened to the first blank page and in her best block lettering wrote *The Kortelisy Escape*. Beneath that, she drew a very serviceable Matryoshka doll separated into halves, showing the innermost doll—the littlest Matryoshka, keeper of secrets. From upper left to lower right, she drew a cone, the flood of a single stage light. On the next page she wrote *For Nate Larson, my grandfather.*

"I'm flattered," I said. "Are you sure?"

She was.

"Will you help me write it?" she asked.

I would not. I was a graybeard fading; she, a young life rising. *The Kortelisy Escape* was her work, not mine. "Tell it any way you see fit," I answered. "Put words in my mouth if you want. It's OK. But if people are going to read this book of yours, tell it all. Even the hard parts. Especially the hard parts. And don't make me look pretty because I'm not."

"Don't worry," she said. "No one could lie *that* much."

Our Tabernacle Tour of New England was over, a distant memory—our first and only traveling magic show. The stress of our last performance had shaken my nerves to such an extent that my hand tremors, which I'd controlled more or less well with medication that summer, grew worse. Rather than frustrate myself when I could no longer perform at my best, I gave up magic, settling instead for the daily wonder of watching Grace, smile by uncertain smile, grow into her womanhood. She excelled in school, planning to become a professional game designer, and favored a young man who for the life of him couldn't figure out *The Vanished Card.* She tormented him with that trick. One Saturday night when I'd padded out of my bedroom and went downstairs for a cookie, I discovered them on the back porch, kissing. I padded away.

From the inside out, my granddaughter stunned me with her beauty. For four years we lived the most ordinary of lives with the Maloneys—which for Grace and me was nothing short of miraculous. No guns, no prison, no prostitutes, no threats of murder, no Mr. Parker. No Petrov. But we did mow the lawn and weed the beds and carry out the trash and watch movies as a family: all the trivial, invisible things that, day by day, add up to a life.

On a Tuesday in the November of her senior year at Cathedral High, I waited for Grace to return from school. I was dressed and ready when she came upstairs to check on me. "Field trip," I announced.

"You look terrific, Nate. What happened?"

"That's no way to greet your . . . Never mind. Ready to learn another trick? It's the best one I know."

I wanted to be very clear about the dangers of *The Barber Shop*. "You've got to be ready," I cautioned. "Old enough. That's why I waited, because this one tends to upset people. But I think you're ready."

I called a cab.

Thirty minutes later we stood in Union Square, the beating heart of Somerville, Massachusetts. Intense but brief snow squalls had blown through the city that afternoon, leaving the cars and sidewalks dusted and sparkling in the street lamps. We stood before a barber shop with a big sign in block letters that read **LOUIE'S**. Outside, bolted into the stonework with iron rods, was a barber pole, its red, white, and blue stripes spinning. Grace and I watched until she said, finally: "The stripes spiral up from the bottom and vanish through the top."

"That's right."

"It doesn't end. It comes from nothing and goes to nothing. Wait a second . . . I think it may come from something and go to something else. I can't quite . . ."

"You can't quite what?"

"I *almost* see it. But if I look straight on—"

"It disappears?"

"Exactly."

I motioned her inside.

"Louie," I called. "I'd like you to meet my granddaughter."

My old high school buddy and I embraced. The shop still felt like the old days with its overhead lights in frosted globes hanging from long poles, horsehair brushes and Clubman talcum powder, and chairs—those gorgeous, complicated iron and leather chairs, six of them, each fronted by a large, round mirror. Louie's father had aligned three chairs and mirrors along one wall with chairs and mirrors on the opposite wall. Perfect symmetry. I asked Grace to choose a chair and sit.

I stood behind her, blocking her view of the chair behind me. "Look into the mirror," I said. "What do you see?"

"I see me and a goofy-looking old guy."

"Excellent. What do you see now?"

When I stepped away, her world shifted and she no longer saw just one of her. The mirror on the opposite wall reflected her reflection. That reflection, in turn, was reflected and so on again and again. She was looking down a corridor of reflections with herself in the center of each.

"It doesn't end, Nate!"

"Louie's dad owned the shop when we were kids. I came every month to get my hair cut. Same chairs, same mirrors, same barber pole outside. I never had much use for God after the war. I got what I needed right here."

She turned back to the corridor of reflections. "There's too many to count," she said, raising her hand and pointing. A thousand million hands pointed.

"This is it? The trick?"

"I'd call it more of an illusion. But, yes."

"It's *beautiful!*"

"I was hoping you'd say so."

"And scary. A little."

I agreed.

"It's a road, I think. A long one."

"It is."

"I'm on it. Alone. Am I alone?"

"You met me and the Maloneys, didn't you? You'll meet others. When you do, remember your hellos and good-byes. It's polite."

I turned to Louie. "Hey there, Louie."

"How's it going, Nate?"

I stepped into the reflections, cutting off her view to the infinite. Her world grew small and cozy again, once more bounded by the walls and mirrors of a little barber shop in Somerville, Massachusetts. Louie shut down the lights, and I bent over and kissed the crown of my granddaughter's head. I grinned as I pointed to the mirrors. "It's like getting pushed off a cliff, isn't it?"

"The mirrors?"

"No. Being born. Living."

Grace Nora Larson swiveled in her chair. She studied me a good long while and said, "Grandpa, you're a very strange man. I love you."

With that, I knew she would make it. She would live and flourish despite the misery of her childhood and despite all my failings. The next evening I vanished. Poof! Gone, cradled once more in the arms of the German soldier. An excellent effect, I must say, a real Tabernacle Moment! My jaw dropped, my breath mingled with other breaths. I smelled lavender. There came a sudden rising, or falling, it's difficult to say. But even if I could say, I wouldn't because magicians never tell and, in any event, this particular vanish is for each of us to discover alone. Still, I'll bend the rules a little and share this: Mama Rachel was right, or nearly right. Our world *is* heaven, only not all at once. Heaven is heaven all at once, every instant of every day. (Yes, there are days and nights here.) It's the best I can do until you arrive and see for yourself. Good-bye, friend, well met along the road! Or as I was fond of saying onstage: Here one moment . . .

THE KORTELISY ESCAPE

1. BEGIN WITH...
   GIRL ABANDONED AND WAR SURVIVED.

D. C. F.

2. HOODLUMS MAKE LIFE DANGEROUS

3. ADD A UKRAINIAN BEAUTY.

4. MIX.

5. TRICK THE HOODLUMS!

6. MAKE FRIENDS.

PERFORMANCE NOTES:

1. TRICK SELECTION WILL DIFFER FOR EACH MAGICIAN.

2. ON ENTERING, BOW. GREET YOUR AUDIENCE.

3. DO SOME MAGIC. WOW THEM!

7. THINK LARGE.

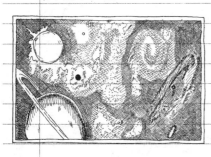

4. YOU MAY BE PART OF A LARGER SHOW. (I THINK I AM.) RELAX.

5. OPTION: PANIC.

6. WHICHEVER, ENJOY YOUR TIME ONSTAGE.

Author's Note

One of the great pleasures in researching a novel involving magic was time spent with magicians. It's no exaggeration to say that even when I knew how a trick was done, these men and women astonished me. One turned scarves into doves. Another somehow placed a cantaloupe beneath a bowler hat when I was expecting a little red ball. Part priest, part technician, and all entertainer, professional magicians are as practiced as surgeons and take their work as seriously. The shows I attended so delighted and mystified me that, novel aside, I wanted to share the experience somehow. The best way to do that, of course, is to urge you to attend magic shows where you live. For my part, I've devoted a page on my website to "Magicians at Work," a video collection of some of the tricks I love best. Go to lenrosenonline.com.

New York based Matias Letelier (magicianmatias.com) introduced me to the world of magic, generously discussing theories and techniques without once divulging trade secrets. His shows leave audiences slack-jawed with wonder—laughter, too—and it was an honor to be taken under his wing (cape?) and included in gatherings with his fellow magicians. Boston-based magician Debbie O'Carroll (debbieocarroll.com) also guided my introduction to magic. Debbie performs for children, surely the toughest of audiences, and kids *never* turn their backs on her—nor do their parents, who watch alongside just as amazed. Magic lovers who find themselves in Cambridge, Massachusetts, will enjoy catching a show at The Mystery Lounge in Harvard Square, as I did on many Wednesday evenings. Touring magicians frequently perform at The Lounge, and the local talent is superb.

Many people commented on drafts of *Kortelisy* or otherwise aided the effort. What deficiencies remain are mine; but I give special thanks to Simon Reinhardt (Simonreinhardt. tumblr.com), the graphic artist who produced Nate's notebook sketches. Thanks also to Aevitas Creative Management, whose Elias Altman, Chelsey Heller, Sarah Levitt, and Todd Shuster proved themselves (yet again) generous with their time and patient beyond reason. With apologies to those I may have overlooked, I am also indebted to Frederique Apffel-Marglin, Larry Behrens, Steve Bennett, Elisabeth Brink, Felicia Campbell, Joe Chen, Bruce Coffin, Tina Feingold, Jill Fletcher, Nancy Gertner, Cindy-jo Gross, Larry Heffernan, Claire Jensen, Shannon Kirk, Kathy Koman, Stuart Koman, Adina Kraus, Allan Kronzek, Claire Lamb, Misia Landau, Lester Lefton, Bruce Levine, Dick Marks, Mike Mayo, Jenny Morrison, Paul Polansky, John Reinstein, Rachele Rosi-Ketel, Hank Phillippi Ryan, David Schmahmann, Jonathan Shapiro, Frank Sladko, Sara Smolover, Doug Starr, Jessie Stein, and David Woodruff. The team at The Permanent Press—Marty Shepard, Judy Shepard, Chris Knopf, Lon Kirschner, Barbara Anderson, and Susan Ahlquist—are valued critics, advocates, and friends who expressed confidence in my work even when confidence on my end was in short supply. I am fortunate to work with them.

As for Linda, Jonathan, Matthew, and Anna, I have no words. The most beautiful magic defies description.

—LEONARD ROSEN, Brookline, MA
lenrosenonline.com